MURDER AT
GOVERNMENT
HOUSE

A VIKING NOVEL
OF
MYSTERY
AND
SUSPENSE

Also by Elspeth Huxley

The African Poison Murders
Murder on Safari
The Flame Trees of Thika

MURDER AT GOVERNMENT HOUSE

ELSPETH HUXLEY

VIKING

VIKING

Published by the Penguin Group
Viking Penguin Inc., 40 West 23rd Street,
New York, New York 10010, U.S.A.
Penguin Books Ltd, 27 Wrights Lane,
London W8 5TZ, England
Penguin Books Australia Ltd, Ringwood,
Victoria, Australia
Penguin Books Canada Ltd, 2801 John Street,
Markham, Ontario, Canada L3R 1B4
Penguin Books (N.Z.) Ltd, 182–190 Wairau Road,
Auckland 10, New Zealand

Penguin Books Ltd, Registered Offices:
Harmondsworth, Middlesex, England

Published in 1988 by Viking Penguin Inc.

1   3   5   7   9   10   8   6   4   2

LIBRARY OF CONGRESS CATALOGING IN PUBLICATION DATA
Huxley, Elspeth Joscelin Grant, 1907–
Murder at Government House.
I. Title.
PR6015.U92M87   1988   823'.912   87-40640
ISBN 0-670-82318-X

Printed in the United States of America by
Arcata Graphics, Fairfield, Pennsylvania
Set in Garamond

To H.H.
What the Doctor ordered

MURDER AT GOVERNMENT HOUSE

GROUND FLOOR PLAN OF
GOVERNMENT HOUSE, MARULA

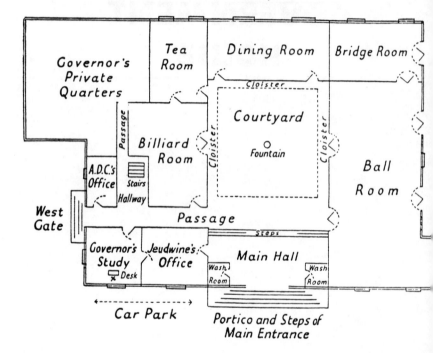

1

Mark Beaton was in that embittered mood that was apt to follow the nerve-racking preparations for a Government House dinner-party. Around him sat twenty people, faintly uneasy in the carefully adjusted armour of tail coats and formal evening dresses. They might like their food, but he doubted whether they could enjoy the conversation. About ninety per cent of them were government servants who already knew each other well — often too well; an official dinner-party presented no opportunity to make new acquaintances. Every one professed to hate these formal functions; but if an eligible official wasn't invited there was hell to pay for the Governor's staff. Mark knew that for the next few days his life wouldn't be worth living because he had put the wife of the Surveyor-General above the wife of a senior-ranking Puisne Judge.

How extraordinary it is, he thought, that the English tradition debars from dinner-table conversation almost all topics that might interest the conversers and insists upon strict adherence to banalities. There was the Governor, Sir Malcolm McLeod, for instance, talking to Mrs Pallett, the Colonial Secretary's wife. He was probably thinking: 'Damn these women! Why should I waste time talking about the Girl Guides' rally, when I've got to think out a plan of campaign for tomorrow's meeting with that old fool Flower?' And Mrs Pallett, who was really a very intelligent woman — at any rate she had taken her mathematics tripos at Cambridge — and enjoyed most of all a discussion on Dunne's theory of the serial universe, wondering: 'What on earth can I say to keep the conversation going? How I hate these gimlet-eyed, domineering Scotsmen, with their literal, practical minds! All he cares about is administering colonies more efficiently than they've ever been administered before. No wonder his wife won't live out here with him. Well, there's always the Girl Guides.'

Then there was Pallett, the Colonial Secretary, a sandy-haired, broad-faced, pompous man in steel-rimmed spectacles. He was probably composing in his mind a dispatch to the Secretary of State about the registration of non-native seamen landing in steam-propelled vessels at the port; and talking to Marvin McLeod, curse him, about the monthly golf medal. Marvin was looking grand tonight; that white dress suited her, and the green ear-rings he had given her went perfectly with it. She was looking pale, but that suited her too; her face was like a pearl, clear, somehow glowing. . . .

'It's a great pity,' said a voice on his left, 'that nearly all the usual topics of conversation are under a taboo in English society. Limits the field so, doesn't it?' It was a penetrating voice; it pierced the buzz rising from the table as the whir of a bombing squadron subdues the hum of bees on a summer's afternoon.

'Among the M'Bole of Southern Nyasaland, for instance,' the voice continued, 'it would be a gross insult to invite a guest to a meal and fail to ask him whether his wives were fertile and if his girl children were still virgins. But I imagine that Sir Bertrand Flower would be quite offended if Sir Malcolm McLeod's daughter were to sound him on such points.'

Mark came back to his party duties with a jerk. 'I was just thinking the same sort of thing myself,' he replied politely. 'No one ever says anything they really think at a show like this. It seems such a waste of time.'

His neighbour glanced at him curiously. 'You seem to be an unusually serious-minded young man, for an A.D.C.,' she said. 'A craving for reality is seldom noticeable among English colonial officials. Perhaps, however, you're in love.'

Mark flushed, and checked an angry reply. Damn the woman's cheek! he thought. A condescending prig, and a prying one at that.

'At least you'll admit that colonial officials are human enough to fall in love,' he replied stiffly.

His neighbour cackled vigorously. A hideous laugh, thought Mark, with satisfaction. She was very unattractive anyway, he considered. She had an untidy mop of black frizzy hair; small, beady black eyes; a round white face, with an alert expression; too heavy a jaw-bone. She must be at least twenty-eight, and looked all of it. Her name, he knew, was Miss Olivia Brandeis; she was an anthropologist who divided her time between field work among Central and East African native tribes and lecturing on functional anthropology at the London School of Economics. (A Communist, probably, Mark thought to himself). She was visiting Chania to study the social structure of the Wabenda tribe. Sir Malcolm McLeod had asked her to stay at Government House on her arrival, and had regretted it ever since. They had taken an immediate dislike to each other.

'A good object-lesson,' Miss Brandeis remarked when she had recovered from her laughter and helped herself to the sweet. 'You advocate the lifting of British conversational taboos; but at the first sign, however faint, of an infringement of the taboos — when I say what comes into my head, which happens to be a personal remark — you think: "Damn the woman, she's got no manners", and kick me, mentally, into the outer darkness where non-pukka memsahibs go.'

Curse her, thought Mark, she's perfectly right. That's just what I *did* think. Aloud he said:

'I thought you were being a little condescending, if you want to know. But I expect being an anthropologist makes condescension a habit. Always in the role of a superior mortal from another sphere, inquiring how the savage and untutored conduct their poor affairs.'

– 3 –

Miss Brandeis's beady eyes seemed to shine a little brighter. 'Call it quits,' she said, 'though I could argue with you over your conception of an anthropologist. I won't, though; and as a reward, please tell me something about the people here tonight. I've been in Chania less than a week, and I hardly know any of them.'

A slim black hand slid round Mark's shoulder and removed a plate of ice-cream with chocolate sauce, half eaten. Mentally he cursed the fate of an A.D.C., condemned to be served last and to surrender his food long before there was a chance to finish it. He turned again to Miss Brandeis. After all, he reflected, she is staying at Government House, so I'd better be polite.

'Well, the dinner's in honour of Sir Bertrand Flower, the Governor of Totseland,' he began. 'You know that, of course. And no doubt you recognize him, sitting over there.'

Olivia Brandeis glanced across the table and saw an elderly man with a fringe of grey hair, a short, grey moustache, and gold-rimmed spectacles. His face was lined; he looked worried and rather ill. A weak face, on the whole, she thought. At first sight the expression might be taken for strength and determination, but obstinacy would probably be a truer interpretation. The visiting Governor sat heavily in his chair, his shoulders stooping. She knew his reputation in England. It was that of a hard-working, competent, but not brilliant administrator, nearing retirement. Over thirty years of undistinguished but conscientious, obedient, and not unsuccessful work in the colonial service lay behind him; a peaceful retirement in the west of England, whence he came, no doubt lay ahead.

'He's visiting Marula, I gather,' said Olivia Brandeis, 'to discuss the proposed federation of Chania and Totseland into one territory.'

'Right,' replied Mark. 'That's a long story, which you probably know. The idea has been floating about in the air for ages. Now H.E. has at last got out a proper cut-and-dried scheme, which the Colonial Office has provisionally blessed, and he and Sir Bertrand are going to discuss it. The first meeting happens tomorrow morning.'

Olivia Brandeis nodded. 'Yes, I know that much. I also gather that prospects of a speedy agreement are not considered very bright.'

'It's not going to be plain sailing by any means,' Mark agreed, warming to his work, now that he had started, rather more than was necessary. 'Sir Bertrand isn't nearly as keen on the idea as H.E. The real snag is the amalgamation of the two railways. Both countries think *their* railway is much the more solvent, efficient, and generally desirable, and that the other fellow's railway is nothing but a collection of scrap-iron, worth about sixpence. If anything's to come of it all, they'll both have to agree about valuations, but I believe Sir Bertrand has suggested some fantastic figure as the value of the Totseland line — which actually doesn't make anything like as good a profit per mile as ours — so there's sure to be lots of fun before it's fixed — if it ever is.'

'Railways are nearly always the crux of economic problems in Africa,' said Miss Brandeis — sententiously, Mark thought. He fell quickly upon his savoury. 'Who's that over there?' his neighbour continued. 'He's got an interesting face.'

'That's the Secretary for Native Affairs, Victor Moon,' Mark replied. 'A nice chap — at least, I like him.'

'Others don't?'

Mark hastily gulped the last mouthful of savoury just as the black hand reappeared behind his shoulder. 'In a small community like this,' he replied, 'you always get internal jealousies and things, don't you? I don't suppose any service is free from them.'

Olivia Brandeis looked again across the table at Victor Moon. He was tall and dark, with a narrow, bony, sunburnt face, deep lines in it although he looked young. His hair, brushed carefully back, was thick and wavy; his eyebrows heavy, his eyes deep-sunk. At that distance he looked proud, reserved, and self-contained.

'I've heard that he's not a great admirer of his immediate senior, Mr Pallett,' Miss Brandeis remarked.

Mark glanced quickly at his neighbour. Shrewd, he thought, with all that damnable self-complacency. And, after all, a bit of gossip. Well, he wasn't going to be drawn. The sharp, at times almost bitter, division of opinion between the Governor and his Colonial Secretary, Pallett, on certain matters of policy, and the Secretary for Native Affairs' support for the Governor's views rather than for those of his immediate chief, were common pieces of Marula gossip. No doubt this inquisitive woman would hear more of them; but it was hardly the A.D.C.'s job to act as a relaying station. He gave a non-committal reply.

'Who's the woman over there?' his companion continued, undismayed. 'The platinum blonde in slinky vermilion satin, who looks like a high-class tart — and, obviously, has blood-red toe-nails?'

'The girl-wife of the Director of Education,' Mark replied.

'Watson?' queried Miss Brandeis, in surprise. 'I've been to see him. He struck me as an exceptionally intelligent man, for a Director of Education.' She observed Mark stiffen slightly at her condescending tone, and smiled. 'He must be twenty years older than she is.'

'He is,' Mark replied.

'How long have they been married?'

'About a year. He brought her out after his last leave.'

Mrs Watson was eating archly. Rhinestone bracelets flashed as she moved her arms. She was making animated conversation with a rather melancholy-looking, dried-up man who was the Colonel in command of the King's African Light Infantry. He did not appear to be a very likely quarry. Her methods seems a little perfunctory, almost automatic.

'Well, I wouldn't give it long,' Olivia Brandeis commented.

'You're evidently an authority of marriage as well as on colonial administration,' Mark said, rather heavily.

Miss Brandeis chuckled. 'That's the second taboo I've offended against. Attempting to pump a conscientious A.D.C. about the personal affairs of his fellow-officials. All right, I won't press the point. And I'll try to be less offensive.'

Queer woman, Mark thought. Seems to have the knack of knowing what's going on in one's mind. Well, she'll find out lots more about Maisie Watson before she's been around this town much longer.

Maisie Watson was, indeed, Marula's principal source of scandal. Her behaviour was a great deal more dashing and less moral than that of any wife of a departmental head within living memory. Most wives of senior officials were middle-aged and unadventurous, their complexions battered by a lifetime in the tropics and their spirits broken by an endless obligation never to let their husbands down. They hated Maisie Watson. She, however, worked hard to maintain her reputation as the top local floozie. And her latest effort had, as one of the junior officials remarked, upped it to an all-time high. Nothing like this scandal had been known in Marula for years. The air, as Mark well knew, was tense with expectation and whispering. To some of Marula's officials these rumours seemed like the mutterings of distant thunder before the crash of an expected storm.

Olivia Brandeis looked down the table at the Director of Education. She saw his profile, bending slightly forward; a high forehead, a finely chiselled nose, closed lips which dipped down at the corners and gave a sardonic expression to the face. He had the ascetic look of a don; but the flesh at the corners of his eyes was crinkled, like a sailor's. Suddenly he glanced up across the table at his wife. Olivia Brandeis saw the muscles around his mouth tighten —

unconsciously, she was sure; it gave Watson's face an implacable, almost a ferocious, expression.

'He doesn't look the sort to take things easily,' she remarked.

.　　　.　　　.　　　.　　　.

The dinner-party was nearly over. Deft and silent native servants whisked away the empty plates and cleared the table of its litter of crumbs and wineglasses. Over them all Abdi, the butler, brooded almost like a spirit — Abdi, the ruler of the Government House entourage for fifteen years, so prosperous that he had, almost alone among his lithe Somali tribesmen, grown fat and portly. His quick black eyes missed nothing; his low, soft voice was more feared by the staff than that of a dozen white men. He made a fine appearance, gliding barefooted over the carpets, dressed in a robe of heavy white silk and a thickly embroidered scarlet and gold waistcoat, with a scarlet sash and fez. Government House needed no white domestic staff while Abdi presided, and no A.D.C. dared to act without his approval.

Dessert was over, and the hum of conversation subsided expectantly. Abdi himself, with his second-in-command, poured port into each guest's glass. Then silence fell, so familiar was the routine, and the Governor rose slowly to his feet.

He stood there for a second, impassively. The wine in his raised glass caught and held the light. It glowed softly, like a small flame, never flickering, so steady was the hand that held it. All eyes were turned to him, rather because he commanded attention in whatever action he took than because of the oft-repeated little ceremony.

He was a handsome man, in a rugged way. The strength and energy of his character were reflected in his features. Keen and steady grey eyes, under the protruding bushy brows common among Scots; high cheek-bones; a sensitive, mobile mouth, a jaw firmly set. Black hair, streaked with grey, with a crisp in it that oil would not erase. A strong face, certainly; lacking, perhaps, in humour and flexibility, and certainly in that easy-going quality in men that will prompt them to compromise with events for the sake of peace and never to press a dangerous case to its conclusion. The face of a leader, of a man who would be generous to his followers but impatient with his opponents; of a man who would be direct and honest in his own dealings and unforgiving to those whose honesty was less than his own. A great colonial administrator, perhaps; his career was only at its opening, and already his reputation stood high.

He had come into the colonial service from the outside. Trained as a doctor, he had gained administrative experience in the organization of a mission to relieve famine areas in China, and practical knowledge of the colonies from service on a commission investigating leprosy in the tropics. He had undertaken an inquiry into native dietetics for the Colonial Office with such success that the Secretary of State for the Colonies had, with unusual imagination, taken a rare gamble and offered him the Governorship of British Somaliland. He had accepted, at the age of thirty-five; and in his five years' term had introduced more reforms and innovations than that little Protectorate had experienced in the whole of its previous existence as a part of the Colonial Empire.

A year ago he had been appointed to Chania, a senior Governorship. Immediately he had adopted the idea, long vaguely discussed, of a federation between Chania and the neighbouring Protectorate to the north, Totseland — a first step, perhaps, towards welding into one confederacy the territories under British rule lying between the Zambesi and the headwaters of the Nile. He had taken his scheme, drawn up to the last detail, home to the Colonial Office for discussion, won the approval of the Secretary of State, and flown back to Chania to put it through. This conference with Sir Bertrand Flower was intended to be the last of the preliminaries. Few doubted that he would succeed to the

Governorship of the new federation. His admirers spoke of him as the coming man in Africa, a fit successor to Lugard and Cameron; his enemies as a dangerous and ambitious theorist, an over-confident amateur.

His voice was pleasantly soft, with a trace of Scots burr. He raised his glass to give the regulation toast. Chairs scraped gently on the carpets as the guests rose to attention and gripped their glasses by the stems.

'The King!'

The company muttered after him, like a congregation, 'The King!' and sipped their port.

'You may smoke,' Sir Malcolm said abruptly, and sat down. There was no one in the room who suspected that he had given 'The King' for the last time in his life.

2

Outside the Government House ballroom lay a carefully tended lawn, kept green with sprinklers so that it was always soft and springy to the feet. Two shafts of light from open french windows lay like bright spears across the dark and shadowed grass. The point of one spear fell on to the bole of a tall acacia and the light shone softly on to the under-sides of leaves and branches. The stars were clear overhead and a splinter of new moon hung unobtrusively among the more flashy companions that it would so soon outshine. Irregular snatches of music from a radio-gramophone floated out over the lawn. The bulk of Government House loomed up like a white sleeping monster, throwing no shadows and yet full of suggestions of shadows in its many-angled depths.

'My God! Just *look* at it!' The voice was bitter, and slightly raised. It belonged to Donovan Popple, who stood with his hands pushed deep into his pockets and his back to the acacia tree, squarely and savagely facing Government House. 'Look at it! I ask you!'

Olivia Brandeis, standing by his side, drew on her cigarette and complied.

'It looks remarkably inoffensive, compared with most colonial architecture,' she replied. 'Rather pleasant, in fact. No particular style — early Californian, one might call it. And I think the courtyard in the middle is—'

'Oh, it *looks* all right,' Popple broke in irritably. 'And by God, so it ought to. Do you know what that little shack cost us — *us*, the taxpayers?'

'More than you think justified, evidently.'

'You're damn right, it did. Sixty thousand pounds. Sixty thousand — and we pay. There was a perfectly good house there before, that was good enough for better men than this damn fool, pocket Mussolini—' Popple checked himself, remembering, as he was always having to do, that he was talking about the King's representative. It was remarkably difficult, he found, to keep on thinking of the Governor as one who dwelt in reflected royalty when he was continually playing ducks and drakes with the country's police and finance.

Popple had been farming and trading in Chania for twenty-five years, and believed that he knew more about its needs and troubles than most of the outsiders who came in at the Colonial Office's orders for a few years, to sit in Marula behind a barricade of officials and tell every one who had to make a living in the colony where to get off. Besides, as the most active of the elected members on the Legislative Council, it was his duty to try to keep official extravagance somewhere within bounds.

'But surely,' Olivia Brandeis said, 'this place wasn't Sir Malcolm McLeod's idea? He's been here for less than a year, and the new—'

'Ah, well, I'll not be accusing him of commencing the project,' Popple interrupted, 'but he didn't put a stop to it when he came. That was bad enough, but, by God, it's nothing to his latest crazy, treacherous, criminal notion, if I've understood it aright!'

Olivia Brandeis had to step out to keep pace with him. He strode excitably across the lawn. She wondered why he was talking like this to a woman he had met for the first time a few hours ago, at a dinner-party. She knew from hearsay that he took his politics terribly seriously. Not that he made anything out of them; on the contrary, he spent most of his spare cash and all of his spare time in fighting the farmer's battles with the Government.

'It's this Japanese concession. You've probably heard talk about it.' Olivia nodded and Popple lit a cigarette. The match lit up a lined and leathery face hardened by sun and wind, and surmounted by a mop of ginger hair. He threw the match down impatiently, took a quick draw at the cigarette and tried to knock off ash that wasn't there.

'H.E. wants to give a big concession to a Japanese firm,' he continued, speaking quickly. 'It's nominally a firm, but of course the Japanese Government's behind it. A million acres of the Maji River — irrigation; cotton, sugar-cane, and so forth. They guarantee to spend half a million pounds.'

Olivia nodded. 'New capital, increased railway traffic, profits to tax, and so — there are lots of good reasons.'

'Damn it, I know that. But don't you understand the Japanese situation? Don't you know what they're after?' Popple grew more and more excited. 'Penetration into Africa, of course; and here's this fool wants to blast a gateway wide open for them. They'll immigrate in thousands — hundreds of thousands — millions. They're doing it now in Brazil. First they'll undermine the British settlers, all of us. Drag down our standards of living. Then they'll start to push the Africans out of jobs, take all the higher paid posts. It's—'

'The Australians,' Olivia interrupted, 'have already made the world familiar with most of those arguments.'

'All right.' Popple threw away his half-smoked cigarette. 'Then at least you'll admit that there *are* no arguments. And now what does this fellow do? Tries to push the whole thing through over our heads, without consulting the country, without debating it in Council, without saying a word to any one. Never gives us a chance to put up our objections. It wouldn't have come out at all if a big British interest at home hadn't got hold of it, from the London end. They say England will never have a dictator, but, by God, we've got one in the colonies!'

'Has the scheme gone through, then?'

'That's the devil of it. I don't know. That son-of— I mean H.E., keeps as tight as a clam. He thinks he doesn't have to talk to any one but God, and only on special occasions to Him. But it's coming up for discussion at this conference with Flower, so I don't think anything's settled. And I'm going to do my damnedest to stop it.' They walked on a few steps in silence. 'The whole future of the country hangs on it.' Popple broke the silence violently. 'If there's anything a man can do to stop him messing it up for good, then, by heaven, I'll do it!'

'Sir Malcolm sounds pretty high-handed, even for a Governor,' Olivia commented.

'He is that,' Popple answered, more calmly. 'I'm afraid I've bored you with all this. It's a shame to throw it all at the head of a visitor. I've got it so on my mind. . . . I wonder if you'll excuse me now?' He looked at his wrist-watch. 'It's nine-thirty and I have some work to do.'

He walked rapidly across the lawn and into the ballroom, through the french window. Olivia noticed the music again. Curious, she thought, how sounds, quite loud ones, cease to register in one's brain when it's occupied with other things, and are picked up again by the brain when it's got nothing better to do. About twenty or thirty people had been asked to Government House for a small informal dance after the dinner-party. Through the french windows Olivia could see couples revolving round the ballroom. The garden, she decided, was pleasanter.

It was very dark and the air seemed alive with delicate movement and the scent of night blossoms. She sat down on a bench standing against a kei-apple hedge, and savoured the mingling smells. One, most powerful, dominated: frangipani. She decided that it had a spectacular sort of scent, a little flashy, the sort of smell that characters in a Noel Coward play would enjoy under a full moon in the garden of a tropical country house.

A couple walked along a path which emerged from a clump of frangipanis near Olivia's bench. The man's stiff shirt-front crackled slightly as he moved. The woman was talking in a metallic voice that Olivia did not recognize.

'I was dreadfully worried,' she said. 'He was such a nice boy and I was so afraid that he'd do something foolish. But I told him that we all had to face up to our responsibilities, whatever tragedies our private lives might hold... One has to give up so much, doesn't one, living out here? One feels so cut *off*. Don't you think so, Mr Moon?'

Moon's voice was quiet and easy on the ear. 'I'm afraid I've lived so long out here now that I'd feel cut off at home.' They walked on towards the ballroom.

'Cut off at home? Why, how could that be? It's the centre of things. I should have thought that a man as *clever* as you are, Mr Moon, would feel so *wasted* out here. After all, with your personality...'

Distance absorbed the words as they walked on. A man came towards them from the house and called out: 'Hello, is that Moon?' He halted in front of them. He was tall and lanky and thrust his head out in front of him as he walked. His voice was high-pitched and a little querulous. Olivia recognized him; it was Jeudwine, the private secretary.

'I've been looking for you all over the place,' he said. 'H.E. can see you right away.'

Moon walked off and the man and the woman stood facing each other on the lawn. Olivia could see their silhouettes faintly againt the ballroom lights. She fished in her bag for a cigarette and reverted to some mental comparisons of the relative positions of the witchdoctor among the Wabenda in Chania and the Nupe, a Mohammedan tribe that she had studied in Nigeria.

Her thoughts were interrupted by a sharp exclamation from the woman on the lawn. Olivia looked up and saw that Jeudwine was gripping her wrist and that she was trying to free herself.

'Let go!' She had raised her voice. 'You've no right to!' Olivia could not hear his reply. He was leaning over, his face close to hers, his body tense.

'I must have been crazy!' she said, almost shouting. 'I'll never speak to you again!' He dropped her wrist suddenly, as though he was throwing it away from him, and she fell back a few steps, starting to sob.

'All right.' Jeudwine raised his voice now, and spoke every word slowly and clearly, as though he was trying to show he wasn't drunk. 'All right. You'll be sorry you said that. Don't think it's the last word.' He laughed abruptly, a note of hysteria in the sound. 'Sir Malcolm may be interested in some of the things I can tell him.' There was a short silence and then Jeudwine turned quickly and walked back — it was a sort of long-striding shuffle — towards the house, his shoulders hunched into the contour of a football.

The woman took a compact out of her bag and powdered her nose in the dark. Then she, too, walked back across the lawn and into the ballroom.

· · · · ·

'Good heavens,' Mark Beaton said, 'I'd no idea it was so late.' The clock on the mantelpiece above the big fireplace in the ballroom pointed to 11.15. 'I must go and do some work.' He stood at the french window with Olivia Brandeis, looking at the dancers inside.

'I expect you'll find her in the supper-room,' Olivia said.

'Damn it, I said work,' Mark answered. 'I have to sweat blood over the dowagers while she spends the evening dancing with a Shell man. Oh, I'm sorry,' he added uncomfortably. 'I didn't mean—I mean, of course, some of the time. . . .'

'Don't mention it.' Olivia spoke a little shortly. 'Insults to anthropologists involve no breaking of public school taboos.'

'Oh, hell,' said Mark. 'Well, I think I'll start with H.E. It's time he was prised out of his files to come and mingle for a bit.' He crossed the dance floor and went out by a door on the opposite side of the room.

The main part of Government House was built around a grassy courtyard with a fountain in the centre. The ballroom ran along the whole of the east side of the courtyard, and the dining-room occupied the north wing. To the west lay the billiard-room and a small sitting-room, known as the tea-room. The southern side of the courtyard was open and gave on to large hall, beyond which lay the main entrance, flanked by cloakrooms on both sides. A stone cloister ran round the entire courtyard.

As you came in at the main entrance, therefore, through a portico guarded by sentries, you found yourself in the hall. Straight ahead you could see the green courtyard and the fountain. A passage ran off to the left. It led past the billiard-room on the right and the offices of the private secretary and the Governor on the left, and ended in another entrance, known as the west gate. Only one door opened out of this passage on the left: the door to the Governor's office. This was guarded day and night by a KALI sentry, and two more sentries were on duty just outside the west gate. The private secretary's office was next to the Governor's room, with a communicating door. The exit from the secretary's office lay through the main hall.

Mark Beaton walked across the courtyard and along the passage leading to the Governor's office and the west gate. The native sentry on duty outside the Governor's door saluted. Mark was attached to the KALI by virtue of his position and wore the uniform of a subaltern when on duty. There was no reply to his knocking and he turned to go.

'How long ago did the Big Chief leave?' he asked the askari in Kiswahili.

'He has not left, bwana.'

There were only two exits to the Governor's office. One was the door into the passage at which Mark was hesitating. The other led into the private secretary's room. The Governor could leave his office by walking through the secretary's room and out into the main hall. Mark supposed that this was what he had done, but thought he had better make sure.

He opened the door and looked in. The office was big and square, panelled in cedar. It contained little furniture beyond some bookcases, a large couch, and a leather-covered arm chair. Opposite the door, at the far end of the room, stood a massive desk. Immediately behind it a window gave on to the driveway. There was another window on the right, between the door and the desk. The only illumination came from a reading-lamp standing on top of the desk.

Behind the desk was a heavy swivel chair and in it sat a man. He was slumped over the desk, his face flattened against its surface. His left arm sprawled across some files and papers. His right elbow rested on the table and his forearm lay limply across the back of his head. A telephone receiver, off its hook, gleamed faintly on the blotting-pad, where it had evidently fallen from a hand suddenly deprived of muscular control.

Mark caught his breath and reached the desk in three strides. He lifted up the head and gazed for a moment of startled horror at a macabre caricature of the features of his master. The face was swollen, blotched, and darkly mottled, the eyes bulging horribly out of the sockets. The half-wrenched-out eyeballs were dark with blood. The head of the late Governor of Chania thudded dully on the wood as Mark, with an instinctive gesture of recoil, let it fall.

Then he noticed a cord knotted round the neck, biting

- 17 -

deeply into the lifeless flesh.

Mark gave a choking cry and sprinted out of the room. In the passage he pulled himself up, retraced a few steps, and said to the amazed askari: 'Let no one in there till I return. No one. Understand?' Then he closed the door and ran on, planning what to do as he went.

There was a telephone in the hall, on a table inside the main entrance. He got through to the Commissioner of Police, explained in agitated phrases. Then he tried the Director of Medical Services, got no reply; dialled the Medical Department with no results; finally, sweating in agitation, got on to one of the leading private practitioners in Marula, who promised to be up in ten minutes. Abdi, the head boy, stationed in the main hall all evening to welcome and dispatch guests, listen unashamedly behind him, his training unequal to curiosity and consternation.

Sir Malcolm McLeod was dead, all right; there wasn't any doubt about that. The Colonial Secretary must step automatically into his shoes. The colony couldn't be without a Governor. Pallett must be found next. And Jeudwine.

Mark crossed the hall and tried the door into Jeudwine's office. It was locked. He knocked without result. He found Jeudwine at the buffet in the dining-room having a drink. Mark had to shake the secretary's arm before he realized that something had happened, and then drag him out of the buffet. Jeudwine was shambling more than ever. His face was flushed, and he had forgotten to wipe the moisture from his thick-lenses glasses.

'For God's sake pull yourself together, man,' Mark said. Jeudwine was clutching a tumbler. He took a gulp and said, 'Whassher matter?'

'H.E.'s been murdered,' Mark said in a low voice. 'He's been strangled. I've got to find Pallett.'

'Murdered?' Jeudwine said thickly. He didn't seem to realize what the word meant. He stared stupidly at Mark, and stepped back, swaying unsteadily. 'Murdered?' he gasped. 'S'impossible. S'flower-bed.'

Mark had no time to waste on a drunken idiot. 'Listen, can't you,' he said. 'Where's Pallett?'

'Pallett,' said Jeudwine. 'Went to Sh-Secretariat. S'down there now.'

Mark left Jeudwine standing vacuously with a glass in his hand, and ran back to the telephone. There was no reply from the Secretariat. He tried Pallett's house. No answer. As he turned round he saw the Colonial Secretary walk in through the main entrance. Mark told him the news in the doorway. He gaped, his round blue eyes wide with horror. Nothing like this had ever happened to him before, in all his twenty years' experience. There was no precedent. Mark led him along the passage and into the Governor's office, to see for himself. He took one look at the dead man's face, and sat down in the leather armchair, breathing heavily.

'We'll wait here for the Commissioner,' Mark suggested. 'He'll be up in five minutes.' He looked around the room. He could see no sign of a struggle. The dead man's desk was littered with papers, but they seemed orderly enough. He must have been telephoning when he was attacked and strangled from behind.

Mark walked over to the door leading to Jeudwine's room, on the right facing the passage, and opened it. Everything was dark. He flicked down the switch and saw that the room was empty. There were no closets big enough to hold a man. The door opposite, leading into the hall, he knew was locked.

They heard a car draw up outside the west gate with a flurry of gravel. Mark went out to meet the Commissioner of Police, Major Armitage, a short, dark, abrupt little man, slightly bald, with a greying moustache and, when he wore his horn-rimmed spectacles, a strong look of Groucho Marx. With him came a younger man in khaki police uniform, whom Mark recognized as the new head of the C.I.D. — Vachell by name. He was a Canadian, Mark remembered; tall and rangy, with sparse sandy hair and eyebrows, light blue eyes, and a bony face which betrayed a Scots ancestry. He had a slow way of speech and an expression which Mark couldn't classify, but which seemed to be at once amused and wary. Two men carrying a camera and flashlight apparatus followed them.

'This is terrible, absolutely terrible.' The Commissioner spoke jerkily, in a gruff voice. 'Couldn't believe my ears. Never, in all my experience—' He broke off as he saw the figure slumped in the chair. He shook his head. 'We'll get the fiend responsible for this if it's the last thing my department ever does.'

The next half-hour was like a confused nightmare. The doctor arrived and made his examination. The Governor had been dead not less than half an hour, not more than an hour, he said. It was 11.30 when he saw the body. Flashlight exposures were made and the room examined. Finally the body was carried by askaris to the Governor's private quarters.

A half-company of KALI arrived in a fleet of lorries and the men were posted around Government House. Askaris guarded all entrances and gates. Pallett, pale and flustered, was driven down to the Secretariat in a police car at sixty miles an hour to dispatch a cable to the Colonial Office. All wires were cleared as the news zipped over six thousand miles of land and sea to a startled night clerk in Downing Street — astonishing news that His Majesty's representative, the Governor and Commander-in-Chief of Chania, His Excellency Sir Malcolm McLeod, K.C.B., K.C.M.G., M.C., had been strangled while engaged in the execution of his duties at Government House.

A telephone message caught the Secretary of State for the Colonies while he was attending a banquet. He remarked: 'Good God! I knew these bloody settlers would be up to something soon, but this is too much!' and scribbled a message of sympathy to the dead Governor's wife on a piece of paper.

Mark, in the meantime, had been sent by Armitage to break the news to the murdered Governor's daughter and to the guests. The first was a terrible assignment. He left Marvin McLeod in her room and returned to the ballroom, getting the gong from Abdi on the way. He struck the gong three times. The music and the talk stopped as though a chill wind had blown all sound out of the room.

'Ladies and gentlemen,' Mark said, trying to keep his voice steady, 'I regret to have to inform you that a very terrible disaster has taken place. His Excellency the Governor has met with—has been murdered.'

There was a sound like a gust of wind striking a pine wood, and then a moment of stupefied silence. A scream followed, and a woman sagged to the floor. Some one caught her before she hit the boards.

'The police,' Mark continued, 'are now in charge. The Commissioner's instructions are that all guests, except those staying in the house, are to return home. They are to leave their names and addresses with a police officer who is stationed in the main hall. Guests staying in the house will go into the tea-room and wait there for further instructions.'

'Also,' he raised his voice, 'any one who saw H.E. this evening after he left the dining-room, whether at an interview or casually, or any person who has any information, however trivial, which might be of value to the police, is to go at once to the tea-room and not to leave the house until he has seen the police.'

3

An outer crust of calm had been restored to Government House an hour later. KALI askaris patrolled the grounds with fixed bayonets and kept all comers at bay. Automobiles had been turned back containing reporters from the daily newspaper, Marula residents filled with curiosity

and excitement, and an Indian undertaker who had heard
rumours in the bazaar and rattled up in a hearse, which
served also as his private car. He was very indignant at
being turned back. 'I early bird,' he exclaimed vehemently.
'I come catch worm. I make famous coffins, please.' Even
the offer of a percentage of profits on the job failed to win
over the sergeant on duty at the gate, and the Indian drove
sadly away. A small group of native idlers quickly collected
at the gate, drawn there mysteriously by the scent of
trouble that spread through the air like some highly volatile
gas. All through the night this silent crowd grew larger,
waiting vacuously for action.

Government House itself lay quiet in the aftermath of
sensation. The shrill and clattering guests were gone. But
an undercurrent of excitement ran through the rooms and
corridors. In the servants' quarters the entire staff, except
for the stately kingpin Abdi, was up and dressed. The
natives stood about in groups; Somalis, turbaned and
outwardly disdainful, saying little, but waiting alertly on
events; Wabenda chattering and animated, prognathous
jaws working double time and white teeth flashing in quick
conversation; Baganda smoking cigarettes and arguing
with fluent gestures; half-grown lads, the ubiquitous *totos*,
squatting round-eyed and amazed on their haunches, awed
by the sound of patrolling soldiers which came to their ears
from beyond the windows.

Already the African quarter of Chinyani, two miles
away, was buzzing with rumours. Already the news was
spreading, more, it seemed, by elemental than by human
agency, along dirt roads and winding paths deep into the
reserves, where blanket-clad natives slept around the
smouldering ashes of their fires. Shortly after midnight a
native servant on a farm thirty miles away told the news to
his white employer. Later in the night the tale spread along
the cultivated valleys and across the pastures of the
Wabenda country, and into other native reserves that lay
beyond. The news skipped swiftly across plain and bush

and forest, over Africa's own radio hook-up, evolved without benefit of science.

. . . . .

Seven people sat in the tea-room of Government House, waiting, for the most part in uneasy silence, for the Police Commissioner's instructions. Superintendent Vachell, after hearing Beaton's story, had the Governor's office to himself for the best part of an hour while Major Armitage personally led a KALI search-party through the grounds, with drawn revolvers, hoping momentarily to find the murderer crouching behind an ornamental shrub. He returned soon after midnight, empty-handed, and sat down purposefully in the leather arm-chair.

'Well, Vachell? What have you discovered?' The Commissioner still felt a little dramatic.

Vachell drew up a chair and sat astride of it, leaning his chin on his hands over the back. He stretched out his lanky legs, pulled a cigarette out of a tin on the desk, and lit it thoughtfully. He slowly thumbed through the leaves of his notebook, the cigarette held loosely between his lips.

'Well, chief,' he said at last, in a voice which retained a little of its native Canadian twang, 'I've got plenty, but I don't know what good it's going to do us, yet. The murderer hasn't left his visiting-card lying around. No hats on the bureau with the name on the band.'

'Quite, quite. You think it may have been a premeditated crime, eh? Most extraordinary. Dreadful.' Armitage's normal jerkiness was accentuated by worry. 'Understand this, Vachell. We've *got* to get the murderer, and get him quickly, whatever it costs, whatever it entails. I needn't explain that to you. If we fail, I shall have to resign, of course, and your position wouldn't be any better. The eyes of the world will be upon us, my boy; the eyes of the world.'

'Sure,' said Vachell. 'Looks like it's going to be a tough proposition. I've had no time to get the facts straightened out, so please pardon a disjointed kind of a report.' He found the place in his notebook and moved an ash-tray to the edge of the table.

'First of all, the body. It was seated in the swivel chair, torso slumped forward, face downward on the bureau. A piece of cord was looped around the neck, tied in a slip-knot. The doctor gave strangulation as the cause of death. Guess it didn't need a doctor to testify to that.

'From the position of the body it looked like H.E. had been telephoning when he was attacked. The other guy came up behind, slipped the noose around his neck, and pulled it tight. Then he hauled on the cord till the job was done. That would need speed, but not a lot of strength. Probably a woman could have done it as well as a man, physically. Sir Malcolm dropped the phone and fell forward, or maybe the murderer pushed him. There wasn't any sign of a struggle.

'That phone call may be important. If we can trace it, we should be able to fix the exact time of death. The supervisor down at the exchange is checking on that.

'Next, the cord. You'll see these windows have blinds as well as drapes. The cord came from that blind over there, on the window behind the bureau — the south window. The cord which works the blind has been cut near the root, and the cord around the Governor's throat fits. It was cut with a sharp knife. The blinds on both windows were drawn all the way down when I got here, and bcth windows were closed and locked. The catches can only be worked from the inside.

'Now for our old pals the fingerprints. The door handles are just a series of smudges. Aside from that, I couldn't see but three likely surfaces that would carry them — the telephone receiver, the whisky-glass on H.E.'s bureau, and the window catches. There's a good set of prints on the receiver and a whole bunch of them on the glass. Just as soon as they're developed I'll get around to identification. We should find Sir Malcolm's prints on both surfaces, of course.

'Now here's a funny thing. No prints showed up on either of the window catches. They're brass and they'd take a print nicely, and you have to handle them to lock the windows. Looks like they've been wiped clean on purpose.'

'May have been a house-boy,' commented the Commissioner, 'cleaning them.' He was chewing his lower lip and plainly feeling impatient.

'Maybe,' Vachell agreed, 'if the windows weren't opened tonight. But it's a hot evening and Sir Malcolm was working in here and—well, we'll be able to find that out.

'Now for the papers. I looked through that pile on the bureau as carefully as I could, though time was pretty short. There are four files stacked on his left, looks like they're waiting for attention. One more file was open on the blotter in front of him. There was a heap of opened mail, not a big one, within reach. And a tear-off pad used for making rough notes. There's nothing on it, but I found one of the torn-off sheets tucked away under the blotting-pad. It has some notes jotted down on it. I have it here: I'd like to turn it in as Exhibit A.'

He handed over a small square of paper to Major Armitage, who glanced at it, frowning. It read as follows:—

> *Memo.*
> 1. Cp rates on Un Pac and C.P.R. rail.
> 2. Est. for inc vet res.
> 3. African Equities.
> 4. Worm powders. B.

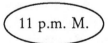

11 p.m. M.

'Well, nothing much there,' the Commissioner said, handing back the slip of paper. 'Go on, Vachell. Remember, every minute may count.' He was clearly fretting for action.

Vachell pocketed the memorandum and continued easily: 'Here's a list of the files on the bureau. The one he was using was M/662, Maji River Basin: Proposed Concession to Japanese Farm Industries, Ltd. It was open at a letter dated last June — that's nine months ago — from the Japanese consul, asking whether Government survey fees on the proposed concession could be paid over a period of ten years, in the event of the scheme coming to maturity.

'Now the files in the stack. Three dealt with the federation of Chania and Totseland: two of these were concerned with the railroad and one with a proposed federal legislative council. The remaining file was all about rinderpest quarantine; pretty technical stuff.

'One last item. There was an empty foolscap envelope, bearing air mail tabs and stamps and cancelled in Marula today, addressed to Sir Malcolm and marked "Private and Confidential", on the floor, under the chair. Postmarked London, E.C.2. Nothing in it. I can't see any letter that fits it lying around, but I guess it's not important.

'Then there's the question of how the murderer got in and out of the room. He couldn't have got *out* by either of the windows, because they were both locked on the inside. That door there, leading into the private secretary's office, was closed but not locked. The door beyond, from the secretary's room into the main hall, was locked and the key has been taken out of the lock.

'That door there'—he pointed to the exit into the passage—'was guarded all evening by an askari on duty. He's a KALI corporal called Machoka. Seems an intelligent chap. He swears he never left his post, and that's confirmed by the sentries outside the west entrance and by the sergeant in charge of the guard. Now he has some dope that may be important. He says he remembers everybody who passed through the door he was guarding this evening. He knows them all by name, too. Here's the list:

'The first man in to see Sir Malcolm after dinner, he says, was Mr Pallett, the Colonial Secretary. He left, and then

Mr Moon, the Secretary for Native Affairs, went in. After him the "big chief from the north" had a turn. That must be Sir Bertrand Flower, Governor of Totseland. This Machoka isn't so good on his times, but he says Sir Bertrand was the last visitor the Governor had. After that, Corporal Machoka is ready to swear by all his heathen gods — most likely he's a Christian, at that — that no one came in or went out by that door.

'Only one person came near the door, he says, between Sir Bertrand's departure and the time Mr Beaton discovered the crime. That was Mr Watson, the Director of Education. He came up a little time after Sir Bertrand left and knocked on the door. Machoka says he just opened it and looked inside. Then he closed it again and walked away. He didn't go in. No one else came along the passage at all until Mr Beaton showed up. That was at eleven-fifteen.

'So if this Machoka's on the level, we know something else — that the murderer didn't come out of that door, unless he was Sir Bertrand Flower, the last visitor.'

'Preposterous!' snapped Major Armitage. 'Confine yourself to legitimate possibilities, Vachell.'

Vachell turned over a page in his notebook without replying. 'That leaves us with quite a little problem on our hands,' he continued. 'How the murderer got out of the room. I had a word with the head boy, Abdi. Been a sort of major-domo around here for fifteen or twenty years, I understand. He says he was stationed in the main hall, right outside the door into the secretary's office, all evening. He says that no one went in or out of the secretary's room while he was on duty, except Mr Jeudwine. He seems like a smart chap. Just the same, I don't believe his evidence is rock-ribbed, because his job was to see guests in and out of the main entrance in proper style — hand them their hats and so on — so he couldn't have been giving his undivided attention to Mr Jeudwine's door. But we can't make much headway along that line until we know the approximate time of the killing. That's my next assignment — if you approve, sir.'

Vachell paused and lit another cigarette. Armitage was still frowning.

'Nothing much so far.' He took out a small cigar and clipped off the end. 'No clues at all, eh? Anything else, Vachell—anything to indicate—well, any—er—clues?'

Vachell grinned. 'I reckon it's pretty hard to tell what's a clue and what isn't, at this stage. Criminals don't make it that easy for the cops.

'There's one more thing I should mention, maybe. I went over the rest of the room as well as I could and found nothing. No sign of a search or a fight; books neatly stacked, curios the same—there's scads of these spears and native daggers lying around. But there's one thing that looks as though something on the bureau had been disturbed. This reading-lamp here.'

Vachell indicated a chromium-plated lamp with a bell-shaped shade, standing on the mahogany desk. It had a flexible joint so that the light could be thrown in any direction required.

'You see how it is — I haven't disturbed it any.'

Armitage eyed it suspiciously. 'Looks all right,' he said. 'Ordinary-looking lamp. What's wrong?'

'These lamps throw a concentrated beam,' Vachell answered. 'Normally you'd expect to find the beam directed on to the writing-pad in front of the guy at the bureau. You see how this shade is fixed? It's directing the light *away* from the desk—throwing it down on to the floor between the bureau and the door.'

Armitage grunted unenthusiastically. 'Anything else?'

'Just one more point. I had a good look outside the windows. The one on the west side of the room looks on to the driveway. The gravel driveway comes right up to the wall. One of the two KALI guards on duty at the west entrance stands within a few feet of that window and parades up and down outside of it all night. I figure no one could get in or out that way without being seen. The guard says no one tried.

'The window in the back of the bureau, the one that looks south, is different. There's a flower-bed right underneath it with quite a lot of junk in it—delphiniums, I guess, and cannas, and some small shrubs. Maybe enough cover for a man to shelter behind for a little, if no one was looking his way.

'You know we haven't had rain in a long while. It's due any day now. The soil is dried out. No chance of finding footprints, even if there were any to find. I had a look around with a strong flashlight and I couldn't get much, but I think there's been some one mussing up that bed recently. Tough break it's so dry; I can't say for certain. It might be just the gardener's hoe.

'I guess that's all at present, chief. The next step is to dope out the evening's schedule and see if we can fix the time Sir Malcolm was knocked off.'

Armitage pulled hard at his cigar. 'Yes, yes, Vachell, quite. But we aren't making much progress, are we? All that'—he waved his hand towards Vachell's notebook—'very thorough, of course, and all that, but where does it get us? We sit here talking while the fiend who perpetrated this outrage is getting away—clean away. We aren't *doing* anything. If we delay it may be too late. We ought to organise a search; rope in the railway people. . . .'

'Search for what, sir?' Vachell inquired, raising his eyebrows; 'that is, for whom? We'd be chasing fleas with a fishnet. For all we know, the murderer may be waiting across the way for us to go and interview him.'

'What? Here? Preposterous!' snapped the Commissioner. 'You're not suggesting that one of our senior civil servants strangled the King's representative, are you?' Major Armitage's brown eyes were wide with amazement behind his glasses. He looked more ludicrously like Groucho Marx than ever. 'No, no. This is the work of some maniac—one of these degenerate, crime-sodden swine from Chinyani, I shouldn't wonder. That's what you'll find. Drugs and drink and sedition—Chinyani's reeking with 'em. Some ex-jail-bird who boasted to his friends he could kill the Governor—by God, Vachell, if we don't catch him the country will never recover from the blow to our prestige!' He got up and strode round the room in his agitation.

'I wouldn't be surprised if this didn't lead to a native rising,' he continued. 'Trouble's been brewing under the surface for some time. This is just the sort of thing to touch it off. The consequences may be greater than we realize—unless we can act at once.'

'Just the same, chief,' Vachell said slowly, 'I've a hunch that this crime isn't the work of a native. There are several things—'

'Nonsense, Vachell, nonsense!' Armitage's face was getting flushed. 'You know as well as I do that native crime is on the increase. You know what they did to that wretched devil Jacobs, and his wife, only a month ago. A double murder, and the brute goes scot-free. I tell you...' He paused, pulled on his cigar, took a turn across the room, and turned decisively to Vachell.

'I'm going down to Chinyani to make a house-to-house search,' he announced. 'See if we can account for all the known criminals down there. Crane's in charge of that division, isn't he? Get him on the phone. Tell him to come up here immediately. He'll know where the most notorious of them hang out.'

Vachell dialled without speaking. The Governor had a private line. All other Government House telephones were connected by day with a switchboard operated by a native clerk. At night this line was normally plugged through to Jeudwine's office when he was using it, and to the main hall when he was not.

'Can't let this slide,' the Commissioner continued. 'Probably some dirty b——'s bragging down there now about his exploit.'

'Guess you're right, major,' Vachell answered. Armitage grunted. He hated being called 'major'.

'I'll stick around and grill the boys across the way,' his subordinate continued, 'if that's all right with you, sir. We've got to establish the time of the murder, if we can.'

'Quite so, quite so,' Armitage replied, picking up his khaki topee with a red police badge in the band. 'Some one must remain in charge here, of course. Report to me as soon as I get back.'

'How about taking one of the boys from the *Courier* along?' Vachell suggested. 'The editor was on the line just now. He's all burned up because the KALI wouldn't let his reporters in. If you take one along he'll get a good story on police activity—'

'Damned newspaper fellers!' barked the major, jerking open the door. 'Always butting in—well, all right, all right! Can't do any harm, I suppose. Tell him to meet me down at Chinyani, then.' A few minutes later Vachell saw the lights of a car shining on the window-pane and heard gravel popping against mudguards as his chief swung an official car into the drive and headed for the native village.

    .   .   .   .

Mr Pallett was annoyed. Two hours earlier he had been Colonial Secretary of Chania. Now, by a violent and unheralded promotion, he was Acting Governor. In him, suddenly, reposed the dignity and authority of the Crown. And his first experience was to be kept waiting for over an hour, without news or consultation, by a policeman.

He, and he alone, was now the supreme authority in Chania. It was his right and his duty to direct the progress of the investigation. He explained this, coldly and precisely, to Vachell, who stood in the doorway of the tea-room, offering apologies.

'I find it hard not to regard this behaviour as an insult to Sir Bertrand Flower,' Pallett continued. 'Sir Bertrand is a guest of Government House and has a right to expect civility, even in these distressing circumstances. Please inform Major Armitage that I wish to see him here.'

Pallett spoke with pedantic precision. He had the smooth, colourless face and bent shoulders of the life-long office worker. He prided himself on a balanced and judicial mind, an absolute discretion, and an encyclopædic knowledge of official procedure and constitutional problems. Hard work, an infallible memory, and an inner driving ambition had won him promotion over the heads of more brilliant and likeable men. Brilliant men took risks, and sooner or later risks got people into trouble. Pallett never got into trouble; or, at any rate, he had not done so since luck had secured him a job in the Secretariat, as a young man, and taken him out of native areas.

The air in the tea-room was heavy with smoke. Pallett and Sir Bertrand Flower occupied the divan. Jeudwine sat at the writing-desk, nursing a telephone. Watson, his face white and expressionless, skulked in a corner. Mark Beaton was leaning against the wall, smoking a pipe, and near him Moon sat upright on a chair, a book on his knee. Miss Brandeis lolled in a chair, a cigarette in her lips. Her beady eyes were fixed on Vachell. When he entered she jumped up in surprise and waved a greeting. They had met before in America, and recognized each other at once.

Vachell explained that he had been left with instructions to interview, in turn, all those in the tea-room. Pallett glowered.

'Major Armitage might have found it possible to conduct his own inquiries,' he said icily. 'But no doubt we have no alternative but to comply with his—ah—commands. Sir Bertrand, perhaps you would like to get this unpleasant ordeal over?'

Sir Bertrand's face looked old and grey. His cheeks were soggy, like the remnants of pricked balloons, his eyes pale and sunken. He was gnawing his lip and twisting knotted fingers in his hands. There was something about his appearance that suggested the crumbling ramparts of a ruin. Clearly the shock had upset him severely. He mumbled an affirmative reply and followed Vachell through the billiard-room and across the passage to the door of the Governor's office. There he stopped dead.

'In there?' he asked. 'Surely...that's where he was... it isn't decent. . . .'

Vachell swung the door open. 'It's the quietest place to talk, Sir Bertrand,' he said. 'I guess Mr Pallett will be moving in here tomorrow.' Flower walked in, hesitating, his eyes glued fearfully on the empty swivel chair behind the desk. He sat down abruptly, and remained perched uneasily on the edge of the shiny leather seat.

'Now, Sir Bertrand,' Vachell began briskly, 'I understand that you were with Sir Malcolm in this room after dinner tonight. What time was this?'

Flower shook his shoulders slightly, as if to pull himself together. He blew his nose, and settled in the chair.

'It must have been about ten-fifteen. I had a word with McLeod, poor fellow, just after dinner. I wanted to clear up one or two points before tomorrow's meeting—I am down here for a conference, as you may know—and Sir Malcolm said that he would be free about ten.'

'You didn't go at ten, however?'

'I rather expected that Sir Malcolm would have sent word when he was free. I waited, therefore, for about ten minutes or so, but no message came, so I walked along to the study and came in.'

'There was no one with Sir Malcolm when you went in?'

'No one.'

'And Sir Malcolm was seated at his bureau?'

'Yes.'

'Can you remember whether the window behind this bureau was open or closed?'

'That window there? I'm sure I don't remember.' Vachell rose and snapped up the blind so that the stars and the pale light of the young moon showed through the panes.

'Was the blind up or down?'

Sir Bertrand frowned and chewed his lip in thought. 'Now you mention it, I think the blind was up. Yes, it was. I remember looking out of the window once or twice, and seeing one or two cars arrive—or leave, I don't remember which.'

'Could you hear the noise of their motors?'

'Yes, yes, and now I remember—the window must have been open. I can recollect that a slight breeze was blowing and that now and then it disturbed some papers on McLeod's desk. They rustled. Yes, it was open.'

Vachell smiled. 'Thank you, Sir Bertrand. That may be a big help. You see, that window was closed, and locked, when the crime was discovered. What was the time when you quitted Sir Malcolm?'

'It was just after half-past ten. I looked at my watch directly I came out of the study, and decided to have a nightcap before going upstairs to my room to do some work.'

'Did you follow out that schedule?'

'Did I—? Oh, I see. Yes, I had a small whisky and went up to my room. I was drafting a dispatch when my personal boy rushed in with the terrible news. I came down at once to see if it was true.'

'You were in here talking to Sir Malcolm, then, from ten-fifteen to ten-thirty. No one disturbed you during that period?'

'No, we were not disturbed.'

'Now, there's another thing, Sir Bertrand. What was the subject of your conversation?'

Flower, his previous agitation under better control, frowned again, this time with annoyance.

'Really, Mr—ah—Vachell, I'm afraid I can't undertake to answer questions such as that. The subject of my discussion with Sir Malcolm can have no possible bearing on his murder, for one thing. And our conversation dealt with official, and therefore confidential, matters, for another.'

Vachell's expression did not change, but he spoke more crisply. 'I'm investigating a murder, Sir Bertrand,' he said. 'I'm not interested in nosing into State secrets. I'm interested in getting at facts. Most likely you were the last man to see Sir Malcolm alive, aside from his murderer. What Sir Malcolm was doing and saying a very short time—a few minutes, maybe—before his death may be very important. I'm asking for your help.'

Flower was evidently taken aback by the abrupt methods and evident sincerity of the young policeman. He was not used to being talked to like that.

'You are wasting your time, young man,' he said, 'but police methods in Chania are not my affair. You ask what my conference with Sir Malcolm was about. I will give you a brief summary, since you insist.

'You may be aware that the Governors' Conference was to open at ten o'clock tomorrow morning. Copies of the final agenda were only circulated this morning, and I observed that the most important matter, the discussion of a draft scheme for the amalgamation of the Chania and Totseland railways, was first on the list. There were several points connected with this proposal on which Sir Malcolm and I differed. I cannot go into the details, but I may say that the purpose of my interview tonight was to discuss these points in a general way, in the hope that some line of potential agreement might suggest itself which could—ah —be followed up in the conference in the morning.'

'Thanks, Sir Bertrand. And did you figure out some sort of a compromise?'

Sir Bertrand seemed uncertain whether to resent this question or not. He looked annoyed, but answered civilly. 'There is—ah—a considerable divergence between the management policies of the Chania and Totseland railways, both as regards capital valuation and rating policy. I am afraid that these differences are not so lightly settled. As I told Sir Malcolm — and I have repeated it again and again

— we *cannot* have amalgamation until a common rating policy has been agreed, and we *cannot* agree on a rating policy so long as Chania insists, for the most ill-founded political reasons, in charging high rates on imported necessities in order to subsidize farm exports by giving them uneconomically low rates. In Totseland our policy is the reverse of Chania's. We wish to raise the standard of living of the natives by giving low rates on cheap imports — cotton piece goods, bicycles, and so on — and let the exports stand on their own feet. But all this is beside the point,' Sir Bertrand added, annoyed at having been led on to a subject evidently much in his mind. 'Railway rates have nothing to do with my poor colleague's murder. Are there are more questions? If not...'

'Just one, I think, Sir Bertrand, if you'll permit me,' Vachell said. He had been scribbling hard in his notebook. 'Was your talk limited to this railway business, or did other matters come under fire? What about this question of a land grant to the Japanese?'

Sir Bertrand looked surprised. 'That concession in the Maji Valley? No, that was nothing to do with me. It is entirely a Chania matter, and Chania politics are not my affair, I'm glad to say. No, it is not on the conference agenda at all.'

'Are you sure of that?' Vachell added.

Sir Bertrand showed renewed signs of impatience. 'I am not in the habit of inventing my statements,' he said stiffly, 'and, in any case, I do not see how these questions...'

Vachell quickly snapped his notebook shut, thanked the Totseland Governor, and ushered him through the door.

4

Mr Pallett was the next to be questioned. He started to protest again, but was cut short by the telephone. The G.P.O. supervisor had, on Vachell's instructions, checked all outgoing calls from the Governor's private line. There was no way by which the time or source of incoming calls could be traced. The last outgoing call was at 4.30 p.m. There had been nothing between 10.30 and 11.30 p.m., and no long-distance calls to or from Government House that evening.

'Looks like Sir Malcolm was answering an incoming call when he was bumped,' Vachell remarked as he replaced the receiver. 'Now, sir, did you call the Governor on his private wire any time tonight?'

Pallett sat polishing his pince-nez, cold and disgruntled. The situation was wrong, somehow, but he was at a loss how to right it. There was no dignity about it all.

'No, I did not,' he replied, his tones precise as ever. 'I had an interview with His Excellency immediately after dinner, and no necessity to consult him subsequently arose. Our discussion was over by nine-thirty or there-abouts, and shortly afterwards I left to attend to some business at the Secretariat. I remained there until about a quarter to eleven, and then returned home.'

'Your discussion dealt with this conference slated for tomorrow morning?'

'It did; yes.'

'Now, did Sir Malcolm seem to have anything on his mind, Mr Pallett? Anything unusual that wasn't run-of-the-mill routine stuff?'

Vachell's blue eyes were fixed steadily on Pallett's pale face. He noticed a slight hesitation and sensed that the Colonial Secretary, Acting Governor now, was about to utter the word most familiar to him of all words, the word 'no'.

'Please think carefully, sir,' he added quickly. 'Some casual remark that doesn't seem to mean anything might give us a valuable line. We need all the help we can get.'

His words had some effect on Pallett. The Acting Governor's eyes swung to the empty swivel chair. Vachell could follow his thoughts. After all, it was murder.

'I have nothing much to contribute,' Pallett finally said, his forehead puckered in a little frown. 'But His Excellency made a remark to me this evening which, perhaps, in the peculiar circumstances, I should repeat to you. On the strict understanding, of course, that you treat this information as confidential.' He cleared his throat.

'Shoot, sir,' Vachell said.

'We were discussing tomorrow's agenda, on which the matter of the federation of Chania and Totseland—ah—figures largely. Without giving away official secrets, I think I can say that the question of railway amalgamation was—ah—a potential stumbling-block to immediate agreement.'

The corners of Vachell's mouth twitched. 'The two Governors were squaring off over railroad rating policy, and ready for the bell. I got that, sir. Go ahead.'

'Quite so, quite so,' Pallett said. 'Though that is hardly—ah—a suitable way to express—however. When His Excellency summoned me to his office, after dinner, he told me that he had received certain information by air mail this afternoon which might have a very important bearing on the discussion on railway rating policy which he anticipated during the conference.

'I must confess I was surprised, as nothing of the sort had come through the Secretariat, and I was not aware that any new information was expected. He added that he did not wish to make use of these new facts, whatever they were, unless he was compelled to do so by the conference reaching a deadlock. In fact, his attitude struck me as altogether—ah—unexpected. He used a peculiar phrase, for instance, in connexion with this information he had received. "It's stinking fish," he said—he had the letter in his hand. "If I have to bring it into the open it will lift the Colonial Office out of their chairs." Sir Malcolm was—ah—forceful in his expressions. He added that he would make every effort to reach agreement without using this information, and that, if he succeeded, he would burn the letter.'

Vachell was writing vigorously. 'Fine, Mr Pallett,' he said. 'Now we're getting somewheres. He didn't tip you off as to where this dynamite came from?'

'I've repeated to you all the information he gave me.'

'But you understood that it was tied up somehow with railroad rates?'

'Yes, distinctly. I assumed that he had secured some new argument in favour of the policy he advocated, perhaps from some expert in England. He had gone to great trouble to prepare a strong case. His Excellency was indefatigable —ah—even ruthless, when engaged in the pursuit of one of his ideas.'

Vachell glanced quickly at the Acting Governor. There seemed to be an undertone of asperity in the remark.

'Would you recognize this letter again?'

Pallett shrugged. 'It was an ordinary typed letter, so far as I could see. I do not suppose that I should.'

Vachell scratched his nose with his pencil and glanced towards the safe which stood in a corner of the room.

'See here, Mr Pallett,' he said, 'that letter sounds pretty important. It may give us a real lead. There was no letter dealing with rates on Sir Malcolm's bureau. Seems to me he'd be pretty certain to put a letter as important as that into his safe. Now, I'd like to search that safe. Who, besides Sir Malcolm, has a key?'

Pallett stood again on his official dignity. It was quite impossible, he said, to allow such a thing. No one had a right to open that safe, with the exception of the Acting Governor. The regulations could not be waived.

Vachell took a chance and was brusque and downright,

pretty nearly rude. American methods, he reflected, not British, and in any case Pallett was Acting Governor and could have him fired. Rather to Vachell's surprise, Pallett crumpled up, after a display of official offended dignity. Vachell suspected that he had hit upon the real reason why Pallett had not yet been appointed to a junior colonial governorship, in spite of his successful career and reputation for industry and discretion. He couldn't stand up to open opposition, to bullying. Vachell knew he could never have handled a man like Sir Malcolm McLeod in that way.

Only two people besides the Governor knew the combination of the safe, it transpired: the Colonial Secretary and the private secretary. Pallett insisted on summoning Jeudwine to be present at the event. Jeudwine seemed sober now. His face was pale and a little blotchy, but no longer glistening.

'Of course, sir,' he said to Pallett, 'you know what's in the safe. There's a very strict rule about any one else having access to it, and even in a case like this...'

'Quite so, quite so, Jeudwine,' Pallett interrupted, while the secretary twiddled the combination; 'Mr Vachell is to remain strictly an onlooker. You will examine the contents of the safe, to see if this particular letter, which only arrived today, has been deposited.' The heavy door swung open, revealing neatly stacked buff files and a series of pigeon-holes full of papers.

'When did you last take a look at this safe, Mr Jeudwine?' Vachell asked.

'A couple of days ago. I put away some files which had been in use.'

'Can you see any evidence that it's been disturbed since then?'

Jeudwine peered about inside through his thick lenses. 'No, I can't; but, of course, there's nothing to show that it hasn't. H.E. may have been poking about in it...wait a moment. Yes, he must have been. This book wasn't here when I last looked, because it's sitting on top of H.E.'s personal accounts, and I put last month's statement in when I opened the safe.'

He took out a small notebook with a battered red leather cover. It looked old and severely used.

'Have you ever seen it before?' Vachell was looking over Jeudwine's shoulder.

'No, I don't think so.' The secretary held it close to his glasses and peered myopically at its pages. The leaves fluttered over. 'It seems to be a diary, written up ... Hello! Nineteen-sixteen, apparently. It's not H.E.'s writing.' Vachell stretched out his hand and took the little book.

'I guess I'll take a look at that,' he said. Pallett glared, and spoke sharply. 'Mr Vachell! *I* am going to conduct this search. You have no authority to abstract any of the contents of this safe. I shall speak to Major Armitage.' It was obvious that he dared not tell Vachell to replace the diary for fear that the policeman would refuse point-blank.

'Okay,' Vachell said cheerfully. He threw the diary on to the Governor's desk and left it lying under the reading-lamp. 'We'll let it lie until the chief returns. Any other finds?'

Pallett, his lips compressed, watched Jeudwine methodically hunting through the papers. The search took time, but no one spoke. Vachell lounged against the desk, hands in pockets, eyes fixed on Jeudwine's fingers. The tramp of the KALI guard outside the windows sounded at regular intervals through the room. Pallett stood by, something tense and unrelaxed in his attitude. His face was pale and tiny beads of perspiration had appeared on his forehead. Once Vachell saw him glance quickly over his shoulder at the empty swivel chair, sensed the current of his thoughts —the recollection of ghastly, staring eyes, blue tortured flesh, the ugly travesty of the chief's fine face.

Jeudwine lifted his hunched shoulders and withdrew his face from the safe, like a lizard pulling back its scaly head after darting at a fly. 'I can't see any sign of the letter you mentioned,' he said. 'Everything seems in order, though of course I can't be certain. I've got a list of all the files that should be in the safe, and if you like I can check that.'

'A good suggestion,' Pallett said crisply. 'That should be done in any event. I should feel easier in my mind if we could make absolutely certain that no official papers were missing.' Jeudwine fetched a typewritten list from his own office and began to check all the files in the safe methodically.

'I must trouble you with a few more questions, sir, I'm afraid.' Vachell still kept up the brusque tone. Pallett seemed in two minds as to his response. Caution prevailed, and he sat down in the arm-chair.

'There were five files on Sir Malcolm's bureau,' the policeman continued. He lounged against the desk and stared down at Pallett's face. It reminded him faintly of a melon. 'Three of them dealt with this federation business. That was the first and biggest subject on the agenda for tomorrow's meeting?'

Pallett nodded.

'One dealt with stock diseases: rinderpest quarantine. Was that slated for discussion also?'

'Yes, it was. The question of rinderpest quarantine is the next item on the agenda. Some—ah—adjustments are necessary to bring the policies pursued by the veterinary departments of the two countries into—ah—alignment.'

'And the Japanese concession?'

Pallett looked startled and annoyed. 'I really fail to see what that has to do with this terrible crime,' he snapped, 'nor do I consider that these questions of high policy are matters for the police. . . .'

'Let me explain, sir.' Vachell was getting impatient, but tried to conceal it. It was terrible, questioning Governors and Acting Governors. 'The files which I found on that bureau covered three subjects—federation, stock diseases, and the Japanese concession. Two of these subjects were fresh meat. They were coming up at this meeting tomorrow. The third subject doesn't seem to be urgent at all. It wasn't on the agenda. Yet it looks like it was the subject Sir Malcolm was studying at the time he was bumped. There may be a slight discrepancy there which I have to check. Now, do you know of any reason why H.E. should study a nine-month-old letter about survey fees on the Maji River section, when he was pretty well sewn up with other work that wouldn't wait?'

Pallett considered, his flat, broad face expressionless, and then shook his head. 'I see your point, Vachell. No, there's no reason that I know of why His Excellency should have perused that file at the present juncture. About a week ago a dispatch from the Secretary of State instructed this Government to take no further steps pending developments at home. I understand that the Premier of South Africa has made representations, and no doubt His Majesty's Government feel that the point of view of the self-governing Dominions should—ah—be taken into consideration.'

'So the matter was dropped?'

'Temporarily, yes. Deferred, perhaps, would be more accurate. You must understand that this information is entirely confidential, Mr Vachell. It it not politic to allow details of this sort to become public property, at the present juncture.'

Vachell sighed and yielded to the temptation to light another cigarette. He had always marvelled at the official mind. This specimen seemed almost too good to be true. He extracted a piece of paper from his notebook and inquired casually:

'There's been some opposition, I understand, to this Jap project.'

Jeudwine, checking the list of the safe's contents against his typed list, turned round and laughed.

'Trust the elected members for that,' he said. 'They'd oppose the millennium if the Government tried to introduce it. You should hear Popple on the subject.'

'Did Mr Popple know that the Jap project had been passed up?'

'Nobody knew, besides Sir Malcolm and myself,' Pallett replied. 'And Jeudwine, of course. But surely you don't think that Popple...'

'I'm not speculating yet,' Vachell interrupted. 'I'm just trying to get information.'

He smoothed out the little slip of paper he had been twiddling in his fingers. 'This was found on Sir Malcolm's bureau,' he said. 'It's his writing, isn't it?' Jeudwine took the paper and raised it close to his face to bring it within the focus of his thick lenses. 'Perhaps you gentlemen could decipher it for me,' Vachell asked.

'"1.—Cp rates on Un Pac and C.P.R. rail." That's pretty clear. Un Pac means Union Pacific, I guess. "2.—Est. for inc vet res." That's shorthand for increased veterinary research, isn't it?' Pallett said, 'Undoubtedly.' Vachell continued: '"3.—African Equities." Either of you know what that is?' Neither of them did.

'Funny,' Jeudwine commented. 'I'm familiar with his stocks, but I never heard of that one. Probably he jotted it down as something to be looked into. Some one may have put him on to it. Sir Bertrand Flower, very likely. His P.S. tells me he's a great one for dabbling in the market.'

Vachell continued to read from the paper. '"4.—Worm powders. B." A less official note there.'

'Hannibal,' Jeudwine vouchsafed. 'His dog. H.E. mentioned yesterday he wanted a dose. I expect he was going to tell Beaton to get the powders tomorrow.'

A sudden silence oppressed the three men in possession of the dead Governor's study. Hannibal's powders, one of the murdered man's last thoughts on earth; his affection for the dachshund, how he used to whistle it to his heels every morning when he went for his daily ride in the hills; the dog's cushion, spattered with red hairs, in the corner of the room. . . . Vachell's even-toned voice continued: 'Then there's one more note. "11 p.m. M.", ringed with pencil.'

There was a silence. 'Well?'

Pallett ran his fingers down the creases of his trousers. 'I expect he wanted to see Mark Beaton then. Or had arranged for Beaton to fetch him back to the ballroom.' His voice sounded tight and strained.

'Not a very good invention, Mr Pallett,' Vachell said. 'B stands for Beaton, when he's to buy worm powders. M for Mark at eleven p.m. That doesn't make sense. You'd better tell me who it is.'

Pallett looked up angrily, and rose from his chair. 'Young man, are you trying to give me orders?' he said heatedly. 'You will kindly remember whom you are addressing! You have wasted enough of my time. Kindly tell Major Armitage that I wish to see him, immediately he returns, at my house.' He stalked towards the door hurriedly. But Vachell hadn't quite finished with him.

'Pardon me, Mr Pallett,' he said. 'Just one more question. You left the Secretariat around ten-forty-five tonight, you said, and you went back home. Now, what caused you to return to Government House at eleven-fifteen, at the time the body was being discovered?'

Pallett swung round, his pince-nez quivering precariously, puffy face like putty, eyes hard as stone. 'Mr Vachell, I dislike your tone, I dislike your manner, I have no belief in your efficiency. Major Armitage shall hear of your impudence. I decline to make myself answerable for my actions to his junior subordinates. Good evening.' The door slammed behind his back.

5

Jeudwine watched the Acting Governor go, smiling. He had a superior sort of smile that was not endearing. Few of his mannerisms were attractive, if it came to that. He gave the impression of dwelling apart with thoughts profounder than those of ordinary men. People said that he was clever, in the tone of voice Englishmen used when they refer to cleverness as a social blemish, like halitosis.

'Now, I wonder what's eating that guy,' Vachell muttered, half aloud, as the door banged shut. 'He certainly isn't too anxious to help along the investigation.'

'For that type of official,' Jeudwine remarked, 'there is no mortification of the spirit so horrible as to take orders from a subordinate.'

'He knew who M. is.'

Jeudwine laughed, a barely audible sound, like the chuckle appropriate to a chameleon. 'So would you, if policemen kept in touch with elementary gossip. Didn't you recognize the symptoms—the loyal English gentleman defending the good name of a colleague's wife? Though "good" is hardly the adjective I'd use.'

The secretary's tone was shot through with malice, like the glint of metal thread in a costly fabric.

'Would you care to enlighten an ignorant cop, Mr Jeudwine?'

'It's Marula's choicest piece of scandal. I can't think how you've avoided hearing it long ago. You policemen must lead very pure lives.'

'I'm waiting to have the facts of life revealed to me.'

'What about *de mortuis*, and all that? It isn't done to talk about a dead Governor's affairs with a lady—even a lady with the morals and decency of a—' Jeudwine checked himself; his voice had risen several keys. 'Oh, well, you'll find plenty of people ready to tell you. M for Maisie. Even a policeman would know that she's been carrying on a notorious affair with H.E. for months. And that H.E. was crazy about her. And that the injured husband was being watched by all the town to see what action he was going to take—a sort of Public Enigma Number One. You police-men do have to be told a lot.'

Jeudwine slouched towards the door. There was evil in his tone, a hint of something festering and unhealthy.

'One moment, Mr Jeudwine.' Vachell's voice was sharp.

'Questions first, please.'

Jeudwine hesitated and then came back. He sat down in the chair, looking hunched and ill. 'I'd be delighted further to enlarge your field of knowledge,' he said.

Vachell asked about his movements that evening. He had retired to his office, he said, directly after dinner. Shortly afterwards the Governor had told him to fetch the Secretary for Native Affairs, Moon, for an interview. Jeudwine delivered the message on the lawn and returned to his office. A little after 10.30 the Governor had buzzed and asked for a whisky-and-soda. Decanters and glasses were kept in a cupboard in the secretary's room. Jeudwine took the drink in immediately. The Governor had been working on the federation question, studying files brought up that morning from the Secretariat.

Jeudwine returned to his office after taking in the whisky, and five or ten minutes later Moon rang up from his house to say he'd left two files behind him in the washroom, and to ask the secretary to send them along right away. Jeudwine left his room immediately and found the files in the cloakroom. He saw Abdi in the hall and said: 'See that nobody enters my office while I find someone to take these.' He decided to send the native driver who was on duty with one of the Government House cars. He found the driver lounging about just outside the main door, gave him the files with suitable instructions, and returned to his room within five minutes.

Then, the secretary continued, he decided to call it a day. He tidied up his papers and knocked at Sir Malcolm's door. There was no reply, so he concluded that his chief had gone. He didn't look in, but quitted his office and locked the door behind him, taking the key. This, he said, was between ten and five to eleven. He went straight to the buffet and had a drink with the Director of Agriculture; he was still there when Beaton discovered the crime.

Vachell digested this story in silence for a little while, strolling about the room, his hands deep in his pockets.

Jeudwine wiped his glasses again. There were beads of perspiration on his pale, unhealthy face, shining in the light of the reading-lamp above his head.

'Let's get this straight,' Vachell said. 'First. You're certain that Sir Malcolm was alone when you took in his drink around ten-thirty?'

'As far as I could see. I didn't look under the couch or behind the curtains, if that's what you mean.'

'You heard no sounds from H.E.'s room between ten-thirty and five to eleven, when you left?'

'If you applied your detective skill to that door, you'd see it was a thick teak object, very well fitted, and designed to eliminate noise. The walls are sound-proof.'

'Are you certain you weren't away from your office more than five minutes when you sent off Mr Moon's files?'

'Have I got to repeat everything I say?' Jeudwine asked, more in pity than annoyance. 'You policemen seem to be remarkably slow in the uptake. That was what I said. It was less than five minutes.'

Vachell sat down on the desk, cocking one leg over the corner, and lit a cigarette.

'We like to get things straightened out properly, Mr Jeudwine,' he replied equably. 'That five minutes may be important. How good a watch did Abdi keep on that door, do you suppose?'

'Abdi's the most reliable man in the house. If he said no one went in or out, no one did. Somalis have eyes in the back of their heads.'

'And you locked the door of your office behind you when you left. You're certain no one else had a key?'

'Absolutely—except Abdi. He's got a master-key of all the doors. I suppose it's possible that some one might have had a key made. I'm told these things can be done from wax impressions.'

'Did anybody visit you in your office here this evening?'

'No, they didn't. I was there for the purpose of working,

strange as it may seem—though, of course, I wouldn't expect a settler to believe anything so far-fetched. I wasn't having an at home for social callers.'

Vachell took no notice of his irritable tone. 'Did you know about this date Sir Malcolm had with Mrs Watson at eleven p.m.?' he asked.

'No, I didn't. But then I never did.'

Jeudwine laughed again, silently. 'I told you they were having an affair. They couldn't do that without meeting, very well, could they? It wasn't a union of twin spirits; on the contrary, entirely corporeal, I should say.'

Vachell continued to pace up and down. He walked to the window behind the desk and looked out. A car was coming up the drive; Armitage returning, no doubt. The head-lamps shone into Vachell's eyes. An idea struck him. He turned quickly to Jeudwine.

'Were there any automobiles parked outside this window tonight?'

'Yes, there was a rank all the way along, from the main entrance to the corner of the wall.'

'There'd be a car parked right opposite here, then, just across the flower-bed?'

'I suppose so. Somewhere there, anyway. Why?'

Vachell didn't answer. The line of cars, he thought, must have formed a perfect screen in front of the study window. The murderer could have climbed in with no risk of being spotted from the drive.

The Police Commissioner's car came to rest opposite the west entrance. The next ten minutes were like a minor eruption. Armitage was triumphant, a little too triumphant, over his search. A Swahili who was suspected of at least two murders, who'd once been employed (he'd been dismissed) at Government House, and who was believed to belong to a Chinyani underworld gang who specialized in housebreaking, was found to be missing from his home. The police kept a fairly close eye on him; and he had been there two days before. There was a mystery about where he had gone. No one knew, or would say. The whole police force was trying to round him up. Wireless messages had already been dispatched to outlying police stations. Armitage was convinced that he had found his man.

.   .   .   .   .

Watson and Moon were still waiting in the tea-room; and neither of them was pleased. It was nearly 2 a.m. Olivia Brandeis had gone to sleep in her chair. Mark Beaton was wondering distractedly how he could help Marvin McLeod. They were all in a bad temper. Armitage barked at his subordinate to finish his damned inquisition quickly and let Miss Brandeis go to bed at once. Vachell opened the tea-room door for her and, on a sudden impulse, asked her to ride with him at seven o'clock the same morning. He had one fixed habit—an hour's ride every day before breakfast. He tried to keep to this, no matter what was going on. It cleared his brain, gave him a chance to sort out ideas. And he wanted to put some questions to Miss Brandeis, too. He had a great respect for her brains. She was surprised, but agreed to borrow a Government House pony and meet him on the polo ground.

Finally Armitage went off to report to Pallett, after ordering his subordinate to be on duty at headquarters the next morning at 9 a.m.

Vachell ushered Watson and Moon into the closely guarded Governor's study, apologizing for the long delay.

'You had some information you wanted to give me, Mr Watson?' he asked.

Watson's face looked haggard in the indifferent light. Pale skin tightly stretched, long sharp features; the face of an ascetic. Yet the crinkles round the eyes gave it a more human look. An intelligent type, Vachell thought. Then he remembered a stray remark he had heard; that Watson's face was his greatest asset. That he looked more intelligent than he was, and that a fine expression concealed a second-rate ability; something of that sort. In any case, he looked the wrong kind of husband for a stupid and promiscuous wife.

'I don't know if it's of much importance,' Watson replied. He spoke slowly, in a measured voice. 'But, as you wished to see every one who had spoken to Sir Malcolm this evening, I thought I had better remain. Though, as a matter of fact, I didn't actually speak to him.'

'I'd like the story, Mr Watson.'

'It's a brief one. I was anxious to have a few words with His Excellency this evening on a personal matter, so at about a quarter to eleven I came along to this office and knocked at the door. I had not made an appointment. I could hear no reply, so I knocked again and then half opened the door to see if Sir Malcolm was there. He was at his desk, telephoning. I closed the door at once and looked at my watch in the passage light. It was exactly ten-forty-eight. I went straight back to the ballroom. That's all. I wouldn't have mentioned such a trivial incident, were it not that I thought it might help you to fix the time of death.'

Vachell nodded. 'Thanks, professor. It sure does. You're positive about the time?'

'My watch is very reliable. I know it registered ten-forty-eight just after I looked into H.E.'s room.'

'Could you hear anything Sir Malcolm said?'

'I only heard him speak a few words into the receiver. I think he was just getting his number. I heard him say, "Hello! Hello! is that—" and then give some number. Then I closed the door.'

'You didn't catch the number?'

'No, I'm afraid not.'

'But if you're sure it was a number he was trying to get—it was an outgoing call, in fact?'

Watson nodded. 'I think so. It sounded like it.'

'No one else was in the room?'

'I couldn't see any one. Of course I didn't go in.'

'Was the window blind up or down?'

Watson frowned and thought. 'I'm afraid I don't remember. I didn't notice. I only just glanced in.'

'Well, thanks, Mr Watson,' Vachell said. 'That may be very helpful. You didn't come back to try to see Sir Malcolm later, by the way?'

Watson shook his head. 'No; I met my wife in the ballroom and she agreed—she said she wanted to go home. She wasn't feeling very well. So we left immediately afterwards—that must have been just on eleven—and I ran her home. Then I decided to come back to Government House on the chance that Sir Malcolm could see me before the party broke up. I got back about eleven-thirty, just after the tragedy had been discovered. When I heard what had happened, I decided to wait and give my quota of information, for what it's worth.'

Vachell thanked him again, and watched him go with a speculative mind. He wondered what business Watson had wanted to discuss so urgently that he had returned to Government House at 11.30 at night to do it.

The Secretary for Native Affairs had taken possession of the leather arm-chair and was turning over the pages of a book he had brought with him from the tea-room. When Watson left he put it down, relit a pipe, and looked inquiringly at his questioner.

Vachell studied his face. Leathery, hard-bitten, the face of a man of action—little of the sensitive flexibility evident in Watson's expression; determination, obstinacy rather, seemed to underlie the clear-cut, somewhat heavy features, and pride to rest behind the deep-set eyes. Not a stupid face, however; the face of a self-assured and decisive man. Vachell knew that Moon's successful career had been of his own making, owing little to luck and none to patronage. Few men in the colonial service, probably, knew more of native customs and languages, had a better understanding of native psychology. Anthropological journals had published his studies of tribal life, although he had had no scientific training. A self-made man, within the limits of his rigid and formalized profession.

'Guess you're last on the list,' Vachell said. 'You know

I'm checking on everybody who saw ·Sir Malcolm after dinner tonight. When did you have your interview, and why?'

Moon replied economically, his voice low and even. 'H.E. wanted to clear up a final point about safeguarding native interests in the Chania-Totseland federation scheme,' he said. 'The Colonial Office had queried one paragraph in H.E.'s last dispatch. Jeudwine fetched me at a quarter to ten and I stayed with Sir Malcolm for about fifteen minutes. I returned to the dance to fulfil a few social obligations, and escaped about ten-thirty. I worked at home for about an hour, when Beaton rang up with the news and asked me to come up to Government House. I got here in ten minutes and waited in the tea-room for nearly three hours. You fellows don't hurry yourselves, do you? Anything more?'

'Did any one see you return to your home?'

'Checking alibis, Mr Vachell? I'm afraid mine isn't water-tight. My boy was up when I got back. He brought me a whisky-and-soda. That must have been at about twenty to eleven. But I'm afraid I'm a bit vague about times.'

'It's just a matter of routine, Mr Moon. There was nothing in your talk with Sir Malcolm to indicate anything unusual—any reference to an important letter he'd received by today's air mail, for instance?'

Moon shook his head. 'Nothing at all. We stuck to native policy. He didn't mention any letter.'

'What about the files you left behind in the men's washroom?'

'Files? Oh, that's right. I brought up a couple of files which I thought H.E. might want to see. But he didn't, and I left them behind in the cloakroom, where I'd put them before dinner. I remembered them as soon as I reached home, and telephoned to Jeudwine to send them along by messenger.'

'What time was it when you telephoned to Mr Jeudwine?'

Moon shook his head. 'I don't know exactly, I'm afraid. I discovered I'd forgotten the files as soon as I got to my study. That would make it about a quarter to eleven, I should think, or a little before.'

Vachell jotted down a note in his book and struck off on a different line.

'I want to ask your advice, as an expert on native customs and psychology, and all that stuff. Sir Malcolm was strangled, as you know, with a cord cut from the blind on the window behind his back. There was no struggle. Now, do you think it likely that a native did the job?'

Moon drew thoughtfully on his pipe. 'It's possible, of course,' he answered. 'Anything's possible, especially in Africa. Say probable, and I'd answer no. Strangling isn't a usual African method of disposing of enemies, although it's not unknown. There was a case of a native strangling an old woman, a European, in Kenya not long ago, I remember. But poisoning, spearing, and stabbing are far more common methods. Smothering is a recognized way of killing witches, for magical reasons generally. But strangling, as a rule, no.'

'That's what I thought,' Vachell agreed.

'Another thing against it's being a native,' Moon went on, 'is that, as of course you've observed, there's quite a good collection of native daggers and swords lying about loose. I collected one or two of those myself on the western frontier twenty years ago. Supposing a native burst in, ready to kill, but apparently unarmed—that's your theory, I take it. Wouldn't he be more likely to seize a sword or dagger, weapons instinctively familiar to him, than to cut off a length of cord from a blind—a thing in itself entirely novel to the ordinary native—knot it into a noose, and do the job in an unfamiliar way? If you look at one of those daggers you'll see they're pretty well designed for a murder, and they're lying ready to hand.'

Vachell walked over to a revolving bookcase by the wall and examined a short, heavy dagger with a clumsily worked iron handle which lay on its top. Its blade was encased in a thick leather sheath. He felt the point; it was sharp as a splinter of broken glass.

'The Timburu use them for throwing,' Moon said, 'or used to. They were wonderful shots, if you can call it that. I can't help feeling a native would be more inclined to grab one of those than to cut a piece of cord off the blind.' He knocked out his pipe in an ash-tray on the desk. Vachell came back to the desk and extracted another cigarette from the tin.

'That makes sense,' he said. 'But I guess some of these detribalized natives who've lived with Europeans might have heard about strangling and be pretty rusty on their dagger-throwing.'

'That's quite true,' Moon agreed. 'I dare say they've even seen strangling practised on the movies. As a method of education, if you can call it that, a night at the cinema equals a cycle of my colleague Watson's efforts in the mission schools. That's why I said it's not impossible that the murderer might be a native.'

Vachell nodded thoughtfully. Moon had struck a topic that interested him and he seemed anxious to talk.

'I've been thinking over the situation from my point of view, Mr Vachell,' he said. 'Naturally, this is going to have repercussions in the native reserves. Rumours and false-hoods may grow out of it, and I'm a bit afraid that it may lead to trouble. Especially at the present time.'

'How's that?' Vachell asked. 'Anything wrong at present?'

'Well, things are more unsettled just now than they've been for a long time. There's been a drought, as you know. Droughts mean hardship, and hardship brings discontent. That's a universal African rule. And discontent, anywhere in the world, generally gets vented on authority. But natives need some special grievance on which to focus their discontent. Generally it has to be something that reaches down into the roots of their tribal beliefs. I think they've found it this time in the Wabenda witchcraft case.'

Vachell's attention was quickly aroused. He sat down on the settee, legs sprawling, and massaged one ear-lobe between finger and thumb, a trick of his when he was concentrating.

He hadn't forgotten the case. It was one of the first he'd had to handle as newly appointed head of the C.I.D. The Wabenda, among whom witchcraft was more strongly entrenched than among most Chania tribes, had put to death an old woman, who, they alleged, was a witch. The woman had stood trial before the elders and chiefs of the tribe, had been subjected to a poison ordeal, and found guilty of causing the death of one of the head chief's wives and the deformity of two of his children. Then, following th custom of the tribe, she had been executed, in a slow and painful manner. Pinned to the ground with spears, but not killed, she had suffered the torments of thirst, sun, and the bites of soldier ants. As life ebbed the vultures had dropped down to her to pick at still faintly seeing eyes and tear at not yet nerveless entrails. It was a horrible death, but meted out after due trial, and for the most anti-social crime in the Wabenda calendar.

The chiefs and elders were put on trial for the murder of the old witch. Forty-five of them appeared in the dock—a special dock built for the occasion. They did not deny that the witch had died under their instructions. They claimed that in ordering her death they were protecting the tribe from sorcery, in accordance with their obligations and traditions. They were found guilty and condemned to death. There was no other alternative under British law; the judges who pronounced sentence did so with reluctance and disquiet.

The Government was in an awkward position. It could not, obviously, execute forty-five respectable old men, many of them appointed to authority and trusted by the Government, who had acted in good faith and according to the customs of their fathers. In the end it had compromised. Thirty-four of the elders had been reprieved and pardoned. Ten had been reprieved and sentenced to terms of imprisonment. In one case, that of the senior chief who had supervised the execution, the death sentence had been allowed to stand.

The case was not yet over. The sentenced chief, M'bola, had appealed to the Supreme Court, lost, and finally appealed to the Privy Council. Feeling in native areas ran high. Agitators had seized upon the case as an example of the tyranny and brutality of British rule. Administrators feared serious trouble should the death sentence be carried out.

All this was familiar to Vachell, as indeed to every European in the colony.

'What I'm afraid of,' Moon continued, 'is this. You probably know that one or two hot-heads among the Wabenda have threatened vengeance if M'bola's hanged. They've talked of using force, and even made wild threats to kill the Governor—our chief for theirs, they said. At the back of it all I believe there may be one of these strange secret societies that periodically crop up among natives, though more often in West Africa and the Congo than here. I can't find out much about it, but I believe that a society has existed for some little time, and that this Wabenda case enabled it to take advantage of native discontent and make a good deal of headway. Its members, I should think, are mostly semi-educated natives who've lost their tribal discipline and for some reason or other are dissatisfied with their existing position; and I think they're definitely anti-European. There's been a suggestion that it is linked up in some way with the Watchtower movement, which was said to have fomented those riots on the copper mines in Northern Rhodesia a couple of years ago. Personally, I believe the Watchtower movement has been exaggerated, and I very much doubt if any such connexion with this Chania society exists, but that's only my own opinion.'

Vachell nodded. The police had come across rumours of this society during the Wabenda witchcraft trial, and had investigated it; but they hadn't been able to find out much.

'Don't they call it the League of the Plaindweller, or some fancy name?' he asked.

'Yes, that's it. I don't know what the name means, and I think the whole thing's probably mainly bluff. We aren't worrying unduly about it. There have been agitations of this sort before, and they're ninety per cent hot air. But here's the danger. It's just possible that these Wabenda malcontents might jump in and claim this crime as their doing. They know enough law to realize that we can't arrest them if we don't think they're guilty. But they might try to cash in, so to speak, on the kudos value—to claim this murder as proof of their power, and to use it as a warning to the Government. In fact, they might raise hell and high water in the native areas.'

Moon paused, and rose to his feet. 'I'm afraid I've talked a lot,' he said. 'I don't want to be an alarmist, but you see how important it is for you fellows to clear up this terrible thing quickly, before political complications can set in.'

'We'll do our best,' Vachell assured him. 'It's pretty important for us too.'

Moon walked across the room and hesitated in the doorway.

'Yes,' he said, 'I know. I've got personal reasons, too, for hoping you'll get your man. I've never struck a better chief to work with than McLeod. Or a finer man.'

Vachell's eyes followed Moon across the room and rested for a moment on a pair of native spears, crossed above the lintel on the wall.

'Parson me, Mr Moon,' he said. 'There was one more question. Just what did you mean by a remark you made a little while back—that you collected some of those curios lying around this room? How did they come to get here?'

'Through Sir Malcolm's brother,' Moon replied. 'I worked under him once, you know—twenty years ago.'

'I didn't know. How was that?'

'Alistair McLeod was in the Chania administration. He came out in — let me see — about nineteen-eight. He'd have gone far. But he died of blackwater on the western frontier—in nineteen-sixteen, I think. I was up there on my first tour, as his assistant. He was a good officer, and he knew how to handle Somalis. Then the war came, and no one got leave, and we all had to do twice as much work with half the usual staff. It's a hell of a climate up there, you know, and rotten with fever. It did for him, poor chap. Queer they should both have died in Chania, when their work was only beginning. . . . Well, good luck, Mr Vachell, and I hope you find your man. Good night.'

Vachell sighed, knowing that there would be no sleep for him during what was left of the night. Four hours to straighten out his notes and his thoughts. He settled into the Governor's leather arm-chair, notebook on knee. Outside the study the tramp of feet indicated the vigilance of the KALI guard, and bayonets gleamed at the gates. But quiet and darkness at last enshrouded the big house. Only the figure of Abdi lurked in the shadows of the carpeted hall—Abdi, disconsolately seated in a tall-backed chair and silently mourning the death of a respected master.

6

The Governor had been murdered on a Tuesday night.

Wednesday morning was bright and fresh. The air had that brittle clarity that comes before the rains. The distant peak of the mountain that overshadowed the Chania highlands towered in delicately pencilled outline against the deep blue of the sky. The white snow-cap was like a chiselled cloud. Above it lay a thick band of smoke-coloured stratus through which the sun had recently climbed; and now sunlight triumphantly flooded the big plain that lay below Marula. The steep hill-sides, green valleys and cool forests of the rolling volcanic country which stretched from the outskirts of the city to the high downland plateau behind it rejoiced with the life of a new day. Sun glistened on the black bodies of natives stooping over their cultivation; sun drenched the compounds, swarming with goats and pot-bellied children; flooded the thatch of rounded hut roofs so that they glowed like blobs of honey.

Vachell and Olivia Brandeis rode together along a native cattle track winding like the trail of a snake on the crest of a ridge between two valleys. At the bottom of the valleys flowed little streams which had eaten their way deep into the chocolate earth so that a steep, slippery slope rose above them on either side. Along the beds of the streams flopped green fronds of banana trees. Small uneven plots of cultivation jostled each other along the bottoms and sprawled up the fertile hill-sides. Squat, loose-breasted women toiled methodically in the cultivation, hoeing and digging and preparing for planting. Goat-bells tinkled gently in the bush, an accompaniment to the subdued twittering of cicadas. Voices shouted easily to each other across the valleys, and smoke rose in feathery spirals from occasional groups of huts.

The polo ponies on which Vachell and Olivia were mounted cantered smoothly along the grassy track, responding instantly to every touch on the reins. The country was open on top of the ridge. Vachell was feeling restored after a hot bath, three cups of coffee, and a shave. He had had no sleep that night, but the cool, crisp air blew the heaviness out of his head. He rode easily, with stirrups unusually long for an English saddle.

Olivia, too, was a good rider. Her mop of frizzy hair stood up on end in the wind, and her normally pasty cheeks glowed with the tang of fresh air. She wore Jodhpurs and a red turtle-necked sweater.

Their last meeting had taken place in Arizona. At the time Vachell had been acting as a guide to tourists in the

Painted Desert and Petrified Forest sections. Olivia had been making a tour of Indian reservations, studying what was left of religious dances, and had hired Vachell as her guide. They had spent four days in the desert on the way to and from a Navajo fire-dance, buying their food at crossroad stores, cooking it over camp-fires, and sleeping out, rolled up in blankets, by the side of the car. They had become good friends. Now, four years later, they had met unexpectedly in Africa.

Vachell gave Olivia a brief outline of his career since then. From Arizona he had gone to Galveston, Texas, and worked for a time for a shipping company, loading cotton into freighters. He spent a winter buying furs from Cajans in the Louisiana swamps. Then a friend in the Canadian police had written to tell him of an opening in the Mounties. They were reorganizing their crime detection bureau, and before going back to Montreal Vachell took a course in detective work with the Department of Justice's Bureau of Investigation in Washington, D.C.

He spent a year in Alberta, and did one spell in the Arctic. Then the itch to travel seized him again. He aimed for India; and good luck got him a temporary job with the Indian C.I.D. at Delhi. On his first leave he came across to look at Africa. He liked it, and looked around for a job. A chance came: the Chania police were reorganizing their C.I.D. to bring it up to date. Cables flew about the world, and he got the job: big promotion for him, for he was put in charge of the remodelled department. This case was his first big break. Failure, he knew, would finish his career as a detective.

'It's a pretty tough case,' Vachell concluded. 'And for this reason. Most of these guys I have to grill are my chiefs. I'm just a bottle-washer to them, and a new one at that. When I start to question them they forget it's a murder case and think I'm getting fresh. I'm telling you, it's a hell of a spot to be in.'

'It's bad luck,' Olivia agreed, 'but I shouldn't worry. No

one will give you the sack until this case is cleared up. If you succeed they won't sack you at all, and if you fail they'll sack you anyway.'

'Well, that's a consolation,' Vachell grinned. 'Do you have any bright ideas?'

Olivia shook her head. 'The queer thing is that no one seems to have any. Or at least, if they have, they didn't produce them last night, when you kept us cooped up in that room like a lot of laying hens. The usual motive for a murder, I imagine, is money, but every one knows that McLeod had practically nothing of his own, so his wife and daughter will be far worse off now that he's dead and there's no Governor's salary to support them. The thing seems to have come right out of the blue.'

'See here,' Vachell said suddenly, 'I'll tell you the truth, and that is, I don't know what in hell to think either. I'm in a fog. You're a pretty smart girl and you're on the outside of all this, and I don't suppose you knocked off H.E. I'd like your opinion—off the record, of course. Care to go through a summary of the testimonies I got last night that I've made out for Major Armitage? And then maybe we could see between us if it all adds up to anything.'

Olivia agreed enthusiastically. They came to a tall fig tree whose thick foliage cast a circle of deep shade round the massive bole. It was a dwelling-place, no doubt, of a locally respected spirit; and a very pleasant one, too, Olivia reflected.

They reined in their ponies. A small black boy, standing sleepily about in a strip of goatskin, was enlisted to hold the reins. Olivia and Vachell sat down under the fig tree, backs to the bole and legs stretched out in front of them.

Vachell handed over some sheets of foolscap and drew a folded copy of the morning paper, heavily edged with black, from his pocket. The reporter had given Armitage a good write-up in his account of the Chinyani raid. Olivia Brandeis read through the notes and handed them back.

'There's one thing,' she said. 'Jeudwine's lying. According to your notes, he left his office at about ten forty-five to find a messenger to return Moon's files. He says he went straight back to his room as soon as he'd found the G.H. driver just outside the front door. Well, he didn't. I saw him emerging from the car park about that time, some way from the main door. I thought he'd been to fetch something out of one of the cars.'

'I was pretty sure that baby had something on his mind,' Vachell commented. 'How did you come to see him there, Miss Brandeis?'

'I'd better tell the story in order,' she replied. 'I went out to get a breath of air and smoke a cigarette somewhere about ten-thirty. I walked round to the driveway in front, where the cars were parked. As you know, they were mostly standing in a line along the front wall of the house—noses to the flower-bed, behinds pointing outwards. I strolled down the line, and stopped to light a cigarette about half-way along. Then our friend Donovan Popple came along. I remarked that it was early to leave, and he asked me the exact time. I happened to be standing just outside a window and there was a beam of light coming through a crack between the blind and the window-sill. I looked at my watch in this beam, and that's why I remember it. The time was just after ten-forty. I hadn't any idea whose window I was standing under then, but afterwards, thinking back, I realized that it must have been H.E.'s study.'

'Swell. That's something definite, anyway. Then the blind was drawn down at ten-forty.' Vachell took a crumpled piece of paper from his pocket and added a note to it.

'We talked for a minute or two,' Olivia continued, 'and then Popple got his car out and left.'

'One moment. Where, exactly, was Popple's car parked in relation to H.E.'s window?'

'It was exactly underneath.'

'Okay. Go ahead.'

'Then I wandered off down the drive for a short stroll, and when I turned to come back I saw Jeudwine. He was emerging from the line of parked cars, about where Popple's had been, and walking towards the main entrance. I looked at my watch again as I went back past H.E.'s window, in the same beam of light—a sort of automatic action based on the connexion of ideas, I suppose—and it was just on ten to eleven.'

'I wondered at the time if Jeudwine was on the level,' Vachell commented. 'He seemed kind of jittery. There's something phony about him.'

'He's a queer cuss,' Olivia agreed. 'Psychologically twisted in some way, I should say. But I can't see him as a murderer, somehow. I doubt if he's got the guts. There's something queer going on between him and the alluring, if predatory, Mrs Watson.' She gave a brief description of the scene she had watched between the two of them in the garden on the previous night.

Vachell listened with interest, and settled himself more comfortably against the bole of the tree.

'The first thing we—the police—have to decide is whether this is a native crime, as the chief believes, or whether some white man had it in for Sir Malcolm,' he said. 'Let's start on the first supposition. There are two possibilities. One, a native gangster from Chinyani. Major Armitage is taking care of that and the whole goddam police force is hunting up this Swahili guy right now. Two, some sort of a Wabenda plot, involving this Plaindweller society Moon spoke about. There's another angle to that: this KALI askari who was on guard outside H.E.'s door last night is a M'Benda, and there's an outside chance he might be mixed up in it somehow. We only have his word for it that no one aside from the people he named went in or out of H.E.'s study last night. Personally, I doubt if any bunch of half-baked native agitators would pull a job like this. Looks like it's a pretty cool piece of work. Just the same, there might be some fanatic mixed up in it with enough brains to figure out a murder and enough guts to put it through. It's a lead we have to follow, I guess. Now, that's where you come in. You're over here to work on the Wabenda anyway, aren't you?'

Olivia nodded.

'You'll be going down to their country, then, and this is what I want you to do. Go down there just as soon as you can make it. Get in with the big shots of the tribe, whoever they are. Find out all you can about this secret society. Get them talking on the murder, and get their reactions. If they know anything, sooner or later they'll get to bucking about how they put a fast one over on the British Government. They'll know you're not connected with the Government, and you might pick up things where one of our own men wouldn't even get to first base. What do you say?'

'A sort of female police spy,' Olivia commented. 'An unaccustomed role, but not a bad idea. I should certainly have more chance of finding out what the Wabenda think than one of your police detectives, though that's not saying much. All right, I'll have a shot at it.'

'Swell,' Vachell said. 'That's settled, then.' He knew she was flattered by his confidence, though she would never admit it. 'Keep this under your hat for the present. The Commissioner doesn't altogether care for my unorthodox ways.'

'Though I don't believe it's a Wabenda crime for a moment,' Olivia said. 'It's much more likely to be a European.'

Vachell got up without replying and broke a twig off the tree. He sat down again and started to peel it.

'There are a lot of things in this case that don't make sense,' he said, 'and one of them is, how the murderer ever got out of the study when he was through. If Watson's on the level, then H.E. was still alive at ten-forty-eight. And Jeudwine was back in his office two minutes later—you've checked on that. No one could get into the room, strangle a governor, search through a lot of papers—for I've a strong hunch something was removed from H.E.'s desk, and it looks like the "stinking fish" letter has taken a walk—and make a getaway inside of two minutes.

'Well, the windows were locked on the inside, so there were just two ways out. He could go through the secretary's room and take a chance on giving Adbi the slip. In that case, either he bumped into Jeudwine or he waited till Jeudwine had gone and then used a duplicate key on the door leading into the hall. Now it seems to me it would be a funny thing to plan a murder so well that you had a duplicate key made so you could escape all right, and then forget to take a weapon along.'

'Yes,' Olivia agreed, 'it does look as though the murderer had decided to act on the spur of the moment, and used the first thing he could see. I suppose that KALI guard on the passage door *might* have been bribed.'

'By a fellow native, possibly,' Vachell said, 'if they were in it together. But no white man with a murder on his hands would have been that kind of a fool. Machoka's going to be grilled all right, you can take it from me. He'll be plenty scared. Suppose the murderer had slipped him five pounds to forget who he saw coming out of the Governor's study around eleven p.m. last night. Do you think that Machoka wouldn't squeal when he knew that the big chief had been bumped and that he was likely to be held for the killing? No, ma'am! He'd kick through with the truth mighty quick, to save his own skin. No white man in his senses would stake his life on the chance of a native sticking to a phony story for the sake of a few pounds, and under a pretty intensive grilling.'

'No, you're right there,' Olivia agreed. 'The white man would have to bear his own burden in a case like that.'

'I have a hunch that if we could get these times straightened out we'd be a whole lot further on,' Vachell continued. 'Take a look at this time-table, will you?' He handed her the crumpled piece of paper on which he had been scribbling during the conversation. On it was written:

Schedule of Events. Night of March 28th

p.m.

9.15-9.30 (approx.).	Pallett visits H.E. in study
9.35 (approx.).	Pallett leaves G.H. for Secretariat.
9.45-10.00	Moon sees H.E. in study; returns to ballroom, leaves for home around 10.30.
10.15-10.30	Sir B. Flower sees H.E. Blind in study still up. Flower retires to own room about 10.40.
10.32 (approx.).	Jeudwine takes whisky in to H.E.
10.40	Blind in H.E.'s study seen to be drawn down by O. Brandeis.
10.45 (approx.).	Moon calls Jeudwine from house to ask for files, and Jeudwine leaves room to dispatch them. Pallett leaves Secretariat and goes home (approx.).
10.48	Watson looks in to study, sees H.E. telephoning. Sounds like outgoing call, but none recorded by P.O.
10.49 (approx.).	Jeudwine seen by O. Brandeis walking away from line of parked cars near H.E.'s window. Returns to his office.
10.55	Jeudwine leaves office, locking door and taking key.
11.15	Crime discovered by Beaton. Pallett arrives at G.H.

Olivia digested this in silence.

'Well, it looks as if either Jeudwine or Watson is lying,' she said finally. 'Leaving the KALI corporal out of it for the moment, that is. Strict adherence to the truth doesn't always seem to be Jeudwine's strong suit, and Watson, I suppose, has got a motive. It'll probably just turn out to be a *crime passionel*, or whatever it's called when the possessive instincts of the male get too much for him. Very prosaic.'

'That's the only motive we've uncovered so far,' Vachell agreed. 'Looks like Maisie Watson never kept her date with H.E. last night. Guess I'll have a talk with that dame today.'

The idea depressed him slightly. He stretched his arms and sniffed the symphony of smells that teased his nostrils—an aromatic shrub, delightfully pungent; hot sun-baked earth; a whiff of wood-smoke; cow dung; the slightly rancid, not unpleasing smell of native bodies. A little way off the ponies stood patiently, heads down, tails idly flicking at flies.

'In many ways,' he heard Olivia intone in a distinctly lecture-flavoured voice, 'the functions of a detective in our society resemble those of a witchdoctor among native tribes. The witchdoctor's job, like the detective's, is to hunt down the enemies of society and prevent them from doing further harm. In my opinion there's a good deal of nonsense talked about the barbarity of witchcraft, except perhaps among certain West African tribes. Sorcerers are killed, of course; but we kill murderers, and that's what sorcerers are, in native eyes. The conviction of a sorcerer is by no means arbitrary. There has to be a long record of suspicion by responsible people—not just an unfounded accusation—followed by a properly conducted ordeal, before a verdict is given. Of course there are abuses, as in all systems, but in nine cases out of ten I believe the victim has been genuinely guilty of anti-social designs. In many ways it's a very efficient method of eliminating the disruptive elements in society. And it has enabled African tribes to maintain for centuries a large measure of social stability, without anything in the nature of a police force.'

'Say, don't you start to put ideas like that into circulation,' Vachell said. 'I might lose my job. Maybe we should get a witchdoctor in to take charge of this case.'

'Their system works,' Olivia retorted. 'I doubt if

Scotland Yard has evolved anything like so efficient a way of extracting confessions as the poison ordeal, for instance. Among the Wakamba in Kenya a suspected wrongdoer is made to swear an oath on a sacred object called the kipitu, made out of a wart-hog tusk. Every one believes implicitly that a false declaration means certain death, and it is said that a guilty man will always break down and confess rather than commit the heinous offence of telling a lie over the kipitu.'

'We could use one of those in our department,' Vachell agreed.

It was past eight: time to start back for Marula. He took a deep breath. It was a lot fresher and cooler up here than in the hot streets of the town. Police headquarters consisted of a wooden building on piles with a corrugated iron roof. And Armitage's liver would be hideous as hell. He helped Olivia up and they walked slowly towards the grazing ponies.

'How about that diary you found in the safe?' Olivia asked. 'Whose is it?'

'It belonged to H.E.'s brother,' Vachell answered. 'It had his name on the fly-leaf, and I guess it was written the year he died—nineteen-sixteen. I went through it pretty carefully, but I couldn't see anything in it. Seems like it was just day-to-day stuff—notes on native disputes, distances covered on safari, names of camps, and so on. Entries start tailing off along about April, and then there's one that says: "Down with malaria" and then a lot of blanks. The last entry comes early in May; it just says: "Temp. 105." I guess he died pretty soon after that. I went through the blank part, too, but there was nothing there, and no missing pages.'

'Well, if anything sinister happened on the western frontier twenty years ago, I should think it would have been cleared up by now,' Olivia said. 'It's rather funny, though, that the diary should be kept in the private safe.'

They halted the ponies and tightened the girths. Vachell

dug into his pocket and extracted a reward for the pot-bellied boy.

'What you need,' said Olivia, 'is a nice motive—apart from Watson, who seems to be the only candidate so far.' She stroked her pony's nose reflectively and delivered a little lecture, apparently to the horse.

'To find a motive,' she said, 'I think you should begin at the other end. People will concentrate on trying to find the cause of the crime. I believe they should also think about the effect. A murder, of course, has several effects, and among them is the vital one that the murderer committed his crime to get. So you've got to ask yourself—which effect is the one the murderer wanted? Then you get on to the scent.'

'That's rather a complicated way of putting things,' Vachell commented, sliding his foot into the stirrup.

'Not if you apply it,' Olivia replied. 'Take this case. What are the obvious effects of McLeod's death?'

'First of all—the conference which ought to have met today, won't. Federation of Chania and Totseland will be delayed—perhaps even dropped altogether. That's one effect. The Japanese concession very likely won't go through. Pallett becomes an Acting Governor, which may help on his promotion, or may enable him to get something done, or to block something in which he had a special interest. Watson won't divorce his wife—yet. Mrs Watson will be free to look around for a new boy friend. Jeudwine wil have an opportunity to destroy any of H.E.'s private papers he may want to. The Wabenda may feel that justice has been done to the head of a Government that persecuted their tribe. And so on.'

Olivia mounted her pony and they rode back along the ridge. In the distance, below them, the iron roofs of the Indian bazaar in Marula caught the sunlight and gleamed like pools of water.

'What I need most,' Vachell remarked, 'is some way to find out what was in that letter H.E. said was "stinking fish", and who has it now.'

'Well, I hope it won't turn out to be a red herring,' said Olivia.

.   .   .   .   .

Vachell found the Police Commissioner in a much better temper. He observed a newspaper, open at the account of the Chinyani raid, on his chief's desk, and guessed the reason. The major wasn't a bad old guy, he reflected; irascible, but not really sour-tempered. Armitage read through Vachell's résumé of the evidence and studied the time-table carefully.

'The first thing we've got to decide,' he said, 'is whether Watson's story is true. On the face of it there's no reason why he should say he saw Sir Malcolm telephoning at ten-forty-eight if he didn't. On the other hand, he's got a motive—obviously. Damned unpleasant, all this coming out. Washing dirty linen in public. For a man in his position, H.E. was rash, very rash. I always said so. However, too late now. You must verify Watson's statements, if you can. Talk to that little bitch of a wife of his. But I don't like it; don't like it at all. Watson's a decent chap—bit of a highbrow, schoolmaster and all that, but a good feller. Not the type to commit a murder, not a bit of it. But we must do our duty. You're in charge of that.'

The Commissioner paused to light a small cigar. A native secretary put his head round the door and announced that Mr Pallett would be pleased if the Commissioner would attend the swearing-in of the Acting Governor at eleven o'clock at Government House. Armitage swore and the secretary withdrew, rightly interpreting an affirmative.

'If Watson was speaking the truth,' Armitage continued, 'and Sir Malcolm was alive at ten to eleven, either the murderer had a key to Jeudwine's office and escaped after Jeudwine had cleared off at five to—which you think is unlikely, and I agree—or else he escaped through the door guarded by Machoka. In other words, Machoka acted as the murderer's accomplice—or committed the murder himself.

'There's your first lead, Vachell. Follow it up. Leave no stone unturned. You'll find Machoka up at the KALI lines; I've had him kept under guard. Go over and question him right away. It's my belief he's mixed up in this damned secret society in some way. You must *make* him talk.'

'I'll give him the works, sir,' Vachell promised.

'Keep in touch, Vachell, and report directly you get something definite. Mr Pallett has been on at us already. The Secretary of State wants a detailed report. For God's sake get something solid, Vachell, and look sharp about it.'

Vachell grinned reassuringly at his boss, but he didn't feel at all confident about the solidarity. The case didn't look like a solid one, somehow.

He found Machoka locked up in a small room in the KALI lines outside the city. The askari was sitting forlornly on a bare camp-bed, and rose when the sergeant let his visitor in.

Vachell sat down on a dilapidated straight-backed chair and studied the native carefully. A good-looking boy, he decided; tall and slim and rather skinny, like most Wabenda, but wiry and well-proportioned. He looked intelligent, too. Vachell knew that he had not been in Africa long enough to tell anything about a native's character from his facial expression. It needed years of association with them to do that. But Africans weren't like Chinese, expressionless and wooden-faced to a European stranger's eyes; their features showed great variation. That, he supposed, was due to their lack of homogeneity; like the English and Americans, they were a mixture of any number of different races. Machoka, for instance, seemed to be a throwback to the almost pure Hamitic type. He was light in colour, almost as light as a Malay, and although his lips were thick they didn't jut out like rolls of rubber. His front teeth, following the tribal custom, were filed into sharp points, and there were raised tattoo marks on his cheek-bones. Among the Wabenda, Vachell knew, tattoo marks on the cheeks were a sign of high rank.

Machoka stood to attention during the scrutiny. He was in uniform, a simple navy-blue sweater reaching half-way down his thighs; khaki shorts; puttees; a red fez; no boots. Vachell told him to stand at ease, and began to question him in Kiswahili.

But Machoka's answers didn't help at all. He denied, again, and with vigour, that any one—apart from the Europeans he had named—had either entered or left the Governor's study through the door he had been guarding the night before. Vachell became stern and warned him of the terrible consequences of telling a lie, trying to convey the impression that the least he could hope for was to be shot at dawn. Machoka was properly scared, but he stuck to his story.

Vachell switched the theme abruptly.

'When did you join the League of the Plaindweller?' He fired the question crisply. It had an immediate effect. Machoka made a little gesture of recoil. His mouth half dropped open and he closed it quickly, licking his lips. His skin changed colour, too. Vachell was intrigued; you couldn't say he turned pale, but something happened to his complexion; it seemed to take on a dirty grey tinge beneath the brown.

Machoka shook his head violently. 'I am not a member, bwana. What League? I do not know the League you name. I know nothing.'

Now Vachell knew his man was lying. He shot out an arm and pointed a finger at the askari. He knew that for some reason this action often disconcerted natives.

'You lie, Machoka. You know the League of the Plaindweller. Do you think we, the Government, are ignorant of it? Our eyes are everywhere; we have eyes that see this League. We know the members. When the day comes that it does evil openly, we shall kill it—thus.' He snapped his fingers.

Machoka shook his head more violently. 'I know nothing, bwana. I am an askari. I do not belong to any league. Such affairs are bad.'

'So you admit that the League of the Plaindweller exists? You admit that you know it?'

Machoka was growing more and more agitated. He shrank back until his legs rubbed against the camp-bed. His eyes were beginning to roll in the peculiar way of the eyes of frightened natives.

'I tell you, bwana, I say'—the words burst out rapidly now—'I know nothing! nothing! I have heard that there is such a league; so much every one knows. I have heard that it has members among my people, and that it has a strong magic. But what is this to do with me? I am an askari. I serve the King. Never would I meddle with such an affair!'

Either he's sincere, Vachell thought, or—well, that doesn't help. Natives *are* good actors, it's well known. A clever native can fool a white man at the drop of the hat.

Machoka knew more than he would say about the League, that much was certain. In his mind Vachell had got it classified as a sort of native fascist society. Not that it had any connexion with fascism as such, of course, but it seemed to be inspired by similar emotions. It was a nationalist movement, in its way; Wabenda-land for the Wabendas, back to the ancient customs of our forefathers, and to hell with the contamination of foreign ideas. He imagined that William Randolph Hearst would find himself at home, spiritually if not in the flesh, at a meeting. Its leaders appeared to regard the Government's attempt to improve the conditions of the natives as a sinister foreign plot to undermine the Wabenda system of government. Probably they opposed Christianity, too, and mission propaganda: they believed that the gods that were good enough for their fathers were good enough for them.

There was no doubt that the League had been disconcertingly active in stirring up feeling against British rule. Could it, Vachell wondered, have dared to execute a plot against the Governor's life as a warning to the whites not to enforce the death sentence passed on the Wabenda chief? Had it found a leader capable of carrying out such a bold and fantastic plan? It seemed ridiculous, and yet... Could it be possible that a renegade white man, perhaps even some one paid to stir up anti-British feeling, had joined forces with this League and planned the murder as a daring coup?...

Machoka shifted uneasily from foot to foot. He was intensely unhappy. Vachell tried again.

'M'Bola is your chief,' he said. 'You know that he is in jail condemned for murder?'

'M'Bola is no murderer.'

'I didn't ask you if he was a murderer. I asked you if you knew he was in jail.'

'I know, bwana.'

'Yes, you know. And you know something else. You know that this League of the Plaindweller has avowed vengeance against the Government because it condemned your chief to death. You know that, don't you?'

Machoka made no reply.

'You know some more, too. You know that this League tried to scare the Government, so that it should turn coward and release M'Bola. And so the leader of your League killed the Governor. And you know who he is. You let him out of the room last night when his crime was done!'

Vachell was speaking intensely, standing up, pointing at the askari's chest. Machoka shrank back even farther against the bed, terror in his eyes.

'No, no, bwana, no! That is not true. I know nothing, nothing. I let no man through. I speak the truth!'

Vachell knew that he was defeated. The askari wouldn't crack. He dropped his arm.

'All right, Machoka. We shall find out. Remember—truth flies in the air like a bird. We cannot reach up our hand for it, but our cunning is a net to tempt it to the earth, and before the moon is old we shall hold it in our hand.' He cupped his hands in front of him as if they held a fluttering bird.

Machoka said nothing and Vachell turned to go. As he opened the door Machoka said, 'Bwana.' Vachell turned.

'You will not find out who killed the Governor.' The askari spoke earnestly and rapidly, in a low voice. 'No one passed through the door that I guarded, in or out. No one came. There was not a man. Therefore you cannot find him.'

'What do you mean?'

Machoka spoke apprehensively, almost in a whisper. 'There are men who do evil while they sleep. The Governor died because they had captured his soul!'

7

There were plenty of jobs waiting for the Superintendent back at headquarters. A couple of local reporters were lying in wait on the veranda. Their spirits had long ago been broken to accepting the official 'no' for an answer, and Vachell got rid of them without much difficulty. He took refuge from further attacks in his office—a small, bare room, furnished with a regulation government desk, two chairs, a filing cabinet, and a book-shelf. His rank did not rate a carpet, but he had provided a gaily coloured North American Indian rug, and modern Indian drawings hung on the beaver-boarded walls.

His first action was to ring up Olivia Brandeis. He asked her if she would interview Machoka. She knew some Kibenda; and it was hopeless trying to talk to natives in a language other than their own. There was just a chance that Machoka would talk to some one not connected with the Government. She agreed to do her best, and Vachell arranged for her to go over to the KALI lines that afternoon to see the secretive askari.

Armitage had detached one of the young police inspectors from routine duties to assist in the big investigation, and at ten o'clock Janis reported. He was a young Chania-born boy who had just been brought down to headquarters from one of the outlying stations. The move had distressed him deeply, because he'd had to sell a cherished pony that he could not afford to keep in Marula, and Vachell had asked for him in the hope that an interesting job might offer consolation.

Janis was told to start with a visit to the telephone exchange to trace the call that the Governor had been answering at 10.48. As it wasn't an outgoing or a long-distance call, the only way to go about it was to get from the supervisor a list of all the calls that had been made in the Marula area—there was only one exchange—between 10.45 and 10.50 on the previous night, to collate the numbers with the subscribers, and then to visit each subscriber in turn. After that the young inspector was to check up, as far as possible, the movements of all the people Vachell had questioned the night before, starting with Watson.

Janis saluted and went out, radiating enthusiasm. He was a tall, loose-limbed boy with a mop of fair hair and a deep tan complexion. He was full of excitement and dreams of promotion, and went out looking as though he expected to bring the murderer back under his arm within the next half-hour.

At eleven o'clock the fingerprint man turned in a report. All the prints on the telephone receiver, he said, were the dead Governor's. The empty whisky glass carried a set of H.E.'s prints, clearly defined, right hand; and another set, not H.E.'s, possible Jeudwine's. And one extra thumb-print, tent type, belonging to a third person. It was near the top, and the peculiar part was that there were no fingerprints to go with it.

'Seems kind of left out in the cold, that thumb—as though some one forgot about it,' Vachell said. 'Suppose the rest of the prints had been wiped off, and this got overlooked? Maybe it's a break, at last. I'll turn in some prints for comparison later on.'

.   .   .   .   .

The abrupt death of the Governor did not affect Marula's outward appearance. A few Union Jacks flapped at half-mast, but life in Administration Avenue seemed as active as ever. A row of angle-parked cars lined the sun-bathed street on both sides, and the pavements were crowded. There were European housewives doing the round of fishmonger, grocer, and market, often with a perky little native boy acting as bodyguard and carrying the basket; well-dressed natives sauntering along, swinging their walking-sticks and gazing into the shop windows; occasionally a bewildered African hayseed from some remote part of the reserve, feeling under-dressed in a bright blanket hitched up over one shoulder; a group of native women, oiled skins shining in the sun, brass anklets and bracelets gleaming, clad in dirty goatskins, hunched almost double under heavy loads of produce slung on their backs; endless numbers of Indians in greasy black caps, shirts hanging down outside their trousers, scurrying to and fro.

A large cluster of parked cars surrounded Marula's tallest and most imposing building, Dane's Hotel. 'Dane's at eleven' was one of Marula's standing assignations. Vachell never went. He didn't aspire to the fashionable life of the town. That morning he decided, on sudden impulse, to stop in for a quick drink on his way up to Government House. He was hot and thirsty, and he'd had no sleep. He parked the car, shouldered his way through the swing doors, and found a seat at a round glass-topped table in the lounge. The room was tall and cool, with blue-distempered walls and a blue and silver carpet.

Dane's was unusually crowded that morning, and the buzz of conversation, he knew, centred round a single topic. There was a sprinkling of settlers, in to see the bank manager or the dentist, to have a farm implement repaired or to buy a new pair of shoes. Most of the men were dressed in tight-fitting suits, cut when they were younger and less muscular, carefully preserved for visits to the capital; the women wore printed dresses copied by the local Indian tailor from a model bought on the last trip to England. The imitation settlers formed a more spectacular group. They wore richly coloured corduroy trousers—chocolate, cream, and bottle-green seemed to be the most popular shades—and equally gaudy silk shirts. One or two of the men carried broad-brimmed black Stetson hats, but the women, whose slacks were on the whole even more colourful than the men's, were mostly bareheaded. The Marula business men and their wives were in more conventional dress. There was a party of rich Americans, attended by camera-men, on their way through to photo-graph big game from a privately chartered aeroplane; a couple of white hunters who had just got in from three months after elephant in the Congo; a group of young men down from the goldfields to play off a tie in the rugger league.

Vachell recognized several of the local celebrities by sight, though he didn't know them. He saw Colonel Horton, his leonine profile and iron-grey hair reminiscent of a retired villain of melodrama, discoursing eloquently on the need for devaluation and the parasitism of the Government. Lady Saffery, dark and dynamic beneath a heavy make-up, came in; Chania's only woman Legislative Councillor, she was famous alike for the hospitality of her parties and the skill with which she manipulated the numerous beneficial committees on which she served. A tall young woman pilot in rust-coloured corduroys who operated an air-taxi entered with the stocky and pug-nacious ex-naval editor of an effervescent up-country weekly paper whom she had flown down that morning to be near the source of news. Several rather tired-looking young men in check shirts surrounded the slim and drooping figure of Lady Constance, who had hurried down with her current house-party from her up-country farm.

Vachell was trying to attract the attention of a waiter when he was hailed genially by a tall man in chocolate-coloured corduroy trousers and a green check shirt who zigzagged across the crowded room and sat down at the same table. His face seemed vaguely familiar: a smooth, well-fed face with an upturned nose, small brown eyes, and a carefully trained Guard's moustache.

'Hello, hello, what?' he said. 'Have this one with me. Know your face, you know, but not the name. Mine's Tollemache. Met before, haven't we, what?'

A waiter in a white kanzu and blue sash approached at last. Vachell hastily introduced himself and accepted the offer of a drink. His host ordered two Pimms.

'Sleuthing the murderer, what?' Tollemache remarked. 'Like in one of those detective stories. Can't read them myself. Get fog-bound in the clues, what?' He laughed heartily and talked at the same time.

'Just got back from Bolshie-land by plane, and what do I find?' Tollemache continued. 'Everything quiet over there, but people shooting up Governors over here like a lot of Bolshies themselves. Bad show, what?'

Vachell agreed and drank down his Pimms. It was fresh and cooling, and he felt better at once. He remembered Tollemache now: a rich up-country dairy farmer with a private plane, who paid more attention to flying than to milk yields.

'Might as well move to Chicago,' Tollemache went on, twirling his erect moustache, 'if this sort of thing goes on. Hope you'll grab the culprit, what? Disgraceful show. Let me know if I can do anything. Always glad to help the bobbies, what? Lend you the bus, if you want it—chase the fellow anywhere you like, any time. Only got to say the word.'

As he rose to go a woman came in through the swing doors and stood for a moment on the threshold, adjusting her blonde curls. 'Here comes the female mastiff, looking for a nice morsel of raw meat,' Tollemache added. 'You watch out. Bites, you know. Bit so hard last time she got a fellow down there was nothing left—even a titbit. Ha, ha! Good luck, old boy. On with the handcuffs.' He waved to Vachell gaily and dodged through the tables towards a party at the other side of the room.

Vachell looked up to see the newcomer poised just inside the door, her large eyes, heavily shadowed in blue, darting over the room. A general studying the disposition of the troops, he thought; looking for the weak spot and deciding where to strike. He suddenly realized that her face was shrewd and cunning below its mask of babyish innocence. She was dressed entirely in black; a large black straw hat and a flimsy, tight-fitting chiffon dress. In one hand she clutched a large black chiffon handkerchief, monogrammed in red.

Her eyes came to rest on him. Her fact underwent some nameless change. The expression of cunning was rubbed out; it vanished into one of dreaminess, faint sadness, and simplicity. Vachell found himself wondering whether he had seen or imagined that fleeting look of calculation. She smiled at him, shyly and a little uncertainly, not quite sure whether they had met before. Then she walked across the room, swinging her hips, to a table at the far end. Several heads jerked up to follow her progress across the room. Vachell decided that he would have known who it was, after last night, even if he'd never seen her before. I'll have to watch my step, he thought as he negotiated the swing door on the way out, when I get to grips with Maisie Watson.

.   .   .   .   .

The ceremony of swearing in the Acting Governor had just concluded when Vachell arrived at Government House. The participants walked out through the hall, led by Pallett, in full fancy dress—a sword dangling ridiculously from his hip, the white plume in his cocked hat bobbing up and down as he walked. He looked more pompous than ever, trying unsuccessfully to conceal his gratification at the assumption of a new dignity.

He passed within a few feet of Vachell, who watched the little procession from the doorway of Jeudwine's room, somehow giving an impression of lounging although he was standing upright, half instinctively at attention. Pallett looked straight through him and then quickly away, without nodding. Vachell knew that his rumpled hair and creased uniform—he had changed in a hurry and couldn't find a fresh pair of trousers—had scored another black mark against him. His bony jaws worked methodically on gum.

Behind Pallett came the Chief Justice, in wig and robes, and Moon, now acting Colonial Secretary. One or two other heads of departments followed, among them Watson, looking tired and grey. Jeudwine was there, walking more briskly than on the previous evening. He had a greasy complexion, faintly repulsive, and in daylight he looked sallow and ill. Popple, in his capacity as a member of the Governor's Executive Council, brought up the rear. His ginger hair was smoothed down with water and he wore a worn dark suit that had once been admirably cut, but for a younger, thinner Popple. There was something springy in his gait that made him seem to bound rather than to walk. He gave off energy like a vibrating coil. Already his combed-down ginger hair was getting out of control.

Irish charm, Vachell reflected, was a stale phrase for an overrated quality, but, in a rugged way, that was just what Popple had.

He stepped forward and touched the settler leader on the arm.

'Pardon me, sir,' he said. 'If you can spare a few moments, I'd like a word with you.'

Popple turned quickly and then smiled, holding out his hand. 'Captain Vachell, isn't it? Of course, if there's any way at all I can help, I'll do it. This is a terrible thing that's happened, terrible.'

They went, at Vachell's suggestion, to the tea-room. Popple sat down on the sofa, hitching up his trousers till an expanse of bare leg showed above the sock.

'May I sit down? Are you getting along well?' he asked. 'Have you found the man? Just fancy the nerve of him—walking in under all our noses as he did, killing the Governor in front of us all! And a fine fellow like Sir Malcolm too. There wasn't a question of policy we didn't disagree on, but you couldn't help respecting him all the same, in spite of his crack-brained notions.'

Vachell leant against a desk and handed Popple a metal cigarette-case. Popple took the case, extracted a cigarette, and conducted a vigorous match-hunt in his pockets.

'I'm checking up on every one who was around here last night, just for the record,' Vachell began. 'What did you do after, say, nine-thirty p.m.?'

Popple finally located a match-box and lit his cigarette. Vachell took back the case and got out his pencil and notebook, ready for action.

'I'm afraid I don't know anything that will help you,' Popple said. 'I never heard nor saw a thing. D'you know what I think? I'll tell you.' He leant forward intently, forearms resting on his knees, and hit the palm of one hand with the fist of the other. 'I think it's Somalis. Somalis.' He leant back impressively.

Vachell nodded. 'Maybe, Mr Popple. We'll get around to that angle in a moment. But right now I'd like to know where you were last night at—'

'Now maybe you'll be saying that a Somali wouldn't strangle a man.' Popple was not to be put off. 'More often they'd stick a knife into him, I'll admit, but they're up to all sorts of tricks, and I'd not put it past them to use the rope. You know McLeod was in Somaliland for five years, don't you? And maybe you know that he was up against the Black Aisa too? And that they swore vengeance on him for

- 83 -

giving an award against them in a big camel-raiding case? And that there was once a band of them that attacked McLeod and had to be driven off with loss of life by the Camel Corps fellows? I had all this from a chap who was up there while it happened, after a frankincense concession. The Government hushed it up at the time—they'd hush up the screams of the tortured in hell—but I know the Black Aisa were after his blood, and they're holy terror, those fellows—if they were after him then, they'll be after him now. They're a murdering lot of devils too, spoiled and coddled by the Government they are, and—'

'Pardon me, Mr Popple, but I've no time to spare for your theories,' Vachell interrupted. 'I want facts, and I want them now. Where were you after nine-thirty last night?'

Popple looked ugly for a moment, but then he laughed: it was an attractive laugh; his blue eyes twinkled, his jaw went up, and his head back.

'Ah, I know my weak spots, Captain Vachell,' he said. 'A loose tongue, a hot head, and a soft heart, and I don't know which gets me into the most trouble. Well, last night, then. Lord knows what made me go to that dolled-up bunfight at all, I don't go looking for boredom and I can't drink that fancy stuff they serve you with at dinner; but I thought I might get a word in with Sir Malcolm about official business, so I put on my bib and tucker and came along to the party—and don't you be forgetting that *we* pay for it all, it comes out of the revenue, and a fine waste of money it is too.

'Well, we sat down to dinner and I found myself between an old hen with a chest as flat as a board and a face like an ant-bear, who—'

'Say, listen, Mr Popple,' Vachell put in. 'I'm not here to get a broadcast commentary on last night's party. This is a murder case. I want your movements from nine-thirty onwards. Kick through now, and make it snappy.' His voice was peremptory. Popple took a quick look at him and relit the cigarette with which he had been gesticulating.

'Impatient sort of chap, aren't you? I'm doing my best to tell you. After dinner now—let me see. I remember young Beaton introduced me to that woman with a haystack of hair, an anthropologist she is, studying native customs they call it nowadays—in me father's time they called it a business trip to Paris, but it comes to the same thing, though the natives here could give two stone and a beating to the natives of Paris, I shouldn't be surprised. D'you know the story of the two anthropologists who met at a party in London, amid a great crowd of people they didn't know, so they got to talking professionally with each other, and one of them said: "Now my natives stand this way when they—"'

'For God's sake, Mr Popple,' Vachell interrupted. He had got to the sharp edge of his patience. 'Can't you understand that I've got other things to do than stand here listening while you put on an act? I want to know what you did last night, when you did it, and why. If you refuse to tell me, okay, but let's have it straight, so I know where I am.'

'Ah, I'm sorry, Captain Vachell.' Popple's mobile face took on a look of real concern. Expressions raced across it as quickly as cloud shadows over the open plain on a windy day. 'I've no consideration. My tongue runs away with the words. Well, after I'd met this anthropologist woman, we walked about outside on the lawn for a little and then I went off to see if I could get hold of H.E. I went to Jeudwine's office, but his door was locked, and then I thought, if I can't see McLeod perhaps I can do some good with Pallett. It was about this Japanese concession that McLeod was backing, you understand. I thought, if H.E.'s anxious to push it on, that's a good reason for Pallett wanting to hold it up. You know how they got along together, like a hawk and a sparrow. Abdi said Pallett had just gone, and I guessed it was to the Secretariat, so I followed him down there and had a talk to him, and all he would do was to hedge and say that "no immediate action was contemplated". Pallett would say that no immediate action was contemplated by God when the last trump was blowing, so, of course, I didn't believe him, and I came straight back here, still wanting to see H.E. before the meeting that was to have been held today.'

Popple paused to light another cigarette. The first had got mangled in his restless hands. He was frowning slightly in the effort of keeping to the point.

'I got back here a little before ten and went to get a glass of whisky, for I hadn't had a drop all evening, and I was talking to a fellow at the bar when I'm blessed if that snake-eyed little tyke Jeudwine didn't come up and offer me a drink. "Have this one with me, Popple," he said. "It's our duty to give free vein to social impulses on an evening like this"—or something to that effect. Of course I wanted to refuse, but I couldn't without being downright rude, so I had the drink and Jeudwine started to tell me his views on women—to tell the truth, I thought he'd taken a drop too much—and before I'd had time to feel more than a little sick, fortunately, Watson came up and started to talk. Thank God Jeudwine cleared off then, the slimy little runt.

'Then, a little while later, old man Flower came up for a tot, but hardly a word would he say to me, although he was a jovial old jackal when I stayed with him up in Totseland for the Customs Conference last year. He looks ten years older, too. I don't know what's come over him, unless it's his wife; they say she dresses up like a Hollywood film star nowadays and dines with all the bigwigs in London, and I bet she makes a hole in his salary you could take the *Queen Mary* through. And I heard that the other day she—'

'Steady, Mr Popple, now. We're getting along fine. What time did you speak to Sir Bertrand?'

'I don't know the exact time, but it must have been about half-past ten, because soon after the old boy went I decided it wasn't any good hanging about on the chance of seeing H.E. any longer. So I got me hat and coat and went home. I know the time then, it was twenty to eleven, for my watch wasn't working right and I met that mop-haired anthropologist outside and asked her the time. Then I got in the car and went home—when I say home I mean the Mazuri Club, you understand, where I stop when I'm in Marula. I had some work to do, so I went to my room and then to bed, and I didn't hear the news until this morning.' Popple stood up and stretched his arms. 'That what you wanted, Superintendent?'

'Thanks,' Vachell nodded. 'Just about. One more thing: did you speak to anybody when you got back to the Mazuri Club?'

'No, I didn't, because I kept away from the bar and the bridge-room; I'd wasted enough time at that damfool party trying to get an audience with his grand panjandrum. It's we who pay him, and yet he's harder to get a sight of than a queen houri in a sultan's harem. I went straight to my room at the club and I didn't meet any one, so if it's an alibi you're after I'm a non-starter, Captain Vachell.'

'I haven't any military rank,' Vachell said, 'and the "a" in my name is pronounced as in baby, but I'm obliged to you for the information.'

'Don't you be forgetting about that Somali business,' Popple added. He walked towards the door, smoothing his now quite undisciplined hair. 'Who was it who first said: "I always get my man?" Mae West, wasn't it? Well, those Black Aisa fellows are just the same, vindictive as a sex-starved spinster. You'll find the Somalis are at the bottom of this.' He went out, leaving Vachell to wonder why Jeudwine, who was supposed to be clever, told lies that were so easily detected.

8

Mark Beaton, sitting in his small office across the way from the Governor's study, was hectic with preparations for the funeral. It was fixed for three o'clock that afternoon.

'I'm up to my neck,' he told Vachell. He was in uniform, with a black tie and arm-band, looking harassed and upset. 'You do have time to make arrangements in England, but it's hell when the corpse won't keep. Do you happen to know anything about rules of precedence in regard to pall-bearers? No, I suppose you wouldn't. It's just the sort of thing one might drop a fearful brick over. And now the C. of E. parson's fighting mad because the Church of Scotland fellow's going to do the service—says it's the official religion, and as it's a Governor's funeral he ought to officiate. And the Timbergrowers' Association have just been on the phone to say that they've heard rumours the coffin is made out of imported timber, and why the blazes don't we use a local hardwood they're trying to push for coffins. And the market's out of flowers and—oh, lots of things. I wish—'

The telephone rang and Mark plunged into a violent argument with Marula's only florist. Supplies had run out and the florist explained that he couldn't execute an order cabled from the Colonial Office to lay a wreath in the name of the King. 'But you don't understand!' Mark shouted. 'It's for the King. Cancel some other order, man. Who's got the biggest wreath? Lady Cape? Well then, send that... Of course you'll get paid... What? You leave that woman out of this.' He slammed down the receiver. 'Can you beat it?' he wailed to Vachell. 'The man says he gets good orders every week from Lady Cape but not from the C.O., and anyway he doesn't suppose the C.O. would pay for them. And the KALI adjutant rang up to say the white ants have eaten the stuff they muffle the drums with, and where can they get some more. My God, this is awful! Is there anything you want? Because if so, make it snappy, will you?'

'Suits me,' Vachell said. 'I want a word with Miss McLeod, if she's up to it. And one answer from you. It's this: you told Jeudwine about H.E. being knocked off last night, didn't you?' Mark nodded. 'Just how did he react?'

Mark Beaton hesitated and stabbed at the blotter with a pen. 'It's funny you should mention that,' he said. 'He was blind as an owl last night—I've never seen him like that before, either—so I don't think anything he said meant anything. But he did behave a bit oddly.' He paused and looked uncomfortable.

'I'm listening,' Vachell said. He handed Mark a cigarette-case. The A.D.C. took it absent-mindedly and then gave it back unopened, shaking his head.

'Well, I don't want to say anything that... I think he was just tight and didn't grasp what I was trying to tell him. I had to shout at him, and even then he stood there like a stuffed fish and mumbled something that sounded like "Impossible", and then said something about a flower-bed. Do you think he can be going batty?'

'Sounds nutty to me,' Vachell admitted. 'Flower-beds. You're sure he wasn't trying to say something about Sir Bertrand Flower?'

An expression of relief came over Mark's pink, scrubbed-looking face. 'Of course, that was it. He must have been trying to say something about Flower going to bed. Stupid of me not to have seen it. Though God knows what that had to do with H.E.'s being murdered. Surely you don't think...?' Mark looked ludicrously shocked. The telephone rang shrilly. He picked up the receiver, listened a moment, and said: 'I'm sorry, but the church won't *hold* five hundred Indian children,' and slammed it down again. 'Come on, I'll take you up to Marvin. She's being absolutely marvellous about the whole thing.'

Vachell had never seen Marvin McLeod before. She

certainly looked swell, he thought. Her face was thin and oval, her skin pale and clear as alabaster, and she wore her blonde hair combed back in a sweep across her head. Her lips were scarlet, but apart from that she used little make-up. She looked slim and fragile in a simple black dress.

Vachell tried to think of the right things to say, but failed. He plunged straight into his questions, putting on his most official manner to make it seem as impersonal as possible. Her answers were much as he had expected. So fas as she knew her father hadn't an enemy in the world. Of course there had been official disagreements, but nothing serious or personal. She had never heard him speak of any threats or fears. The tragedy, she said, was inexplicable.

Vachell was usually relentless in his cross-examinations; but he felt a strong reluctance to ask Marvin about Maisie Watson. He had almost decided not to raise the subject at all when she dragged it in herself. It was obvious that she hated doing so, and she kept her eyes fixed on a pencil that she twiddled in her fingers.

'I said just now that there wasn't anything in my father's private life that could possibly—that led to his making real enemies,' she began. 'That's absolutely true, but there's been one thing, lately... people may think...' Her voice trailed off and she swallowed nervously, fingering her throat.

'You mean Mrs Watson?' Vachell prompted. She nodded. 'I hate to pry into Sir Malcolm's private affairs, Miss McLeod. But you understand I have to. Was it true, what was said about his relations with Mrs Watson?'

'He only spoke to me about it once,' she said. She looked acutely miserable. 'You know mother's got very delicate health, and she has to spend a lot of her time in sanatoriums. Father wouldn't let her come out here, though he missed her awfully. You couldn't expect him never to... to live like a monk for the rest of his life, could you?'

She paused, without looking at Vachell. He said nothing,

fingering a tin of cigarettes.

'Do have one,' she continued. 'There's a match on the table. He wasn't in love with Maisie Watson, but she's awfully attractive to men—you've seen that, of course—and she made a dead set at him. It's rotten luck being a Governor. People in ordinary jobs can get away with anything and nobody minds, but if you're a Governor you're supposed not to have any ordinary feelings. I don't see why he shouldn't have done what he liked in his private life.' She was speaking quickly now. 'Maisie Watson simply threw herself at him. Of course in his position it was unwise and rash, but my father never gave up doing anything because it meant taking a risk. It made him do things all the more.'

Vachell caught the note of pride in her voice. 'I see,' he said, 'and thanks a lot. There's another angle to it, though. Where did Mr Watson stand?'

Marvin shifted in her chair. 'That's just it,' she said. 'That's what's worrying me. He must have known what people were saying. Mark told me every one gossiped about it in Marula. But I don't think he ever said anything about it to father. I suppose he just accepted it. And yet—somehow he doesn't seem to be the sort who *would* sit still and do nothing. That's what I'm afraid of...'

There was a moment of silence. 'Did you know,' Vachell asked, 'that Sir Malcolm had a date with Mrs Watson at eleven o'clock last night?'

Marvin looked up quickly, meeting his eyes for the first time. 'No, I didn't. Eleven o'clock—just about the time—' She broke off and gripped the edge of the table. Vachell could see that her hands were trembling. 'Do you think that he...'

Vachell smiled at her. 'Go easy, Miss McLeod. We haven't got as far as thinking yet. We don't even know whether that date was kept.'

He switched quickly to the most impersonal topic he could think of, and asked if she knew how Alistair

McLeod's diary came to be in the private safe. She was able to explain that. The Governor's old mother had died six months ago and her private possessions had been sent out to Marula to her only surviving son. Alistair's letters and diaries, which she must have treasured for twenty years, had been among them. Sir Malcolm had sorted them out and destroyed most of them, but he had kept his dead brother's last diary and had given it to Marvin to read, remarking that it threw an interesting light on the difficulties with which administrative officers had struggled during the war. She remembered his saying that they often had a harder time than the men who joined the fighting forces, and they got no thanks for it. She had looked through the diary and returned it to him, and thought it quite likely that he had put it away among his private papers for safe-keeping.

That was about all Vachell could get. He asked her if she had ever heard of African Equities. She shook her head. If it had anything to do with Chania, she added, it couldn't have been one of his investments. He was scrupulously particular not to put money into anything even remotely connected with any of the colonies in which he served. 'That was typical of father,' she said.

.   .   .   .   .

The headquarters of Chania's administration were not imposing. They consisted of a long, low, tin-roofed building on stilts, stuffy in hot weather and draughty in cold, more like a Brobdingnagian rabbit-hutch than a Government office. Indeed, to Vachell, the scurrying clerks appeared strangely rabbit-like, darting in and out of their burrows, and he sometimes caught himself seeming to see the flick of a scut as the back view of a bureaucrat disappeared through a doorway. He imagined them living on a diet of files, the crisp, buff lettuces of their curious world. Then, too, he could see them crouching, startled and ready to bolt, at some indiscreet request for information, almost palpitating like a rabbit at the explosion of a cartridge. On the other hand, he couldn't see them gamboling light-heartedly on a sunny hill-side, playfully twitching their ears.

He found himself, his mind still engaged in such comparisons, being ushered into the Colonial Secretary's office, in answer to a summons from the Acting Governor. He wondered whether Pallett's first glance would be towards his unpressed trousers. Irrelevantly, he remembered a letter he had once seen from a man in India, describing a visitor from England he had recently entertained. 'When I tell you,' the letter had said, 'that he's the sort of man who wears the same tropical suit two days in succession, you'll know what he's like.' Vachell had often wondered what the man really had been like. The sentence seemed to him one of the more cryptic summings-up of history.

Vachell saluted as he entered. Pallett nodded and glanced down at the Superintendent's trousers.

Armitage was there, seated in an arm-chair beside the desk. The only furniture consisted of two other chairs, cane-seated. The wooden floor was partially covered with a worn and faded rug, the walls hung with maps. Pallett's plumed cocked hat lay incongruously on a window-sill, like a collapsed chicken.

Armitage explained that a progress report was to be drawn up immediately for the Secretary of State, who was to make a statement in the House the next day. The C.O. wanted full details, for the Opposition were expected to press for information and to raise various other matters of Chania policy at the same time, such as the security of native lands, the extension of workmen's compensation to kitchen-boys over fourteen, and the case of a native alleged to have been fined six goats by a District Officer for allowing his oxen to stay on the administrative centre's nine-hole golf course, thereby ruining two of the greens.

A draft report covering almost every contingency, but giving practically no information, was finally hammered out. Nothing was said, to Vachell's surprise, about Armitage's pet Swahili suspect from Chinyani for whom so vigorous a search had been made. He learnt later that the Swahili had been traced. The ex-criminal had recently obtained an honest job with the Urban District Council, collecting night-soil in the surrounding suburbs, and his absence from home at two in the morning was therefore understandable.

Vachell grew more and more depressed as the interview went on. Plain-clothes native detectives were being drafted immediately to the Wabenda reserve to trace all natives suspected of being likely members of the League of the Plaindweller. That would put every native in the reserve on the alert. He had seen plain-clothes police in action—huge, beefy men of military bearing, accustomed to uniforms and fezzes and belonging to strange foreign tribes, reluctantly wearing a blanket which they clearly despised. They were a standing joke among the unsophisticated natives with whom they attempted to mingle. Small boys shouted the equivalent of 'Yah, flatfoot', at them as they strode purposefully about a primitive village. Pallett turned down a suggestion of the Commissioner's that a thousand shillings reward should be offered to tempt some native to disclose the secrets of the League, on the ground that such expenditure could not be authorized without the prior approval of the Treasury, and possibly of the Secretary of State. If the Acting Governor takes a hand, he thought, this investigation will go haywire.

.   .   .   .   .

Moon's office was almost identical with Pallett's, except that both rug and desk were one size smaller, to denote a lower rank. The Acting Colonial Secretary was smoking a pipe and sat in his shirt sleeves, his coat thrown over a chair. Vachell explained that he wanted a list of all the files that should have been in circulation up at Government House the night before. He wanted to make sure that nothing was missing from the Governor's study.

'You'd better come along to the registry,' Moon remarked. 'I think Fernandez, the head filing clerk, can give you what you want.' He put on his coat and they walked along the narrow, creaking wooden passage to a large room where all the files were kept.

Vachell felt that he was gazing at the dynamo that provided motive power for the whole colony of Chania. That was the wrong metaphor, though; there was something essentially non-dynamic about a roomful of files. More like the centre of an immense spider's web, perhaps. Threads reached back from these dusty stacks to the remotest corners of the still half-tamed country. If an ailing cow lay down to die on some distant trackless plain the condition of its intestines might become immortalized in a neatly typed minute, puzzled over by departmental heads, discussed at conferences. If an untutored savage disagreed with his father-in-law about the number of goats to be paid for his bride, a file, minuted by legal experts and even pondered by under-secretaries in distant Downing Street, might record the dispute for posterity.

Outwardly, however, the registry showed no signs of the dramatic destiny with which Vachell's imagination endowed it. Two or three clerks sat at littered ink-stained desks or strolled about the stacks to extract or replace a file. At one end of the room stood the index cabinets. Fernandez, a melancholy-looking Goan with a meticulous memory and, in private life, a passion for billiards, paused here to give a little lecture on the card index system. It was a very simple one. Each file was classified under a letter which indicated the subject, and a number, and its movements were recorded on its card. The reference numbers of all files which went up to Government House from the Secretariat were noted on a special card. When the files returned, a clerk ticked them off to show that they had gone back to the stacks. It would be a simple matter, Fernandez said, to make out a list of all the files which should have been at Government House on the day of the crime. He put a junior clerk on to the job at once.

Fernandez continued his personally conducted tour of the registry. 'That door over there,' he said, 'leads into a small room where the confidential files are kept. I have no key.'

'Who has?' Vachell asked.

'The Colonial Secretary always keeps the key,' Moon put in. 'Pallett handed it over to me this morning—the insignia of office, as it were. There's nothing much in here, as a matter of fact. Most of the really secret files—military defence and so forth—are up at G.H. Some of the confidential dispatches from the Secretary of State are down here, and the rest are mainly P files.'

'What are they?' Vachell asked.

'Personal. Every officer in the administration, from the C.S. to the most junior forest ranger, has a personal file. It deals with conditions of service, pay, reports from senior officers, and so forth. When a question of promotion comes up the files of the people in the running for the job are gone through by the head of the department concerned. Otherwise they're not used much, except to keep them up to date on leave movements and so on.'

'Do these files get marked on the card index when they go out, same as the others?' Vachell asked.

'Oh yes,' Fernandez replied. 'All files coming through the registry are marked on the cards, P files as well.' His tone implied a rebuke to Vachell for making the rather scandalous suggestion that a file might move in any direction without strict tabs being kept on its progress in the registry.

Vachell thanked him, and took delivery of a now completed list of all files marked out to Government House. He strolled back with Moon along the passage, discussing the Plaindweller League. The Secretary for Native Affairs filled his pipe and Vachell handed him a metal match-box. At the door of Moon's room the policeman took his leave.

As he walked down the creaking wooden steps of the veranda into the shaded gravel courtyard below, a large car drew up in front. It flew a little Union Jack from the radiator cap and carried a large tin crown on the front. A native driver sprang smartly out and opened the door. The first thing to emerge was a crest of flowing plumes which fluttered gaily in the breeze. A uniformed and bemedalled body followed shortly. It was Sir Bertrand Flower, and he was having trouble with his sword. The native driver had to free it from the doorway before Sir Bertrand, puffing from the effort, could extract his legs. Decorations on his chest dangled like ripe fruit from a hanging branch. As he descended, the plumes, falling forward over his face, overbalanced his cocked hat, and it fell with a soft thud on to the gravel drive.

Vachell jumped forward and retrieved the hat. He handed it back and saluted.

'Ah, thank you, thank you,' the Governor said. 'Very clumsy things, these plumes. Inconvenient in a wind.' He adjusted the hat while Vachell studied his face. He looked tired and ill, grey-skinned in the bright sunlight, but he seemed to have recovered from the shock of the night before.

'I trust that you are making good progress in your task,' he continued. 'I suppose that you are satisfied that it is the work of some half-demented native? Something to do with this terrorist League that I have heard rumours about?'

'We're investigating that just as fast as we can, sir,' Vachell replied.

'Very distressing business,' Sir Bertrand went on, tugging the belt of his white tunic into position around a somewhat fleshy middle. The white plumes on his restored hat fluttered in the breeze. 'It may, I fear, have serious repercussions. I have always supported the right of natives to form associations to protect their own interests, but this appears to be something quite different. It is, perhaps, hardly a coincidence that this movement should have originated in Chania. Now in Totseland I think I may claim that our native policy is such that the incentive to form these societies *sub rosa* is lacking. However, that is another matter.' Sir Bertrand pulled himself up, hitched his sword a little farther to the back, and took his gloves from the driver.

Vachell remembered that there was something he wanted to ask Sir Bertrand, but he couldn't call it to mind. Something that Beaton had said—no, Jeudwine...

He recalled it when Flower was half-way up the steps. 'Oh, excuse me, sir,' he said. 'Might I ask just one more question? I believe you know a bit about the stock market. Could you tell me if you've ever heard of African Equities?'

Flower had turned at the question, and Vachell, for the first time since the case broke, received a shock. The mention of African Equities seemed to hit the Governor like a physical blow. His jaw dropped slightly open and he clutched the railing of the steps with one hand. His face, already grey, went ashen. Vachell was afraid he was going to have a heart attack, and stepped forward, ready to catch him if he fell.

But after that one involuntary action the Governor recovered his control. There was a moment of silence, and his voice, when he replied, was almost normal.

'I have never heard of it in my life,' he said. 'And what, if I may ask, makes you imagine that I have?'

Vachell looked up at him, his helmet tilted over one eye. His lean face was quite expressionless. 'From something we found among Sir Malcolm's documents,' he replied slowly, drawling more than usual, 'we concluded that you would be likely to know.' He kept his eyes fixed on Sir Bertrand's face.

This time the Governor's control was better; but the knuckles of his hand turned white as they gripped the rail.

'I have no idea what you are talking about,' he said. 'I

have never heard of the stock you mention, and your subsequent remark is, therefore, meaningless to me.' He turned away, mounted the remaining steps, and disappeared into the Secretariat without looking back.

9

It was pleasantly peaceful at police headquarters that afternoon. Every one was at the funeral. The streets of Marula were quiet and deserted, save for a few natives wandering aimlessly about or lolling sleepily in the sun. All the shops were closed, and Marula's inhabitants, white, black, and brown, poured in a steady stream towards the Scottish Church, or lined the streets to watch the solemn profession, led by the KALI band with partially muffled drums, go by.

Vachell sat at ease in his office and munched a chicken sandwich and a jam puff by way of a belated lunch. He watched, with interest, a battered Buick touring car, full of Indians, draw up in the road outside his window. One of the occupants stood on the step and addressed the native loiterers squatting in the shade of the gum trees. A small crowd collected round the Buick and when they dispersed a few moments later Vachell observed that each of them wore a white calico band round his upper arm. A smart piece of salesmanship, he reflected. White men were wearing black arm-bands, so obviously black men should wear white arm-bands—they showed up better. At five cents a time the Indians would clean up a nice little fortune.

The fingerprint expert came down to headquarters at 2.30 in response to a telephone call. Vachell emptied his pockets and handed over two flat metal cigarette-cases and a metal match-box, carefully wrapped in separate handkerchiefs.

'Take the prints on all of these,' he instructed. 'There'll be some more just as soon as I can figure out a way to get them. Compare these with the thumb-print on the glass, and let me know if there's anything right away.'

The assistant nodded. 'The other set on the tumbler was Mr Jeudwine's all right,' he said. 'That just leaves the extra thumb. I'm having that matched with all the sets of known criminals in our records. Nothing to report yet, but they haven't finished.'

The next step was to dispatch a cable to Scotland Yard. It read:

Please send all information available about company known as African Equities Limited including names directors and principal shareholders if known and financial position. Should appreciate immediate reply.

It went off in code, at priority rates.

Government House, Vachell reckoned, would be deserted while the funeral was in progress. He wanted to have a quiet look round before things were too badly disturbed. His old box-body Chevrolet rattled noisily up to the porch and the two KALI guards stood to attention as he walked in. No one was home, as he expected, except Abdi, who seemed to be a fixture. He materialized, apparently, out of the air—certainly Vachell neither saw nor heard him approach—as unruffled and dignified as ever. The only concession he had made to the occasion was to clothe his portly chest in a more sober waistcoat. He wore one of black and silver.

Vachell decided to go over the ground again with the Somali head boy. Abdi did not go back on any of his previous statements. He had been on duty in the hall from ten o'clock onwards. He was certain that Jeudwine had not been away from his room for more than five minutes, and equally certain that no one had entered Jeudwine's room during his absence. Just before the secretary had returned the Chief Justice and his wife had come into the hall from the ballroom and Abdi had helped him into his coat.

'You have a key to the cupboard in bwana Jeudwine's

room where the whisky is kept?' Vachell asked.

'Yes, bwana. It is always kept locked. Every morning I see that clean glasses are put into the cupboard, if glasses have been used at night, and then I lock it up again.'

'How about yesterday? Did you put clean glasses into the cupboard in the morning?'

Abdi thought for a moment, and then nodded slowly. 'Yes, bwana. Yesterday I put two glasses into the cupboard, according to custom.'

'You brought them yourself, from the pantry?'

Abdi's face was bland and expressionless, but it somehow managed to convey an impression of mild contempt.

'Who else would bring them?' he asked. 'And where from but the pantry?'

Vachell could think of no answer to this rather devastating question. He explained that he wanted to take another look at the Governor's study. Abdi led him in dignified silence to the door and opened it with his master-key.

The blinds were still drawn down as they had been the night before. Vachell flicked them up and let in a flood of sunlight. A beam glinted on the blade of one of the spears hanging on the wall. There was a smell of stale tobacco smoke in the air. Petals fell silently in a little shower from a bowl of roses on the desk. A glance told Vachell that nothing had been disturbed.

He sat down at the desk, propped his knees against the edge, and considered the situation, his khaki helmet with its red police badge tipped over one eye, a cigarette in his lips, his eyes half shut. This is a hell of case, he thought. The music goes round and around, but it won't come out. He tried to picture the scene that had taken place less than twenty-four hours ago in the room where he was sitting. He imagined a man—black, he wondered, or white?—stealthily worming his way in through the open window, inch by inch so as not to disturb the unsuspecting victim buried in his work on the desk. Then, the quick pounce, thin, hard cord biting into soft flesh, the choking, convulsive threshing of a helpless man's body, the stillness, the search. . . .

No, that couldn't be right. For Olivia Brandeis had seen the blind drawn down at 10.40, and the killer couldn't have got in through the window once the blind was down without disturbing the man at the bureau. And Watson said he'd seen the Governor alive at 10.48. If Janis could trace that phone call H.E. was supposed to be answering when Watson saw him, it would prove the story. If not, then things would look pretty black for Watson. . . .

Vachell turned his attention to the desk and made a thorough search among the papers in the drawers. He found only one that seemed to be of interest. It was a letter from a firm of solicitors called James & Durstine, of Tower House, London, E.C.2; and it read:

March 15th

Dear Sir Malcolm,

I have your letter of March 6th and I will do my best to send the information you require. This is not, naturally, the sort of inquiry we are normally prepared to deal with, but since you ask it as a personal favour I will do what I can. I hope to let you have a brief report, covering the points you mention, in about a week's time. Yours sincerely,

Charles Durstine

Vachell put the letter in his pocket and strolled across to Jeudwine's office. A quick run through the desk yielded nothing. It was piled high with telegrams of condolence and draft replies, and the waste-paper basket was overflowing with torn-up papers. He upset it on the floor and sorted carefully through the contents. Nothing but telegrams and crumpled yellow envelopes. He didn't know what he expected to find, anyway.

At the bottom of the heap he came upon some fragments of burnt paper which dissolved into ash as he disturbed them. When he blew at the papers quite a cloud of ash rose from folds of the twisted scraps. He went through the heap again, but found no recognizable fragments. The burning job had been well done. The final result of the search was one corner of a sheet of paper with no writing on it. It was light blue, good quality note-paper. Vachell scrutinized it carefully and compared it with a sheet of Government House embossed note-paper lying on Jeudwine's desk. They were the same.

He turned to the desk again and unearthed an ash-tray from beneath a heap of telegrams. It contained a small pile of charred matches and the stubs of two cigarettes. Vachell picked up the stubs and examined them closely. One bore traces of lipstick round the edge. He took an envelope off the desk, placed the stub inside and put it in his pocket.

Car wheels sounded on the gravel outside. The funeral party was returning. Vachell replaced the waste paper in its basket and slipped out by the west entrance, unseen.

.   .   .   .

Janis had just come in to report when his superior got back to police headquarters. He was full of excitement and reminded Vachell of an enthusiastic Great Dane.

'I think I've got something, sir,' he said breathlessly. 'It's this phone call you told me to check up on, the one Mr Watson says he saw H.E. in the middle of. Well, he couldn't have, because there wasn't one.'

'Say, is this a mind-reading test?' his superior said, grinning. 'Let's have the story with a dash of grammar in it. Go ahead.'

'Well, I got a list of all the calls made through the Marula exchange between a quarter and five to eleven last night,' Janis went on, a little abashed, 'with the names and addresses of the people who made them. Apparently there's very little going on at that time of night, and there were only five recorded. Two were made by Indians ringing up their pals for a chat, one was a call to a doctor from a woman who started having a baby, another was from the manager of Dane's, who rang up Imperial Airways to find out if the northbound plane was going to start on time the next morning, and the last was from a woman at a bridge-party in Parkside, asking her husband to come and fetch her home. I've seen all the people who made the calls—except the woman with the baby, and her doctor verified that—and I'm certain they're all genuine. So H.E. couldn't have been answering a phone call at ten-forty-eight last night!' He paused excitedly, watching his superior's face.

'Good work,' Vachell said. 'That certainly busts Watson's story wide open.'

'I went straight down to the Watsons' house to find out what time he got home,' Janis went on, 'but of course, as you said, the boys were hopelessly vague, so that was a washout. What they did tell me was, that Watson just dropped his wife at the house and went straight off again in the car, which means he could have got back to G.H. soon after eleven.'

'That certainly puts Watson in bad,' Vachell said. 'Anything else?'

'I didn't see what more I could do about Watson for the moment, so I started on the other statements. The head filing clerk at the Secretariat, Fernandez, happened to have gone back that night to catch up with some work, and he says Mr Pallett got down there at a quarter to ten and left about an hour later, though he couldn't specify the exact time. And Mr Moon's story is okay too. The exchange have got a call charged against his house number at ten-forty-four. He lives by himself, and his boy says that no visitors came to his house all evening, so Mr Moon must have been at home at that time to make it. That's all I've had time for so far.'

'That lets Moon out, I guess,' Vachell agreed. 'And maybe Pallett. You've done a swell job. Now here's something else. See this list of files?' He handed Janis the list that Fernandez had given him at the Secretariat. It read:

A/991.	Witchcraft Ordinance: Draft to Amend No. 86 of 1931.
G/73.	Parliamentary Commission on Colonial Economic Development: Recommendations *re* Chania.
D/827.	Revenue Estimates: Customs and Excise Receipts.
R/56.	Indian Franchise: Dispatch from Government of India.
B/329.	Mbale District Council: Proposals for Sewage Disposal.
M/662.	Maji River Basin: Proposed Concession to Japanese Farm Industries Ltd.
H/27.	Federation Proposals: Chania and Totseland Railways (Discrepancies in Rating).
H/29.	Federation Proposals: Chania and Totseland Railways (Valuations).
H/33.	Federation Proposals: Chania and Totseland (Federal Council).
V/154.	Rinderpest Quarantine: Agreement with Totseland.

'Take a look at it,' Vachell told him. 'Anything about it strike you as screwy?'

Janis read it through slowly, his forehead puckered in a frown. 'No, sir, I don't think so,' he said. 'Ought it to? I mean, it just seems to be a list of files.'

'Sure, it's a list of files. It's the files that were marked out to G.H. from Secretariat. I want you to check on the first five to find out where they are. They may still be up at G.H. or they may have gone back to the registry. The last five have been taken care of already; they were all on H.E.'s bureau. I want you to make sure there's nothing missing.'

'Okay, sir,' Janis answered. He took up his helmet and made for the door. 'But is there anything wrong? I mean, you said...'

'Forget it,' Vachell said. 'Guess it was just my imagination.'

.   .   .   .   .

He drew a pad towards him and drafted another cable to London. It was addressed to James & Durstine, Tower House, London, E.C.2, and said:

> *Did you dispatch letter to Sir Malcolm McLeod Government House Marula Chania by airmail leaving London March twenty-second. Please cable reply immediately together with indication contents. Letter may have important bearing McLeod murder.*

.   .   .   .   .

The most obvious solution of a murder case, Vachell reflected, was generally the right one. It could have been Watson, of course. He had no alibi. His motive was a knock-out. He was the only person who claimed to have seen the Governor alive after 10.30.

You could reconstruct it easily. Watson had seen Jeudwine leave his office to attend to Moon's files, slipped in while Abdi's back was turned, strangled the Governor, and got out again before Jeudwine returned. He had noticed the missing letter, the 'stinking fish', on the bureau, and taken it with him, replacing it with a file, in the hope that its loss would provide a motive to distract the police.

Then he had gone straight along the passage, opened the Governor's door, and invented the clumsy story that he had seen his victim telephoning in an attempt to make the crime appear to have been committed later than was really the case. Of course he had established an alibi after that. It was all as obvious as a haystack; the case was over.

Vachell ought to have been satisfied, but he wasn't. He didn't quite know why. Perhaps it was because the whole case was a little too obvious, like a stage piece. Perhaps because he wondered whether Watson really cared enough for his wife or her fidelity to work himself up to the pitch of strangling her lover. Or perhaps because it seemed strange that an intelligent man like Watson should have invented such an unconvincing tale. It would have been far better to have said nothing. Oh, nuts, thought Vachell, he just lost his head.

He looked in the drawer of his desk for a fresh supply of Beechnut gum and noticed a set of the police photographs of the Governor's corpse and the room where the crime had been committed. An idea came to him. He examined the pictures carefully under the unshaded light of the bulb dangling above his blotter.

One of them, taken from the doorway into the passage, showed the desk at the other end of the room; the reading-lamp; a dark, hunched mass, which was the body, behind; and the closed window and drawn blind beyond that. Vachell propped it up against the inkstand and studied it with a frown of concentration. Yes, the idea was all right. He could use it. He would ask Watson just one question. And Watson's life, probably, would hang upon the answer. One reply would prove his innocence. The other would not definitely condemn him, but it would make his guilt a hundred-to-one chance. Everything depended on that one reply.

He had reached the door when the telephone called him back to the desk. It was the fingerprint expert.

'I've been trying to get you for the last hour,' he said. 'I've got some news. I took the prints from those three metal surfaces you gave me, and one of them fits the thumb-print on the tumbler. I thought you—'

'For God's sake!' Vachell exclaimed. 'You what? Say that over again.'

The voice at the other end repeated the sentence. 'There's no mistake,' he added. 'You got a beautiful thumb impression on the metal. It's a perfect tent. Shall I bring them along now for you to identify the case?'

'Sure,' Vachell said. 'Bring them right away.'

He hung up. This was something entirely new. He had taken the prints as a matter of routine, to start a collection. He hadn't expected to make a bull.

Beaton, Popple, and Moon. The tumbler had been locked in the cupboard until Jeudwine took it into H.E.'s study less than half-an-hour before the murder. And no one had touched it after the crime was discovered.

The fingerprint expert came in briskly, carrying two metal cigarette-cases and a match-box, each bearing a tag.

'This will make me late for dinner,' he said, 'but I thought you might like to know.'

'Which case had the print on it?' Vachell asked.

'This one.' He dropped one of the cigarette-cases on to the blotter.

It was the case that Vachell had handed to Donovan Popple.

.   .   .   .   .

Major Armitage was feeling, the next morning, exceedingly pleased with the way things were going. Only one full day since the murder, and already it began to look as though they had found their man. Scotland Yard couldn't beat that record. His moustache looked more bristling and aggressive than ever.

Vachell reported at headquarters at nine o'clock. He had already put in an hour's work at Government House, inquiring a second time into the history of the tumbler. Abdi refused to be shaken on his story, and Jeudwine swore that he had not opened the cupboard where the glasses were kept until he had mixed his dead chief's drink at 10.30 on the night of the murder. There didn't seem to be any loophole for a mistake.

'Looks as if Popple sneaked into Sir Malcolm's study to air his views on the damned Jap business,' Armitage said, 'and then lost his head and attacked H.E. Always was a hot-headed sort of a feller, making these tommy-rot speeches against the Government. Damned bad form.'

They found Popple having breakfast at the Mazuri Club, which stood in a pleasant, shady suburb of Marula, with a golf course in front of it and tennis courts behind. The room looked bright and cheerful, with the sun streaming in through open french windows. Their suspect was not allowing qualms of conscience to interfere with his appetite. He was tackling his second kipper when the police arrived. They went straight to his table and Armitage asked, in his most impressive manner, if Mr Popple would be so good enough to see them on an important matter.

'Sit down, gentlemen; sit down,' Popple said. 'You'll forgive me for not coming outside, I hope. I do love kippers, and we can't get them out on the farm. That's the real reason I waste me time on the damfool Council, if you want to know.' He grinned at them and stuffed his large mouth full of kipper.

Armitage felt this reception to be in very bad taste. One shouldn't guzzle kippers in a club dining-room while practically being accused of murder. He cleared his throat, made a short introductory speech, and stated the facts briefly and clearly. 'I should like to hear your explanation, Mr Popple,' he concluded, 'of how your thumb-print got on to the glass found in Sir Malcolm's study, and I must warn you that anything you say may be taken down and used in evidence against you.' He looked across quickly at Vachell, who took the cue and drew out his notebook.

Popple was either a superb actor or his surprise was genuine. He abandoned his kipper and stared at Armitage with his mouth half-open in amazement.

'Well, I'll be...,' he said finally. 'I never heard the like of it in all my life! How in the world could the mark of my thumb ever come to be on that glass?'

'That's what I'm asking you,' Armitage replied.

'Then I'll tell you the answer, and it's not so difficult,' Popple retorted, his face resuming its more ordinary expression of indignation. 'The print of my thumb was never there at all. You take my fingerprints by some piece of cheap trickery and then you come up here while I'm eating me breakfast and tell me I'm a murderer! And that's what we pay the police for! They're so damned incompetent they'll even muddle up a simple test like this one—and to think that I supported a rise in the police vote last year! You'd have found that thumb-print belonged to President Roosevelt or the Dionne quintuplets if you'd played your bloody-fool tricks with a cigarette-case on them!'

'Will you stop abusing the police force, sir, and answer my question!' Armitage made the spoons and forks jump as he banged his fist on the table. His face was flushed with anger. 'This is not one of your damned political meetings! Your thumb-print was found on that glass, and it's useless to deny it. When did you have your hands on it?'

Popple's sunburnt face went a deeper shade as he flung his napkin on the table and jumped to his feet, spilling coffee as he jolted the table.

'I'll not be spoken to like that by a policeman or by any one else!' he exclaimed. 'This is my club and I'll ask you to leave it. If you want to arrest me you can get your damned warrant and come back and do it, and to hell with you! I never handled that glass in McLeod's study for the good reason that I was never inside there at all, and if you don't believe me you can go to the devil.'

He strode out of one of the french windows in a tearing rage, his ginger hair flaming in the sunlight almost as vividly as the crimson bougainvillea that climbed up the side of the house. Armitage swore angrily, and an expressionless African replaced the spilt cup of coffee with a clean one. Several members of the club who had been watching the scene with fascinated attention resumed their breakfasts.

'Come on, Vachell,' the Commissioner said. 'I'll have him arrested for this, the damned impudent, hairy-heeled bounder, if it's the last thing I do on earth.' They drove back to headquarters to a running accompaniment of furious mutterings. 'Not safe to leave him at large,' Armitage barked. 'Might do anything. No control. Insolent, tub-thumping, muck-raking politician! Always knew the feller was a wrong 'un. Got megalomania, if you ask me. Well, he's gone too far this time.'

'There's no evidence yet, sir,' Vachell ventured. 'You can't hang a man on just a thumb-print. It will be pretty hard to pin anything on him, I'd say.'

'Nonsense, Vachell. Get him under lock and key and he'll collapse like a pricked balloon. You'll see. I know his type. All fireworks and no guts. The yellow streak—all murderers have it.'

Vachell looked surprised, but forbore to dispute the point. They found police headquarters picketed by local pressmen, stirred to action by cables from the London newspapers for whom they were correspondents. Vachell managed to get rid of them all except an Indian, who reiterated his demand for a statement from the Chania police as to what steps were being taken to safeguard the lives and property of British Indian subjects. When asked what newspaper he represented he replied with dignity that he held a watching brief for the Government of India.

.   .   .   .   .

Pallett had summoned the two police heads to a 'progress conference' at eleven. He greeted them with a nod, and waved a podgy hand at the two dilapidated chairs. He was looking harassed and feeling bad tempered. Two rather brusque cables from the Secretary of State had just come in. Boiled down to plain English, they explained that it was very important to arrest the murderer at once, a fact which he felt he had already grasped for himself.

The Secretary of State, for his part, was thoroughly annoyed. The English press, he considered, had given undue prominence to the unfortunate incident. It had even gone to the length of suggesting that the crime might be a symptom of discontent with Colonial Office rule.

Several more questions were down for answer in the House that afternoon, and things seemed to be brewing up for an acrimonious debate. A Labour member was to ask whether it was a fact that threatening language against the Governor had been used at a recent meeting of the Ngombe Farmers' Association following the Chania Government's decision not to reduce the railway tariff on rock-salt, and whether any connexion existed between these inflammatory statements and the recent outrage committed in Marula. Another was to inquire whether the Secretary of State was satisfied that order could be maintained in Chania so long as Africans were precluded from holding senior positions in the police force and Judiciary. Three Tory members were to ask whether, in view of the apparent spread of terrorism and political violence within the British Empire, the Government would not declare that it would in no circumstances whatever consider ceding any part of the Colonial Empire, whether mandated or otherwise, to a foreign power.

Armitage plunged straight into an account of the case against Popple. 'I think we've got our man, sir,' he concluded. 'He's threatened Sir Malcolm's life on more than one occasion, before witnesses. You know yourself what a state of mind this Japanese concession had got him into. There's no doubt in my mind that he broke into Sir Malcolm's study on Tuesday night, had an argument about the Jap show, and lost his head. The feller's always seemed unbalanced to me. A wild light in his eye. But, as Vachell says, we haven't got enough evidence to hang him yet. A strong presumptive case and a thumb-print, and that's about all. But we'll get it, sir, I can promise you that. I shall leave no stone unturned.'

Pallett brightened noticeably during the Commissioner's report. At the end he remarked that the whole business was most unsavoury.

'We must not, however, allow our personal feelings to blind us to our duty,' he added. 'Popple is, as I have long considered, a most subversive influence in the colony. The attacks that he has frequently made on the Government are not only in the worst possible taste but show evidence of—ah—unbalanced judgement. I must confess that, unpleasant as it is to believe a European guilty of such a brutal and—ah—disloyal crime, I am not altogether surprised to hear that Popple is—ah—under grave suspicion.'

'Unless he can explain away that thumb-print, sir, we'll get him,' Armitage said.

Pallett frowned and played with a pencil. 'The last thing I should wish you to do would be to influence your judgment in any way,' he continued. 'At the same time I feel bound to remind you that on more than one occasion he has given vent to the most ill-chosen, I might even say seditious, utterances. He once went so far as to compare the late Governor with some American gangster then being much publicized, and the heads of departments to the gangster's—ah—molls, I believe the term is. He went on to propose that the settlers should create a force of—ah—G-men to "break the racket"—I think that was the phrase he used. G-men, he said, were accustomed to "act first and argue after"; and he advocated a similar course for the settlers. I must confess that it never occurred to me that he might mean these threats seriously; but in the present circumstances it is our duty to recall the fact that he did utter them.'

'He said that, did he?' Armitage exclaimed. 'Infernal impudence! Talking like a damned Red.'

'I shall, of course, leave you free to act as you think best,' the Colonial Secretary continued. 'But I would urge you to remember that the murderer is a desperate man, and that you are the—ah—custodian of the public safety. It is only fair to warn you that any further trouble would have serious repercussions—very serious indeed. The Secretary of State takes a most—ah—grave view of the situation, and he might even call for resignations were he not satisfied that everything possible was being done to apprehend the criminal and to preserve the peace. You will, I am sure, bear this in mind.'

He nodded a brief dismissal, in the manner of an old-style headmaster releasing two prefects from his presence.

10

When Vachell got back to headquarters he found a decoded cable from Scotland Yard waiting for him there. The message said:

> *Your inquiry twenty ninth. African Equities registered July 1935. Chairman Sir Felix Landauer directors Lord Hoxted Major Eric Fripton-Scoresby L.T. Parrot George Hewson. Company holds shares in following firms all engaged trading enterprises eastern and central Africa including Chania Totseland. Burton & Rutherford The Great Lakes Export Corporation and Blackett Brothers. Business mainly export cotton textiles largely low priced piece goods. Financial position believed excellent. Shares held by directors no public issue capital. No reason suspect any irregularities. Do you require further information.*

On the strength of this cable, Vachell put through a radio telephone call from Marula to London.

It was a long chance, a ridiculously long chance, but Vachell felt pretty certain that Popple would spend that night in jail, and his hand was forced. If the idea turned out to be a flop the Treasury would be down on his tail like a ton of bricks. He ought to get their authorization for a radio call first anyway, but he knew they wouldn't give it, so he didn't try.

The service had only recently been installed. Calls were still a rare event. The Marula supervisor spent most of the morning getting through. He was not yet blasé about the thrill of exchanging remarks with a far-off voice in St. Martin's-le Grand. 'Bit foggy here this morning,' the voice said. 'How's things over your way? Nice and bright? Ah! I envy you. Clap your hands and a nigger comes along with a glass of something to cool you off. I know! Mansion House supervisor, that's right. . . . All clear. . . . Just a moment, here's your party.'

Vachell got through to Charles Durstine, head of the firm of James & Durstine, and explained his authority in official and impressive words. Durstine had received the cable half an hour ago.

'You were right in assuming that I dispatched a letter to Sir Malcolm on the twenty-second,' he said. 'But I am afraid that I cannot reveal the contents. They were strictly confidential.'

'It's a matter of vital importance in our investigation of Sir Malcolm McLeod's murder,' Vachell said. 'On behalf of the Government of Chania, I ask you to tell me the contents.'

The lawyer hedged again, and Vachell wasted a minute of precious and expensive time trying to convince him that it was his duty to his dead client to talk.

'You are forcing me to commit a breach of confidence,' Durstine said finally. 'Hello? Are you there?'

'I'm here all right. Shoot, please. Just what did Sir Malcolm want to know?'

'He wrote to me for information regarding a certain company,' the voice began, resigned now to the distasteful task. 'Since we specialize in company legislation we have a wide—'

'Skip it, please, and let's have the facts. What—'

The line crackled furiously and then buzzed. A voice said suddenly, 'Johannesburg. Germiston supervisor?' and then there was silence. London came through again. 'Are you there? Can you hear me? What?'

'Go ahead, I'm here. What company?'

'A company called Blackett Brothers. I understand it has

a big cotton-piece export business to Totseland. He asked for information about its financial ·position and the distribution of its share capital. I feel I can hardly—'

'Go on, please. I want details. What did you tell him?'

'The controlling interest in Blackett Brothers has recently been acquired by a holding company, African Equities. I told Sir Malcolm that to the best of my knowledge the company was in a very sound financial position. The recent improvement in the world economic situation—'

'That's swell. I sure am pleased to hear about the economic situation. But I'm not spending two pounds ten a minute of somebody else's money for a talk on economics. What more did Sir Malcolm want to know?'

'Well—er—Inspector, it's hardly... I don't feel that over the telephone...'

'This is a *murder*...' The line went dead again and Morse signals started to cut in. A voice said: 'Have you finished?' Vachell shouted, 'No,' and got no reply. More buzzing, and then he heard London again.

'...have any bearing on Sir Malcolm's death. Perhaps, if you undertake to keep the matter entirely confidential... Hello? Are you there?'

'Hello! Yes. Go ahead with the story.'

'Well, Sir Malcolm wanted to know whether any of the Directors of African Equities were newcomers to the Board.'

'And were they?'

'One of them, yes. Major Fripton-Scoresby. In order to qualify as a director he recently acquired a block of thirty thousand one-pound shares. They were transferred from the Chairman's holding—Sir Felix Landauer.'

'And who's this Major Fripton-Scoresby?'

'I understand that he is a retired Indian Army officer, and that his address is Clayton Fells, Western Avenue, Salcombe. He has not, I believe, held any directorships in the City before.'

'All right, go ahead, what else was there?'

'That was all. Sir Malcolm said—'

A voice broke in: 'Hello! Marula. Your time is up.' There were several clicks and then London came back on the line. 'I must ask you on no account to make public the information...' The voice faded and the line clicked again.

'Was it all right?' the Marula supervisor said. 'How did you hear?'

'Not enough,' Vachell answered. 'But the line was swell.'

He hung up and scratched his head. 'Major Fripton-Scoresby,' he said aloud. 'Now who in hell is he?' Then he realized that there was a perfectly simple way to find out. He composed a cable to Scotland Yard and sent it off at once.

.   .   .   .   .

Vachell had told Janis to report at three o'clock and it was nearly that before he was through with his overseas telephone call. Shadows from the red-flowering gum trees had already begun to fall across the lawn outside the office. He sighed regretfully for a lost lunch and dug some more gum out of his desk.

Janis came in at five-past, taking the steps three at a time, still looking enthusiastic, though hot. He mopped his forehead and tried to smooth down a dishevelled mop of blond hair.

'I've checked on those files, sir,' he reported. 'They're all present and correct. There was one with the A.G., one at the Treasury, and one with Mr Pallett, and the other two had gone back to the Secretariat. So there's nothing missing, I'm afraid.'

Vachell smiled and offered his assistant a piece of gum. 'We can get along without anything else being swiped,' he said. 'It was just a precaution.'

'I think I spotted what you meant when you said there was something funny about this list of files, sir,' Janis went on. 'All the files except one were about important things like the Totseland federation, and the budget, and so on. But there was one on a very minor subject, a sewage disposal scheme for Mbale township, and it was funny that an unimportant file like that should have gone up to the Governor. Is that right?'

'Say, you'll make a smart detective,' his chief said. 'You scored a bull. Nine times out of ten, little inconsistencies like that don't mean a thing, but just occasionally you get a break and they lead some place. So they're worth watching out for.'

Janis flushed with pleasure under his tan. 'I'm afraid there's nothing in it this time, sir,' he said. 'The sewage file was ticked off on the registry card index to show that it came back from G.H. yesterday, and I asked to see it to make sure it was okay. It was in the stacks all right. Then Fernandez—'

He broke off as the telephone rang and Vachell lifted the receiver. It was Crane, the officer who had been put in charge of the League of the Plaindweller inquiry. He was speaking from the KALI lines.

'Something very unfortunate has happened, sir,' he said. 'I'm afraid Corporal Machoka has given our man the slip. Machoka failed to turn up for a parade at eleven this morning. The man I put on to watch him has been hunting high and low, but he can't get any lead at all. Apparently no one has seen Machoka since late last night. He seems to have vanished completely.'

Vachell listened without interruption and gave brief instructions to concentrate every available man on a comb-out of Chinyani, and to send a small flying column down to the Wabenda reserve.

'If Machoka got scared and took a run-out powder,' he said, 'ten to one he's headed for his home, wherever that is. If it's something else—well, I don't know. Go over those waste meadows in back of Chinyani where the refuse dumps are, and keep an eye on the morgue.'

He hung up and looked at Janis. 'This case gets more

balled up all the time,' he said.

'So Machoka's got the wind up and run, has he?' Janis said. 'Gosh, that's a development. Perhaps he knows something.'

'Maybe too much,' Vachell said.

.　　　.　　　.　　　.　　　.

The Education Department was one of a line of dusty wooden buildings which flanked a gravel road, shaded by tall eucalyptus trees, generally known as Bureaucrats' Row. A clump of jacarandas in full flower shielded it from the road and provided a dash of vivid violet colour against the drab background of light monotonous dun.

Vachell found the Director of Education in his office, behind a desk littered with papers and scientific journals. Sunlight fell in a barred square on to the worn carpet, and motes of dust danced formlessly in the sharp light. The click of distant typewriters broke the stillness of the hot afternoon. Watson greeted his visitor without any visible sign of surprise, pleasure, or hostility. His face gave very little away. Signs of fatigue would in any case be masked by the deep vertical lines running from nose to chin. But his eyes looked tired and restless, and he fidgeted a lot with his hands.

Vachell dived into the middle of the subject without preliminary explanations.

'Listen here, Mr Watson,' he said. 'I'm going to describe to you exactly what you saw when you looked in through H.E.'s door on Tuesday night. If there's any detail wrong, however small, I want you to pull me up. I want to get the picture exactly right, just as you saw it when you opened the door.'

Watson raised his eyebrows and leant back in his chair. He nodded to Vachell to proceed.

'You knocked on the door and H.E. didn't reply. You knocked a second time and got no answer. So you opened the door and saw H.E. way over at the other end of the room, sitting behind the bureau. He had the telephone in his right hand, and he was talking into it. You only heard him say seven words and you couldn't hear those distinctly. The top light was switched off, but the reading-light on the bureau was on. It threw a beam of light on to the blotting-pad on his bureau, and on the pad was an open file. He was turning over the pages with his left hand—'

'No, that's not right,' Watson broke in. 'I never saw what you're describing now. I don't know what was on the desk; in fact, now I come to think of it, I don't think the light was shining on to the desk at all.' He frowned at the floor in an effort at recollection.

Vachell's eyes flickered and he breathed a little more deeply. He felt the excitement of a hunter taking aim for the critical shot after a long and cunning stalk.

'Think carefully, Mr Watson,' he said. 'Keep that scene in your mind's eye. Think of that beam of light from the reading-lamp. You don't believe it was directed on to the blotter. Where was it directed, then?'

He leant forward, his body tense with expectation. Watson went on frowning at the carpet. Then he looked up.

'I remember now,' he said. 'I had a vague feeling when I opened the door that something wasn't quite right, but I didn't realize what it was until just now. The light was directed away from the desk and on to the floor in front of it. There was a pool of light on the carpet. One would have expected it to be shining on to the top of the desk, naturally. That was what struck me as peculiar when I opened the door, but the sensation was so momentary and superficial that it faded immediately. A very interesting example of the remarkably slipshod manner in which the conscious brain records, or fails to record, impressions photographed on the retina of the eye, while the sub-conscious, nevertheless, retains them. What is the significance of this, Superintendent? Does it prove anything?'

'You bet it does, sir,' Vachell answered, getting to his

feet. He felt so pleased that his test had worked out that he laughed. 'You should go buy yourself a drink. If your retina had held out on you Tuesday night I guess you'd have been arrested for murder tomorrow morning.'

Watson's surprise was expressed by raised eyebrows, but he moved no other muscles of his curiously mask-like face, and he asked for no further explanation. For a moment Vachell wondered, as he rattled away in his car, whether he wasn't being a little premature. He went back to the beginning of his chain of reasoning and thought all the way along it, testing every link.

He arrived at the same conclusion. The Governor had been strangled a few minutes before 10.48; and Watson had looked into a room which held a dead man and his murderer.

That evening, at five o'clock, Donovan Popple was arrestd by the Chania police for the murder of Sir Malcolm McLeod.

.   .   .   .   .

Chez Raoul's generally surprised visitors to Marula. Here, on an equatorial plateau in the heart of Africa, surrounded, figuratively speaking, by rhinos and lions, they found a typical small French restaurant with genuine, and good, French cooking. There were plush seats around the wall, small cramped tables, *vin ordinaire* in carafes. Even the dusky waiters, who struck the only note alien to Soho, seemed to hurry more than usual, bearing steaming dishes under tin covers. Raoul himself, a genuine Marseillais, was always there, showing clients to their seats, and sometimes juggling with a special sauce or an order of *crêpes suzettes*. The wines, and particularly the hock, were good.

The restaurant was packed to capacity on the evening of Popple's arrest. Although there was no evening paper, the news had gone through the town like a veld fire. It was a greater sensation, even, than the news of the murder had been.

The immediate reaction was one of incredulity. From the stray remarks which he heard as he waded through the tables on his way in to dine with Olivia Brandeis, Vachell suspected that disbelief in Popple's guilt would soon grow into indignation at his arrest. Up to now the police had been in favour; they were thought to be acting with speed and vigour. But public opinion might well swing round after this. Every one knew Popple; he was a sort of public fixture. Marula, with its population of Government officials and business men, disapproved of his sometimes rather startling opinions, and had often repudiated his actions. Some people actively disliked him. But no one thought him capable of premeditated murder.

Olivia Brandeis, who was leaving at seven o'clock the next morning for the Wabenda reserve, seemed to be almost the only person in Marula who thought that Popple might be guilty.

'Chania settlers are always flying off the handle over something, and Popple's the worse of the lot,' she said. 'His views on native policy are pernicious and offensive as well. The sooner the League mandate system is applied to all the African colonies the better, so long as there are still Popples about. People like that don't think; they run on prejudice. He probably lived up to his threats against the Government, for once. What excellent mushroom sauce this is. You don't think Popple did it, I suppose?'

'Too many darned people in this murder,' Vachell said, with feeling. 'I could make out a hell of a good case against at least three—four, if you count in a Plaindweller plot. I know which I'd pick, but I can't prove it.'

Olivia looked surprised. 'Who—Watson?'

Vachell grinned at her over a raised fork and jerked his head in the direction of a table behind her. 'If you aim to become a detective you'll have to learn to soft-pedal your voice,' he said. She flushed slightly and turned to scrutinize the other diners. Maisie Watson was seated two tables away, in a tight black satin frock and a hat with an eye-length veil. She was dining with an Imperial Airways pilot who was waiting for the southbound, which had come down somewhere in the Sudan and couldn't get up again, to arrive. He was a newcomer to the African route. The old stagers already knew Maisie too well; one of her names was Pilot's Pleasure.

'She couldn't hear,' Olivia said shortly.

'Just didn't want to disappoint her,' Vachell answered. 'If Watson took the rap for this she'd make the front page all the way from London to San Francisco. Think what a kick she'd get out of that. Most likely she has her costume all figured out for a personal appearance on the stand. But I'm no gentleman: I have to let the lady down.'

'Are you trying to say that you *don't* think Watson's guilty?' Olivia asked, this time in a lower voice.

Vachell ordered fresh peaches and cream and refilled the glasses with Liebfraumilch before replying.

'You remember Watson said that he saw H.E. alive and telephoning when he looked in to the study at ten-forty-eight?' he asked. Olivia nodded. 'He was the last person who claimed to see the Governor alive, and he hadn't any proof in the world to support what he said. On the other hand we had rock-ribbed proof that his story wasn't true, because the exchange records showed that no call, either in or out, went over H.E.'s line that night.

'Right there it began to look like a clear case against Watson. It looked like he knocked off H.E. and then came back to fix a phony alibi, by making out the Governor was still alive after the job had been pulled. The only thing that bothered me was, it seemed so crude. I figured an intelligent guy like Watson should be able to think up a better play than that, and at least have sense enough to know that telephone calls can be checked as easy as pie.

'I think you overestimate the subtlety of the official mind,' Olivia said. 'But go on.'

'Well, you may remember in those depositions you read, I mentioned that when I looked the study over, I noticed that the reading-lamp, instead of throwing a beam on to the blotter, was shining down at the carpet in front of the bureau. Now think a moment. Suppose you opened the door to the study and looked in, and the top light was switched off. There was a man behind the bureau way across the room and a bright light shining down on to the floor between you and the bureau. What would you be likely to see?'

'You mean the reading-lamp would prevent you seeing the man behind the desk,' Olivia said. 'Or at any rate you couldn't see his features. You'd probably get the impression there *was* a man there, but that's about all. Yes, I grasp that. But if H.E. was dead he could hardly have been telephoning, could he?'

'Hardly. But wait a minute. All Watson said he heard was a query, and then the number—"Hello, is that two five eight six," or whatever the number was. D'you notice how non-committal that sentence is? There's nothing to give any one a line on who was at the other end of the wire or what it was all about.'

'Now suppose, for the sake of argument, that the guy we're after isn't Watson and that he's just completed a nice strangling job and is all set to go, when he hears a rap on the door. He's got to think fast. If he bolts he's finished, because the man outside the door will come in and discover the crime and the hunt will be on before he has a chance to get clear. He's in a spot. There's just one chance—to bluff it through with the ace that most visitors wouldn't care to disturb a Governor if they see he's busy on a job.

'So he seizes hold of the reading-lamp and twists it around to throw the rays forward, leaving the chair in deep shadow. Then he kneels down behind the bureau and puts his hand over H.E.'s limp dead one and lifts the phone out of its cradle. The guy outside raps a second time and opens the door to look in. Sir Malcolm seems too busy to notice him. The murderer has to say something to make the bluff stick, though he knows his voice will knock the props from under the set-up if he talks too much. So he makes out the Governor's just getting his number and says over a few figures, pitching his voice as near to Sir Malcolm's tone as he can get. He has to take a chance there, but the visitor expects to hear Sir Malcolm's voice, and he isn't likely to get suspicious unless the difference is very pronounced.'

Vachell paused to order two coffees and old brandies and to light a cigarette. Olivia puffed hard at hers and considered carefully.

'Yes,' she said, 'I should think it would be possible. Ears, taken as a whole, are not at all dependable. Your self-possessed murderer could, I imagine, alter his voice to the same pitch as H.E.'s without having to be a mimic—provided, of course, that he was familiar with it.'

'Well, let's suppose it worked, anyway,' Vachell continued. 'Watson, seeing the Governor busy and being a well-trained civil servant—even if Sir Malcolm *is* making passes at his wife all the time—decides to postpone his interview, and beats it. The killer must have had a pretty bad few minutes. When it's over he doesn't even wait to replace the telephone in its cradle. He knows the passage door is guarded and there's some one outside the window, so he has to take a chance on Jeudwine's room. That's where he gets a break, because the secretary's out. So he slips through the hall and into the ballroom to join the merry throng, and everything is fine and dandy.'

'He was lucky to find Jeudwine's room unoccupied,' Olivia said. 'He took rather a chance there.'

'You have to take chances when you bump people off,' Vachell said. He rolled the brandy in his glass and sipped it slowly. The restaurant was emptying rapidly; it was time for the movies. Vachell watched Maisie Watson gather herself together and walk out with the pilot, adjusting her curls. As she reached the door she glanced round at him, tilted her head back slightly, and smiled a little wistfully.

'It's quite a good theory,' Olivia added. 'But I don't see how you can prove it.'

'I figured it this way,' Vachell said. 'Suppose Watson told us the truth. Then he ought to remember the way the light from the reading-lamp fell on to the floor. He hadn't put it into his picture, but that might be because it hadn't stuck in his memory. But suppose he really was the killer, and his story about the telephoning was just a play to fix a phony alibi. In that case the picture Watson would give us would be a busy, healthy Governor right on the job, sitting at his bureau with the light from the reading-lamp shining on to the papers in front of him. No sane, live Governor would sit in the dark with the light turned on to the carpet out in front.

'So I got to this point. If Watson remembered how the light fell down on to the carpet then I'd know he'd told the truth. But if he remembered that the light fell on to the blotter, then I'd be pretty well certain that his story was a stall, and I'd go to work to pin the murder on to him.

'Well, Watson remembered that the light shone down on to the carpet. So I've crossed him off my list.'

Olivia thought for a few moments, frowning slightly, while her companion ordered two more brandies. 'I can't see any flaw in it,' she said finally. 'So after all that, you're back where you were.'

'It eliminates Watson,' Vachell replied, 'and it lets Popple out too. You saw him leave G.H. in his car a few minutes after ten-forty. I'm counting on you as regards those times. Well, we know the killer was in the study and through with the job at ten-forty-eight. Popple couldn't have ditched his car somewhere in the grounds, got back to G.H., found a way into the study, and knocked off H.E. all in about five minutes. It isn't physically possible. And Moon's out of it too, so far as I can see. He was at his home, telephoning, at ten-forty-four; the exchange gives him his alibi. And the fact that the murder was committed earlier than it looked at first puts Pallett in the clear, I'm afraid. I'd like to pin his ears back. He hates me like I was a rattlesnake. But Fernandez at the Secretariat gives him an alibi up to around ten-forty-five, though he wasn't any too definite about the time.'

'It's funny to reflect,' Olivia said meditatively, 'that millions of people in Chania probably think that Pallett has inherited Sir Malcolm McLeod's spirit. I don't imagine it would be very comfortable for either of them. The belief that a sort of divine essence passes from one chief to the next is not at all uncommon. Among the Shilluk of the southern Sudan, for instance, the young men used to go the length of killing their chief when his ability to satisfy his numerous wives began to wane, on the principle that a chief's spirit should never be allowed to lose its vigour. One can well imagine how welcome a good, reliable aphrodisiac would have been to an ageing chief. . . .'

'Did you hear that Corporal Machoka has skipped out?' Vachell put in quickly, while Olivia paused to light a cigarette. 'Just vanished into air. Last night. I guess that puts him way up on top of the betting, for an accessory at least. I reckon he's likely to have made for home, if he's alive, that is, and it looks like he may be mixed up in this Plaindweller business after all.'

'You don't really think this ridiculous League has anything to do with it, do you?' she asked. 'It's only a silly alarmist balloon blown up by the Popples of the country to make people think it's the *Hindenburg*.'

'Maybe so,' Vachell said, 'but there isn't any doubt that the League does exist, and it isn't impossible to imagine a situation where some of these communist agents who go around stirring up trouble among natives might tie in with it somehow. Until recently, anyway, the Comintern had a press in Moscow that printed pretty obscene leaflets in a dozen different native languages—it aimed to line up a regular black anti-capitalist front—and a Greek Jew who was a communist agent was deported last year for stirring up racial animosity.'

'Bogey, bogey,' Olivia said. 'Fancy meeting my old friend the Red Menace again.'

'Sure,' Vachell went on. 'Communists are very swell people, and they've practically got around to having rotary clubs by now. Well, there are others who like to fish in troubled waters. Maybe the fascists are on the job. I don't know. But I do suggest that it isn't impossible that some trouble-shooting white man—maybe just a guy who's sore at the Government because he got fined for forgetting his dog licence or something—has got a hold on this Plain-dweller League and is using it to stir it's not impossible, though I'll admit it sounds a little wild, that he decided a good way to shoot the white man's prestige to hell would be to put the Governor on the spot, and then to spread the word around that the League had shown the Government where it got off on account of this Wabenda witchcraft case. That's only an idea, but I think it's a possibility we have to consider.'

'Are those the only ideas you've got?' Olivia asked. 'Because if so...'

Vachell grinned. 'I have one more,' he said. 'A big one. But if you think the other is a bit screwy, you'd regard this one as just plain nuts. So I'll keep it under my hat for the present.'

.   .   .   .   .

At ten-thirty Vachell ran Olivia up to Government House in his car. A young moon was rising over the trees when they drove up to the big white house standing squarely among its smooth lawns. Vachell slowed down and, on impulse, parked his car under the window of the Governor's study, where Popple's car had been on the night of the murder. The window was shuttered and dark.

'Let's stage a little reconstruction,' he said. 'Show me just where you stood when you saw Jeudwine and when you looked at your watch in the beam of light from H.E.'s window. Wait a minute, we'll get this right.'

He disappeared indoors to borrow the master-key from Abdi, and went into the Governor's study, switched on the lights, and drew the curtains. He let the blind up a little so that a gap showed at the bottom, and rejoined Olivia outside in the drive. A broad, thin shaft of light came out from the chink between the blind and the window-frame and fell across some delphiniums in the flower-bed beneath the window. Beyond that it lit up small clods of earth in the bed in sharp relief.

Olivia walked to a position at one side of the window, about six feet from the wall of the house.

'I was standing about here when I was talking to Popple,' she said. 'When he drove off I stayed where I was for a moment, and then looked at my watch again, more or less for something to do. I couldn't see the figures clearly, so I stepped forward to look at it in the beam of light from the window.' She repeated the action, and the narrow ray fell on to the face of her wrist-watch. She was standing immediately beneath the window. 'It was exactly ten-forty. Then I decided...'

She stopped abruptly. 'Wait a moment. There's something else. As I looked at my watch, like this, I heard a sound. . . . It's coming back. Yes, it was a telephone. Dialling. I heard the sound of a number being dialled in the study. What a fool I was not to remember before!'

'Are you certain of that?' Vachell's voice reflected subdued excitement.

'Yes, I am. I hardly noticed it at the time, but now I remember perfectly. It was just as I looked at my watch. A burr and a click. Then another. There's nothing else it could have been.'

'You didn't hear any one speaking?'

'No. I walked away before the dialling had finished, I suppose. Then I came back about five minutes later, as I told you, and saw Jeudwine emerging from the gap left by Popple's car. It's extraordinary how one's ears play tricks. Just as the sound of a waterfall or a drum. . . .'

Vachell was not listening. He stepped over the flower-bed and leant down to peer through the crack under the blind. The window-ledge came to his hip. He could see the top of the desk, about ten feet away, and the gleam of the black telephone. It would be easy enough to climb in silently over the low sill, if the window was open and the blind up.

'This case is going haywire,' he said. 'That's the second call that's supposed to have been made on this line while H.E. was getting himself strangled that hasn't gone through the exchange.'

He stood gazing at the window for some time, his hands deep in the pockets of his dark suit. Olivia began to feel cold. She had on a short-sleeved printed cotton frock and no coat. Then Mark Beaton came out to offer them a drink, and they went into the billiard-room and had whiskies. Marvin McLeod was there, looking pale but more composed.

Mark suggested a game of slosh. 'Olivia and I will take you two on,' he said. 'She's hot stuff at slosh.'

'Thanks for the compliment,' Olivia remarked. 'Don't say you're beginning to discover that anthropologists have human attributes after all.'

Mark chalked a billiard cue and smiled at her. 'Honestly, I'd entirely forgotten you were an anthropologist at all—and that's high praise. What ought we to give them, do you think?'

They played slosh for a hundred up, and Mark and Olivia won easily. After the game the victors practised billiard shots and argued amicably as to whether Charles Laughton or Gary Cooper was the better actor. Vachell and Marvin stood in the doorway looking at the fountain, which had been floodlit for the Jubilee and remained so ever since. Two photographic studio lamps threw their beams on to the tumbling water, making the fine spray shine like liquid silver.

Sir Bertrand Flower, Vachell learnt, was flying back to Totseland the next morning, and Jeudwine was helping him to clear up some papers. Marvin was only staying on for four days more. She invited him to come up to Government House on the following Sunday for a ride.

'I'm flying to Paris on Tuesday,' she said. 'Mother's there and wants me to join her. I'd like to hear the latest news before I go, if you can tell me. You're not a bit what I expected a police detective to be like, Mr Vachell. It's so much easier to ask you things.'

Vachell felt a glow of pleasure, as though he had swallowed a glassful of liquor at a gulp. The way Marvin did her hair, he reflected, combed back in a sweep across her wide forehead, suited her just right. It wasn't often you saw a girl with such a pale, clear skin, and such finely moulded features. And she looked swell in black. . . . He remembered that it was rude to stare and finished off his drink.

He said good-bye to Olivia, and wished her luck. 'If you run into a real smart witchdoctor down there, send him over,' Vachell told her. 'I guess a poison ordeal is about the only thing that will crack this case open. The only condition I make is that I fix Mr Pallett's shot.'

11

For the fifth night in succession Olivia Brandeis sat over her camp-fire and listened to the rhythmical mutter of the drums. The sounds beat persistently on her ear-drums like the soft patter of rain on a dark grey English afternoon; as inescapable, and as remorseless. They were hollow, deep, and compelling.

She shifted irritably on her folding camp-chair and threw a log on the fire. A cascade of sparks sprang up like spray from a golden waterfall. The deep sky glistened with stars and a young moon threw faint formless shadows across the grass. The night was hot and oppressive; still no rain. The rains were several weeks overdue. The earth lay in a dry and sterile trance of expectation.

For some unaccountable reason Olivia felt disturbed and apprehensive. Almost from the moment of her arrival she had sensed a feeling of uneasiness and disorganization in the air. The natives to whom she made overtures were apathetic, even suspicious. They treated her courteously, but with unusual reserve. And at times she had heard, strolling about the little stockaded groups of huts, sharp evidence of altercation and abuse. Without doubt, nerves were edgy. Some disturbing ferment was at work beneath the placid surface of Wabenda existence.

And then there were those drums. That was the most unusual phenomenon of all, at this time of year; just before the planting. When the harvest was gathered in, the noise of drum-beats up Wabenda valleys was as common as the rumble of lorries on the Great West Road. Drums summoned young men and women to dances, girls and boys to circumcision ceremonies, elders to the marriage feasts of their children. That was the time for feasting, gaiety, and ceremonial. But in April people, normally, worked hard in the fields all day, hoeing and planting, and came home too tired to brew beer or to dance. Besides, food was growing short and there was no surplus for feasts. But now, for five nights running, there had been drums.

Olivia strolled over to the nearby village through a yielding wall of darkness. It wasn't really a village, but a group of huts occupied by different members of a single family. The head of the family was a junior chief, Kyungu: one degree in rank lower than M'bola, the imprisoned head chief. Olivia had selected his village as a starting-point, on Victor Moon's recommendation. Kyungu, Moon had said, was an intelligent, helpful chief, always ready to co-operate with the Government, and with modern ideas. Olivia had found Kyungu anxious to help, but not as effective as she had hoped. He was a plump, youngish man, with a rather Jewish-looking face, and was a little too Europeanized for her taste. He claimed to be a Christian, but he had three wives.

Olivia rapped on the wall of his head wife's hut and called out a greeting in Kibenda. There was no reply and she knocked again. After her third attempt the planks propped up against the doorway were pulled to one side and she found herself looking down into what she could sense, rather than see, was a human face. Faint scuffling sounds came from the back of hut—goats and small children, Olivia knew. There were no windows.

'I search for Kyungu,' she said. 'Is he here?'

The woman, crouching in the low doorway, made no reply. Olivia repeated the question twice. Finally the woman said shrilly: 'Kyungu is not here,' and replaced the boards over the doorway. A goat bleated sharply inside the round, smoke-filled hut; then there was silence once again.

Olivia tried one more hut. It belonged to a withered, monkey-faced old man called Silu. He was Kyungu's maternal uncle and, Olivia suspected, more of a real power in the district than his nephew. He had no foreign education, he dressed in old-fashioned goatskins, and he was hung about with snuff-horns, wire necklaces and charms; but he was the local witchdoctor, a man whom even the callow sceptics of the sophisticated younger generation hesitated to offend. Silu was not at home either.

Olivia lit a cigarette and strolled thoughtfully back to her fire. She had a shrewd idea of what the trouble was all about. Witchcraft, she thought; the leitmotif of Africa. There were evil spirits abroad, sorcerers at work. The atmosphere was charged with black magic as with electricity; evil jumped out suddenly on the unsuspecting as sparks will crackle out of the air when hand and metal touch.

That was what was causing the sullenness, the uneasiness, the high-strung nerves. The Wabenda believed that they were being tormented by evil spirits and that unknown sorcerers were bewitching their crops, their children, and their stock.

Olivia was stoking up the fire for the night when she

heard a commotion break out in Kyungu's compound. There were shouts, yells, and a woman's wail. Then silence. Five minutes later a small boy came running to her tent. He told her, breathlessly, that a child had got burnt and would she give it medicine.

She seized her emergency first-aid box and ran down to the huts. The child, a boy of three or four, was lying in his mother's lap on a heap of skins which comprised the bed. He was mercifully unconscious. His mother was rocking backwards and forwards, her face curiously taut, making no sound. Round her squatted a group of four shiny-limbed, sloe-eyed women, clad in goatskins. They, too, were silent. The dim light of the cooking-fire illuminated the scene. No one was trying to dress the burns.

The child was badly injured. It had fallen face foremost into the fire. One chance in ten for its survival, Olivia thought. She dressed it as best she could with tannic acid jelly and bandaged it loosely. 'Keep the child absolutely quiet and wrapped in blankets,' she told its mother. 'He feels no pain.' The woman did not seem to listen or understand.

Olivia was uneasy as she walked back to her own camp. The women's behaviour had been very strange. Usually a turmoil of lamentation broke out when incidents of that kind occurred. Tonight the women had been more frightened than dismayed. If the child died, she supposed, they would attribute its death to sorcerers. Olivia undressed slowly and crept into her fleabag. She fell asleep with the persistent throb of drum-beats echoing softly in her head.

·　　·　　·　　·　　·

Heavy, low-banked clouds obscured the sunrise next morning. They lay on the horizon in sullen inertia. The air felt sluggish and flat. The country looked lifeless and sad without the sun, and lack of rain had parched the grass to a colourless dun.

Early in the morning small boys drove flocks of goats to

pasture without enthusiasm. Later the women, each carrying a meal of maize and beans in a plaited basket, trudged silently to the plots of cultivation, hoes in hand and babies slung over their backs.

After breakfast Olivia went in search of Kyungu. She found him at the court-house, a rectangular, cement-floored building divided into a main assembly room and, behind, an office. Here a native clerk was working on case records which he entered in a large book. A tribal policeman, dressed in a navy blue blanket with a smart red binding, lounged on duty by the door. He stood to attention as Olivia came in.

Kyungu was seated at a desk, wearing a striped shirt and khaki trousers and an unnecessary pair of horn-rimmed spectacles. He and the clerk, a neatly dressed man in a collar and tie, rose to greet her, and Kyungu offered her his chair. It all seemed very civilized, very remote from the dark magic currents that seemed to flow beneath the even stream of Wabenda life.

Olivia explained that she had come to see the court records, and Kyungu readily agreed to show them to her. They discussed Wabenda tribal law for a little, and then she asked if she could speak to the chief alone. He sent the clerk off on a bicycle to negotiate the collection of a fine of goats from a man who had committed adultery with a neighbour's wife, and Olivia sat down at the empty desk.

She told the chief what she had seen and heard, and how she believed that the fear of witchcraft was paralysing Wabenda life. 'Tell me what's going on, Kyungu,' she concluded. 'I thought that those old ways were finished here, now that your young men are educated and go out to see the world. Are you still ruled by spirits?'

Kyungu looked acutely uncomfortable. Small beads of sweat appeared on his forehead. He licked his heavy lips, fumbled with the white topee lying on his desk, and gave evasive answers. Of course, no one took such things seriously any longer; witchdoctors were not allowed to make magic any more. Wabenda was very up to date indeed. They had a big new hospital at Taritibu, two more dispensaries last year, a seed farm just down the valley; and many children now went to the new Government school to learn English and football. . . .

Olivia suddenly realized that Kyungu was the perfect Rotarian. She could imagine him, translated to another continent and colour, saying: 'Now this is our residential section, where we have some very lovely homes. They call our city the Athens of the West. . . .'

She agreed with Kyungu that the Wabenda were very up to date and progressive indeed. 'But it is difficult to change old customs,' she said. 'The old men stand in the way.'

Kyungu agreed heartily with this. He was clearly bewildered, and uncertain what to do. Something was on his mind. Finally he gave up, and poured out his soul to Olivia in a torrent of words.

Wabenda, he said, was being plagued by sorcerers. Of course he knew that it was all uncivilized superstition and that the spirits of dead ancestors had no power to work evil, being undoubtedly in hell because they had not been Christians. But there were many ignorant and obstinate old men. They believed that tribal ancestors were offended with the Wabenda and were sending spirits to punish them.

It was certainly true that for two years the rains had been small and had fallen at the wrong time, and the crops had failed and hunger had followed. And then many children had died because bad magic had been made against them—at least that was what ignorant people said—and the cows would only get bull calves, and this season, for the first time in history, the bees had not come to the hives set over by the Beridi River, where the richest honey harvest was always taken. . . .

Kyungu shook his head despondently. 'It is all true,' he said. 'How can all this happen if it is not the anger of the spirits? The white man talks of luck. But is not luck the temper of the spirits?'

'And what do the Wabenda people propose to do about it?' Olivia asked.

Kyungu looked embarrassed and distressed. His podgy face was moist with sweat. 'I do not know,' he said. 'They do not trust me. I am their chief, but they see my clothes'—he spread his hands in a gesture of resignation—'and they hear me speak, and they say that I am like a white man, that I am no longer a M'Benda. What can I do? They think it is my fault.'

'Your fault! They don't think you're a sorcerer, do they?'

Kyungu's eyes rolled in sudden panic. He was sweating freely now. 'No, no, no,' he said. 'It is not that. They think our ancestors are angry because of me. Because I, who am a chief, have not carried out the ritual as demanded by our custom. It is true, I have not, because I have been taught by Europeans that many of the things we did were wrong. So I have tried to alter the ritual to avoid the bad things that the white man told me about. And because I have done this the old men say that I have angered our ancestors. And that is why our ancestors have sent evil spirits to trouble us. The old men are all against me. How can I keep the Government's authority when they spread such beliefs? They even think I keep a witch alive in my own family.'

'What do you mean?'

'In the old days, before your people came, we had many customs which protected us from evil spirits. One of them was this. If a child was born, and if the teeth came from its upper jaw before the teeth from its lower jaw, it was believed that the child would grow up to become a witch. So it was killed, that the people might have security.'

'Yes, I know that.'

'Such a child was born to me,' Kyungu went on rapidly and in a low voice, 'out of my second wife. When it was six months old the teeth from its upper jaw came out. I told my wife: "That is an old and foolish custom, and, besides, it is against the white man's law. If you kill the child you too will be killed. So the child shall live." The child lived, and now she is ten years old, but I had to beat her mother to make her suckle the child, and today the women forbid their children to play with her in the fields, and she must eat only out of a cracked calabash so that the evil power can escape from the vessel.'

Olivia did her best to console him. A chieftain's lot, she agreed, was not a happy one. 'Aren't your people afraid to kill witches,' she asked, 'when they see that even the great chief M'bola is taken by the Government when he breaks the white man's law?'

Kyungu shook his head. 'They believe that M'bola will not die. They think that our ancestors will help him, and that they have already avenged his unjust arrest and made a strong magic that will destroy any man who tries to destroy M'bola. A very strong magic—stronger than the white man's medicine.' He stopped abruptly, as if he had said more than he intended.

'You mean,' Olivia asked in a puzzled voice, 'that it was this magic that killed the Governor?'

Kyungu shook his head violently. 'I did not say that. I do not believe such simple, foolish things.'

'But the ignorant people do?'

Kyungu seemed reluctant to reply. 'It is the old men,' he said at last. 'They say, because the Governor wished to kill M'bola, our ancestors made this magic and the Governor died.'

'But they know the Governor wasn't killed by magic. He was strangled with a rope.'

'They think the magic gave some one power to kill the Governor with a rope. That is how magic works.'

'Some one, you say. Do they know who that some one is, then?'

Kyungu shook his head. 'No, I do not think so. But that does not matter. They do not know what the magic was, either. They would prefer to know that.'

Olivia switched abruptly to another theme. 'What do

you know about the League of the Plaindweller?'

Kyungu almost jumped out of his chair. He gave a half-stifled gasp and his topee toppled out of his hand and rolled across the floor. He leant down to pick it up without speaking, obviously making an effort to recover himself. Then he denied all knowledge of the League's existence, emphatically and several times over.

It took Olivia about ten minutes to break down his resistance. She knew by now that he was a weak character, easily browbeaten—too easily for a chief—and she persisted mercilessly. In the end he admitted that he knew of the League's existence, but that was about all. He refused to mention its name and his eyes rolled with fright every time she used the words of its title.

'It is very secret,' he said, 'and very evil. They are bad men. There have been cases where the herds and flocks of wealthy elders have dwindled overnight, but they have lodged no complaint before the tribunal and said nothing of their loss. Yet they bought no brides for their sons nor sold beasts to pay taxes. Where did the goats and sheep go to? No one knows. But there are rumours. There is magic that can be too powerful to defy.'

'But don't you know who the members are?'

Kyungu shook his head violently. 'No, no.'

'Do you think Silu is a member?'

'Silu? No, never. I know Silu. He is old, and he is a witchdoctor, and he does not like the new ways, but he follows the law—Wabenda law. This other is different. No men like Silu are part of it. It is said that they are young men, with a knowledge of white men's ways. Perhaps they have been in the city. At night they wear strange clothes and do evil magic. Be careful, lady, how you ask about them. It is better not to ask. Those who are not members know nothing; and those who belong know fearful curses. To mention that name to a member is to give him power to lay on you a terrible curse. That is, the ignorant believe so,' Kyungu added hastily. 'I myself do not believe this, naturally. But they are evil, and bad for the Government.'

'They are against the Government, then?'

'I have heard so.'

'Do you think that they might have killed the Governor?'

Kyungu shrugged his shoulders. 'It is said that they have a strong magic. I do not know.'

Olivia realized that she had got all she could out of Kyungu. She got up to go.

'It is courteous of you to answer,' she said. 'There is one more question. Do you know Machoka, an askari from Wabenda who joined the KALI?'

'The askari. Yes,' Kyungu replied. 'He is a cousin. I have not seen him for many years. He has been away. I do not think that he is a very good man.'

Olivia was surprised, but she could not get any more information. Machoka was not in the reserve, Kyungu was sure. 'Ask Silu,' he added. 'If any one knows, it should be he.'

'Silu? Why?'

'Silu is his father,' Kyungu replied. 'Two days ago the District Officer sent policemen from Taritibu to look for him at Silu's house. But he was not there. Silu says he does not know where Machoka is hiding.'

Olivia thought she detected a slight note of disbelief in Kyungu's tone.

'Thank you, Kyungu,' she said. 'You have told me much that is useful. I hope that the ancestors of the Wabenda will soon recall the evil spirits. If they don't, what will your people do next?'

'I do not know,' Kyungu answered. His look of worry had returned. 'It will be very bad.'

'A witch hunt?' Olivia asked.

Kyungu shook his head. 'We hunt witches here no longer,' he said. 'We do not believe such things any more. The law says: "There are no witches." We obey the law.'

He spoke without conviction. He doesn't believe what he is saying, Olivia thought; he is afraid that there will be a witch hunt. He's in a cleft stick. He draws a Government salary, and his job is to stop all witchery; and he's also a hereditary chief, whose job is to conduct witch hunts.

She thanked Kyungu once more and left him alone in his office, reading a letter from the District Officer about the installation of a new maize cleaning machine in the local native market.

.   .   .   .   .

When Olivia went down to Kyungu's compound later in the day the door of the hut in which the injured child had been lying had been boarded up, and she received no reply to her repeated knocking. A few small children were playing round the huts. They stared at her silently, and made no answer when she questioned them.

Finally a woman came out of one of the huts, crouching to get through the doorway, and asked Olivia what she wanted. 'The child,' Olivia answered. 'I have come with medicine for the burns.'

'The child is dead,' the woman said. She stared at Olivia for a moment without expression and dived back into the hut.

With that Olivia had to be content. The women were out in the fields, the men mysteriously absent. It was hot and stuffy. Low clouds pressed heavily on a dispirited earth.

That night there was a fire in the open space in front of Kyungu's huts and a small group of men, closely wrapped in blankets, sat around it. The women squatted in the doorways, plaiting baskets out of strips of tree bark and listening to the men's talk.

Silu greeted Olivia, and invited her to sit down with them. As far as he was concerned, a European woman didn't count as a woman at all. Olivia he treated as an elaborate and quite inoffensive joke. He offered her a pinch of snuff out of the antelope horn hanging round his neck. She accepted it, placed it on her forefinger and sniffed. Silu roared with laughter, and the others, a little uncertainly, joined in. The only man she recognized was the tribal policeman. He hawked loudly and spat. It was a sign of goodwill.

Olivia questioned Silu about the customs of his tribe and he responded gravely, though with an undercurrent of tolerant amusement at her curiosity. She learnt that the price of brides had gone up recently; a good one was now worth about twenty goats, three cows, a couple of all-wool blankets and a barrel of honey. They were much cheaper in the good old days when cattle were to be had for the raiding from the Wabenda's less warlike neighbours. He himself had been a great warrior then, he said; but when the Europeans came he had taken service with the Government and seen the world on the western frontier (he said as a guide, but she suspected as a porter), on the Totseland border, and even at the coast. Then he had returned to his own village and settled down to practise as a witchdoctor. Of course, he had always possessed magical powers; a witchdoctor was invariably born with a peg in his hand, as a sign from the spirits.

The subject of witchcraft was introduced cautiously. Tonight there seemed to be a slackening of the tension, and Olivia asked him tentatively about his charms. Did he sell many of them, these days?

There was a hush, and Olivia felt a ripple of disapproval pass over the group. Silu slowly took a pinch of snuff and sniffed deeply. Ornaments jingled on his arms as he did so. From his neck hung a little leather bag which she recognized as a charm.

'You ask me things of which I cannot speak,' the old man said. 'Do you now know that your Government has forbidden the making of magic? Your people say there are no spirits. Therefore, of course, no spirits exist.'

'I do not come from the Government,' she explained for the twentieth time. 'I come from England to learn your customs, because we who live so far away are interested to know how you live.'

– 142 –

'What is it you want, then?' Silu asked.

'I would like to see the magic that you sell to thwart the evil spirits.'

'Very well.' Old Silu was solemn now. 'You shall see.' He rose to his feet and disappeared into his hut outside the firelit circle. No one said anything. The policeman looked uncomfortable, and rearranged his blanket.

Silu returned with a cloth and a long stoppered gourd. He spread the cloth on the ground and gently upset the contents of the gourd on to it. 'See,' he said.

Olivia examined the magic carefully. There were some polished pebbles, some beans, and a heap of small bones—avian bones of some sort. She was surprised that he showed the magic so openly and with so little protest. She touched it with a finger, and even then he did not stop her.

She heard a sort of gasp from one of the men by the fireside and looked up. The tribal policeman had both hands clapped over his mouth and an expression of agony on his face. He gave a snort like a rhino and doubled-up on his hams. Then he rolled on the ground in an uncontrollable fit of laughter.

She looked at old Silu. He was grinning from ear to ear, the heavy pegs of wood suspended from his pendulous, holed ear-lobes shaking violently as he gave way to his mirth. 'Chicken bones!' she heard the policeman gasp, between guffaws. The joke, she understood, was on her. She had been shown junk, not magic.

Olivia laughed with as good a grace as she could muster and waited for the party to recover from its mirth before reopening the conversation. Before she left she dropped one more social brick, deliberately.

'I hear Machoka has been here,' she said.

There was another embarrassed silence. Silu shook his head slowly. The firelight shone on his numerous copper and bead ornaments as he moved, and on one bare, shining shoulder. His face looked like the withered mask of a monkey.

'Does the antelope who finds young grass return to the bare plain where the grass is dry?' he asked. 'Machoka does not return here any longer.'

'He has left Marula. Where should he come but to his father's house?'

Silu made no reply. The silence continued. This time she had offended badly against good manners. The friendliness of the atmosphere faded like the glow of a coal taken from a fire. Olivia rose to go.

'The police think that he killed the Governor,' she said.

Silu spat deliberately. 'Can the hare kill the bull elephant?' he asked. 'Machoka has not killed. The police have seized a white man, but he has not killed the Governor either. They will not find the man.'

'From your words it seems that you know who he is,' Olivia remarked.

'The hunter who slays elephants across the river will return to the same pastures to hunt,' the old man replied enigmatically. That was all he would say. Olivia said good night and walked slowly back to her camp.

She was both surprised and relieved that things had quietened down so quickly in Kyungu's compound. She had been afraid that the child's death might precipitate a sudden outburst—even a witch hunt, ordeal by poison, murder, and then the intervention of the Government. But the Wabenda appeared to have kept their heads, and tonight things seemed normal once again.

At two o'clock in the morning she was woken up by hyenas howling close to her tent. Some goat or ox must have died there yesterday, she thought sleepily. She pulled the flap of the fleabag over her head and dropped off again into slumber.

That was the only sign that came to her notice of the execution of Kyungu's ten-year-old daughter as a witch. It took place within three hundred yards of her tent. The girl was pinned to the ground with fork sticks while two men held her nose and mouth until she suffocated. This was to prevent the evil spirit from flying out of the witch's body and entering one of the spectators. Afterwards, Silu purified the executioners, and the crowd dispersed silently into the night. Justice had again been done.

12

The next morning dawned fine and clear. A long, low range of hills to the east stood out sharply and seemed to have moved in closer during the night. They were hills that the Wabenda refused to visit, because departed spirits were believed to inhabit them. As the day grew older the heat increased and the flies became so sluggish that they could be knocked away with the hand. For the first time, it felt like rain.

Olivia decided that she would drive the twenty miles to Taritibu in her lorry to call for mail and to ask the District Officer if there was any news of Machoka. There was no road into Taritibu, only a rough cattle track through the bush. The lorry lurched about in the long grass, clambering over stones, annihilating acacia bushes, and churning its way through the sandy bottoms of dried-up river beds.

It was nearly lunch-time before she reached the administrative centre. She drove straight to the District Officer's headquarters, a low-roofed wooden and corrugated iron building standing back from a dusty main street fringed with pepper trees. There was a green lawn and a bed of flaming cannas in front.

The D.O. was a slim, self-possessed young man with charming manners and sleek fair hair, dressed in a neatly pressed khaki suit with a white collar and black tie. He approved very highly of anthropologists and referred in complimentary terms to one or two of Olivia's articles in *Africa*.

'I hope you'll be able to take the time to study us really systematically, Miss Brandeis,' he said. 'We haven't been put under the microscope since Gerberhalt's time, and that's twenty years ago. An up-to-date monograph would be a tremendous help to the Administration. I only wish that something on the lines of Brown and Hutt's experiment among the Hehe could be arranged.'

He asked Olivia to lunch and over the meal she tried to find out more about the witchcraft situation.

'We had a spot of bother over the M'bola case,' the D.O. admitted, 'but I think it's all blown over now. It's just a matter of time and education, you know. I've a lot of faith in our younger generation. They're very fine chaps, on the whole. You must let me show you our new central school after lunch. It cost ten thousand pounds, all put up in our own district. It's really a very fine show.'

There seemed to be a strong boosting movement, among black and white alike, in Wabenda, Olivia thought. She repeated Kyungu's story of the plague of sorcerers. The D.O. listened attentively, and explained that there was always a reactionary element in tribal affairs.

'I expect old Silu's at the bottom of it,' he added. 'We've had no end of trouble with the old boy—he's a regular Colonel Blimp. But you shouldn't take everything Kyungu says too seriously. He's a good chap, and keen as mustard—a very pretty half-back, too, when he was at school—but a bit inclined to panic. Thanks very much for telling me about it, Miss Brandeis. I appreciate your help.'

Olivia felt as if she was the vicar's wife being thanked for opening a flower show. She found herself saying 'Not at all,' automatically, and inquired if there was any news of Machoka. Vigorous comb-outs, the D.O. said, were still going on, so far without result. He felt sure that the missing askari hadn't got to Wabenda.

'There's another thing,' she continued. 'Do you know anything about this Plaindweller League?'

The D.O. looked slightly shocked. 'I've heard of it, of course,' he said. 'But I'm sure it's been exaggerated a great deal. Rather like one of those American college fraternities one reads about, don't you think?'

'Kyungu admitted that it exists,' Olivia replied. 'It seems to operate a highly successful racket by exploiting the fear that any one who opposes it will become the victim of a fearful curse. There's a theory in Marula that Machoka may be a member. If he is, and now that he's disappeared, it might be possible that the League is mixed up in H.E.'s murder.'

'Now, really, Miss Brandeis,' the D.O. said, 'don't say that you're running away with the idea that a native school-boy secret society is responsible for Sir Malcolm McLeod's murder! That's almost worthy of a settler.'

'I haven't the least idea who's responsible,' Olivia said shortly. 'But I should have thought that as this League seems to have started down here it might at least be worth finding out about.'

For the rest of the meal the D.O.'s courtesy was greater than ever, but Olivia knew that his respect for her scientific attainments had fallen sharply. She felt better after she had lectured him on the significance of sweat-houses among the British Columbian Indians and caught him out about the seasonal variations in the protein content of *Eleusinium corecana* forming the staple food of the Bemba in Northern Rhodesia.

After lunch he insisted on showing her the native school, the hospital, and the sports ground. There were several football fields and a cricket pitch, but the D.O. had not been very successful, he admitted, with cricket. 'I'm introducing polo this year,' he added, brightening up. 'Most of our fellows own donkeys which I'm sure we could train. I think we might work several teams and have a polo league one day. One's got to introduce something to replace the old thrills of tribal war, you know, and to give the young men some incentive to keep fit.'

Olivia conferred whole-hearted praise on the school, the hospital, and the sports ground. It was nearly four o'clock before she climbed into her lorry to return to camp.

'I think I'll run down your way tomorrow,' the D.O. told her before she drove off. 'I'll have a talk to Kyungu, since he's so down in the mouth. I expect he needs bucking-up a little. I'll see if I can persuade the A.O. to bounce Marula into paying half the cost of that maize cleaning machine he wants.'

. . . . .

The afternoon was hot and steamy. Low thunder-clouds were piling up over the hills. They were black and ominous and moved swiftly. Olivia drove absent-mindedly, and at about five o'clock she steered the lorry too much to one side of the track and the off-side wheels sank deep into a patch of loose sand. She tried reversing, failed to move, and stalled the engine. And then the self-starter jammed. The front wheels were in too deep to swing the crank handle, and she didn't know enough mechanics to repair the starter. The lorry was stuck for the night.

Olivia cursed a little and decided to walk back to camp. It couldn't be more than seven or eight miles. Luckily she had a torch, and there was half a moon. For a moment the thought of lions came, unbidden and unwelcome, to her mind. She dismissed it with an effort, took a box of fifty cigarettes from the lorry, and started out.

She walked steadily for a little over an hour, and then paused to watch the sun go down in a lurid bed of orange and indigo thunder-clouds. A long streak of pale sky showed through between the horizon and the hanging floor of the clouds, and the red sun hung there for a full minute, like a huge bloodshot eye suspended in the middle of a wink, before it plunged under the dark hills. Thunder was rumbling from the other side of the sky. 'God is shouting,' the natives called the thunder. Tonight they would believe it was because He had heard their prayers for rain.

Olivia walked on down the track. The bush was fairly thick. Once she caught sight of a small herd of impala, black in the fading light, leaping high over a belt of bush. She heard a jackal barking out of sight, and later almost stumbled over a slow-witted nightjar which flopped off clumsily into the rapidly accumulating night. She crossed a small river bed and some guinea-fowl squawked at her from the acacias that fringed it. Their dark shapes were just visible against the sky, hanging in the branches like enormous fruit. As night fell it grew much colder.

By about seven o'clock she began to wonder if she was getting near the camp. It was hard to recognize landmarks in the darkness. The storm-clouds blotted out the moon.

By eight o'clock she knew she was lost. She was also hungry and had a blistered toe. The night seems to be getting darker. She crossed a couple of dry river beds which she knew she had never seen before, and several times the track seemed like petering out in thick bush and she had to cast round with the torch to find it. Once or twice there was a faint silver flash of sheet lightning. She cursed herself for not staying in the lorry.

After considering the situation over a cigarette she decided to go on. She was on a path of sorts, and it must lead somewhere. She had passed no huts for about an hour. It was probably going to pelt with rain, and she had better look for shelter.

She plodded on for another long hour. Once a violent rustling in the bush a few feet away made her jump. The beam from her torch caught nothing but the quivering of disturbed branches. She was beginning to curse herself for not turning back when she saw the glimmer of a light in the distance. Thank God! she thought. Huts at last.

The bush thinned out and Olivia found herself at the edge of a natural clearing. The light she had seen came from a hurricane lamp hanging on a pole. That was unusual. She was surprised to see, behind the lamp, the dim shape of a rectangular house. All native huts in these parts were round.

She walked on slowly, and the shape of the house

became clearer. It was quite large. There were lights inside, for a beam shone through the open door and fell across the short grass in front. Olivia halted. There was something wrong about it. Of course! It had no windows. It couldn't be a mission house, then.

She approached closer, unconsciously on tiptoe. A tingling sensation ran up and down her spine. This is ridiculous, she thought. It's probably an evening class in a bush school. In the stillness the sound of voices from within the house came to her ears. She listened carefully. A soft mutter of thunder drowned the sound and she came closer, hardly breathing, edging towards the side of the house farthest from the open doorway.

At the opposite end of the house, at the back, there was a small opening. It was high up and a square of light shone out of it on to the grass below. She crept up cautiously, feeling as if she had swallowed a stone. She flattened herself against the mud wall of the house and peered through the roughly carpentered aperture on a level with her head.

The sight that met her eyes was so astounding that she felt as if every muscle in her body had been paralysed. She stared, uncomprehending, forgetful of the light falling on to her white and startled face.

Down the centre of the room ran a long table made of planks propped on rough trestles. It was covered with a cloth of cheap calico. Three hurricane lamps suspended from the ridge-pole lighted the scene. Round the table sat a group of a dozen natives dressed in costumes so fantastic that Olivia felt as if she were another Alice translated into an African wonderland.

At one end of the table presided a man dressed in a white calico tunic with gold buttons, white tennis trousers, a broad red sash to which a genuine military sword was attached, and a cocked hat made of cardboard and surmounted by an enormous ostrich feather. Rows of coloured ribbon were sewn on to the breast of his tunic. He wore white cotton gloves. On either side of him sat two male natives in women's evening dress, obviously discarded from some European wardrobe. Their faces were smeared with white and grotesquely rouged.

Along the table on either side sat alternate men and men dressed as women. One wore a navy-blue tunic and a pair of blue plus fours, a wooden imitation sword, and two golden curtain tassels fixed on to his shoulders in a manner suggesting naval epaulettes. Another wore a real highland kilt and sporran with a short red mess jacket, a dirty starched shirt, and a white tie without a collar. Opposite him was a man in an old, shiny frock-coat and a parson's dog collar, with an ecclesiastical shovel hat on his head. There were two men in disintegrating dinner jackets, stiff collars and black ties. One of the imitation women wore a moth-eaten fur coat; another fiddled with a diamanté-studded evening bag. The man at the head of the table was smoking a big cigar.

On the table itself was an extraordinary array of crockery. There were tin and china plates of all shapes and sizes. Ground ivy was strewn about in imitation of smilax. Two glass jugs half full of red liquid stood in the centre.

While Olivia gazed incredulously several natives in the long white kanzus worn by servants cleared away the plates and stacked them in a corner. They took round tin mugs and a few cracked glasses, placed one in front of each guest, and filled them with red liquid from the jugs.

Then Olivia received another shock. The man at the head of the table rose to his feet, his cigar still in his mouth. His cardboard hat fell off and he replaced it carefully. No one smiled. He rapped on the table and the others also rose. He lifted his glass, touched it with his thick protruding lips, and said:

'Genelmens, the King!'

Glasses were raised all round, and there was a noise of sucking. One of the party spluttered and choked. The man at the head of the table sat down and the others followed suit.

For several minutes no one spoke. The silence was broken by a voice which said, in English:

'The reason why the rise of the Greek republics is the Greek peninsular separates from rivals with high mountains and sea preventing attacks enablinating cultures blossom.'

This remark was received in dead silence. After a short interval the man in the kilt wrinkled his face in concentration and announced:

'Charles first was unheaded to reserve rights by people refusing scribe divine right of kings.' There was another long silence.

Olivia felt a little delirious. She couldn't possibly be seeing all this in real life. She wondered if she had got fever and was actually lying unconscious in a hospital ward.

She was not sure how long she had watched this nightmarish performance before the president again rapped on the table with the head of his sword. 'Ladies now leaving genelmens,' he ordered. The men dressed as women filed out of the door and did not return.

'Genelmens,' said the president. ''Shun!' They all stood up. 'Bishop, you bring sac'ament.' The man in the frock-coat and dog collar saluted and went out. As he did so a clap of thunder startled the silence. The storm was drawing closer.

Those who remained crossed their arms and joined hands round the table, assuming the conventional British position for singing 'Auld Lang Syne'. The bishop returned carrying an old tin cash-box which he set carefully on the centre of the table.

'Genelmens,' the president announced again, 'we now make worship to sac'ament, asking sac'ament give us white men's magic, making strong as white mens.' They jerked their clasped hands up and down three times and the bishop, wearing white gloves, flung open the lid of the cash-box.

Olivia peered down through the window, so fascinated

that she abandoned caution in an effort to catch a glimpse of the assorted contents of the box. In the centre lay an unidentifiable cigar-shaped object wrapped in newspaper, resting on a small book. Round it was arranged a rifle cartridge, an object which looked like a marble but which Olivia decided was a glass eye, and a pipe.

The assembled company bowed their heads before the fetish, and as they did so there was a flurry of wind, a loud clap of thunder overhead, and a soft rush of raindrops on the thatched roof. One of the men, the highlander, turned his head towards the single window and looked straight into Olivia's peering face. With a sudden shock she recognized him — Machoka, the missing corporal.

He gave a horrified cry and snatched his hand away from the circle of arms. Olivia waited no longer. She turned and catapulted herself away from the wall and towards the bush. Terror propelled her legs at a speed they had never before attained. She had seen their fetish, and she knew that capture would mean death. As she reached the edge of the bush a streak of lightning stabbed the sky. She looked back to see a dark rush of figures pouring round the angle of the house. Their mouths were open, like running hounds, but a sharp clap of thunder drowned their shouts. They were hunting her in a pack, and mob madness drove them on in frenzy.

The rain started in earnest, lashing down in a violent, stinging fury. Olivia plunged into a wall of bush that ripped the coat of her light drill suit. She rammed her thick felt hat low over her forehead to protect her eyes and went at the bush like a charging buffalo. The whine of the rainstorm drowned the noise of her pursuers. She seemed to be running in a void, neither forward nor back, but enclosed in a nightmare barricade of thorns and branches. The bush was endless, malignantly alive. It gripped her thrusting shoulders with relentless arms. She fought it, her breath coming in gulps, until she slipped on a wet log and tumbled head forwards into a tangle of undergrowth.

From all sides came the persistent beat of rain on leaves and branches. There was no glimmer of light. Olivia listened between panting breaths and the pounding of her heart for the crackle of branches that would herald her pursuers. There was no sound. She lay still in her refuge of bush, soaked and scratched and bleeding, but apparently safe.

.   .   .   .   .

How she got back to camp the next morning, Olivia never knew. She spent the night, cold, shivering, exhausted, and frightened, alternately cowering on the muddy ground and forcing herself a few paces through the bush to keep her circulation from giving up altogether. When a watery dawn lightened the sky she started to push her way out, steering east by the sun; and at eleven o'clock, guided by a small boy whom she encountered herding goats, she staggered into camp, limping, stiff, and sick.

Her flimsy tent looked to her as solid and secure as the battlements of a castle. Her boy, amused rather than disturbed at her condition, brought water for the canvas bath, and tea with poached eggs and bacon. She lay down on a warm, dry bed, and fell into an exhausted sleep.

The D.O. arrived early in the afternoon. He had left his driver to fix her lorry and bring it in. He sat on the edge of her camp-bed and listened incredulously to her story, staring at her as though she was delirious.

'I know it sounds ridiculous, but I'm not a victim of delusions,' Olivia snapped. Her eyes and throat were burning painfully and she was shivering in spasms. 'Have you ever heard of the Ntambwe Bwanga?'

The D.O. shook his head.

'It's a native secret society in the Belgian Congo—or used to be. I don't know if it still exists. Its object was to provide a native understudy for every white man in the Congo, from Governor down to engine-driver, so that when the Europeans left—and it was all based on a prophecy made by a famous witchdoctor that the white men would leave of their own accord to fight a war in Europe, and never return—every place could be filled by a black substitute. It had some sort of fetish that was produced at meetings, and was supposed in some way to represent the white man's magic, or secret of power.'

'And you think the performance you say you saw last night was a branch of this society?' the D.O. asked, as though humouring an invalid. He wore a tolerant smile.

'No. An imitation,' Olivia answered shortly. 'Whoever started this thing in Chania probably got hold of a garbled version of the Belgian society and adapted the idea. Each one of those men last night evidently represented some important European official. The man who presided was obviously meant to be the Governor, and I think the whole thing was a fantastic imitation of a Government House dinner-party—an affair which natives may very likely feel has some ritual significance. It's simply a form of sympathetic magic, like nearly all primitive fertility rites. In this case the idea is that by imitating the white man, and behaving as he does, the imitator will acquire some of the white man's magic. Clothes, of course, are very important. And the cash-box contained the fetish, the secret of the white man's magic, which is evidently mixed up with the Christian sacrament in some way. It's very interesting.'

The D.O. looked about half convinced. Put that way, it did sound more feasible.

'Those men were semi-educated natives who'd had some contact with Europeans,' Olivia added. 'They all knew some English. I expect they find it a profitable sideline to terrorize the local natives and make them hand over cattle and goats. I dare say it doesn't concern you, but I thought you'd like to know that I saw Machoka there.'

'It was very good of you to let me know, Miss Brandeis,' the D.O. replied, his manners unshaken and serene. 'We'll certainly investigate at once. The first thing, I think, is to find the hut. I'll put a couple of my lads on to that right away.'

Olivia gave him such directions as she could remember.

'And as soon as my man gets back with your lorry,' he continued, 'I'm going to send you straight into Marula in my car. No! Don't argue. You've got fever; it's no good denying it.'

In spite of violent protests from Olivia, the D.O. produced a thermometer and almost forced it into her mouth. Her temperature was 103. Her face was flushed, her head buzzed, and her throat felt like sandpaper.

'You go straight to bed with thirty grains of quinine,' he said, 'and don't stir till I pack you off in the car tomorrow morning.' She felt too weak to struggle with his efficiency, and crawled reluctantly into her fleabag.

.   .   .   .   .

The D.O. did not return until late that night. It was raining again, steadily and hard. Towards dusk one of his search-party stumbled on a mud-and-stick house in a natural clearing answering to the description given by Olivia. There was a hole in the floor, covered up with planks, and in a rough cellar underneath the D.O. found a jumbled pile of old clothes—women's evening dresses, high-heeled shoes, old frock coats, tunics, kilts, top hats. There was no sign, of course, of the fetish.

It was very upsetting, and not at all part of the scheme of things. The D.O. felt like the headmaster of an exclusive school who finds his prize prefects drunk on port with a party of cinema usherettes. His chaps had definitely let him down. It looked as if Machoka had been in the reserve all the time, too. And Kyungu was silent, unenthusiastic, and moody, quite unlike his usual self. Even a reference to the maize-cleaning machine had no effect. Old Silu, on the other hand, seemed even more self-satisfied than usual. He answered several questions in riddles, took a great deal of snuff and merely denied, as before, all knowledge of

Machoka's movements. The D.O. tried hard to be fair to Silu, whom he treated with the respect due to an elder of the tribe, but he couldn't help finding the old man a bit exasperating.

The D.O. said good night to Olivia, whose temperature was about the same, and strolled back to his tent, pipe in mouth. Thank God the rains had come at last, he thought. Things ought to settle down now. He would like to see regular weather forecasts, made by expert meteorologists, posted up every week in the district council halls. That would bring it home to the native that rain was a natural phenomenon, predictable by scientific means, and not a whim of the gods to be influenced by sacrifices and a lot of ritual.

A white object gleamed in the wet grass, and the D.O. idly kicked at it with one foot. It rolled away, and he saw that it was a small skull. He picked it up and examined it. It was a fresh relic, picked clean by hyenas. Some wretched kid, he thought, chucked out of the hut in the last stages, to die in the bush. He tossed the fragile skull away and wiped his hands on his trousers. This problem of infant mortality...

.   .   .   .   .

Olivia's temperature was down a little the next day, but the D.O. still insisted, in spite of her protests, in sending her in to Marula. She dressed and went down to the huts to say *au revoir*. She felt shaky at the knees, and wore several woollies. It was a clear, bright morning, and the sun shone freshly in a cloudless blue sky. The earth had soaked up the rain thirstily and looked clean and spruce. Olivia heard the women laughing and chattering as they went out early to plant maize. The rain had come, the evil spirits were gone, and all was right with a kind and cheerful world.

Old Silu was sitting on a stool outside his hut, whittling a block of wood with a clumsy knife. He was making a toy for his grandchildren. He greeted her with a great display of friendship—no doubt, Olivia reflected, because he knew she was about to leave.

They exchanged polite remarks about the weather and then Olivia, moved by a desire to shake his complacency just once before she left, said:

'I have seen Machoka, and nearby. You are not a very good witchdoctor, Silu, when you have so little knowledge that you do not know when your own son is in the district.'

Silu went on whittling the stick in silence. After a little he said:

'Machoka is afraid of the injustice of the white man. I know that he did not kill the Governor.'

'You seem to know everything,' Olivia remarked.

'Not everything,' Silu admitted, 'but I have seen much, and I understand.' He tapped his forehead. 'He who follows the path of the bushbuck knows where the kudu goes to lick salt.'

'In that case,' Olivia said, with heavy sarcasm, 'you might tell me who killed the Governor.'

Silu put down his stick and gazed up at her gravely. He rearranged his blanket about his doubled-up knees. His wrinkled face looked at once cunning and amused.

'Very well, I will tell you,' he said. Olivia laughed. She was feeling feverish and irritable, in no mood for jokes.

'Don't be silly,' she said. 'You could not know.'

'I will tell you a riddle,' Silu said. He paused to take a deep pinch of snuff. 'It is this. What is it that swallows at noontime he who is swallowed by night? He who swells and grows little.' He returned to his block of wood and his knife.

Olivia's eyes were swimming and her head had started to throb. She didn't feel like any more sparring with the old man. Besides, he was an old charlatan, trying to impress her with his supernatural powers like that.

'Good-bye, Silu,' she said. 'I shall return soon.'

They shook hands solemnly. 'I wish you good fortune,' he said, and spat. He hitched his blanket up over his right shoulder and sat down again on the low brass-studded stool. Olivia climbed into the seat beside the uniformed Government driver and the car jolted off towards Marula.

13

On the morning that Olivia left Marula for the reserve, the press started to catch up with the case. Vachell found a bunch of them waiting down at his office when he got there at nine o'clock. Besides the local *Courier* reporters, an *Argus* man had arrived by plane from Johannesburg, British United Press had sent a man across from Palestine, the Cairo correspondent of the *Mail* had got a lift down in a plane going through to Capetown, and a woman stunt flyer had turned up to cover the case for another famous London daily. There was an Indian among them whom Vachell recognized as the man with the watching brief for the Government of India. He was still trying to find out what steps were being taken to safeguard the lives and property of British Indian subjects.

The B.U.P. man wanted a story on an imminent native rebellion and the *Mail* correspondent, who had covered the Spanish civil war, kept on asking for anti-Red headquarters. The woman flyer hopped off for the Ngombe plateau at once to get a story on Popple's home life.

Pallett issued a press *communiqué* announcing Popple's arrest, and cabled fully to the Secretary of State. The reply was not as enthusiastic as he had hoped. 'Relieved hear speedy arrest,' it said, 'but would like assurance you are entirely satisfied Popple guilty beyond all reasonable doubt. Feel confident unnecessary warn you unfortunate effect on unofficial opinion should Crown be unable to establish case.' This was the Permanent Under-Secretary speaking. The Secretary of State himself remarked: 'Locked up that jackass Popple, have they? He once called me "a grotesque figurehead without even the attributes of beauty or extreme antiquity". Serves him damned well right.'

When Vachell had got rid of the newshawks he decided that his next move had better be to get Popple out of jail. It seemed a pity to spend his time trying to make his own department look foolish, but he supposed it had to be done. He spent some time wondering how he could best bring Armitage round. Then he went in search of Maisie Watson.

It was eleven o'clock by that time, and he drove straight to Dane's. A roar of conversation hit him in the face as he opened the door. Only three drinks and one topic this morning, he guessed: gimlets, Pimms, beers; and Popple. 'Of course he didn't,' he heard a girl's voice say decisively, as he entered. 'He breeds prize Sealyhams.'

There was a vacant swivel stool at the bar and Vachell occupied it and ordered a large iced lager. A voice behind him said:

'Hello, if it isn't the bar-crawling bobby again! Do the Big Five allow you out to play in Marula's den of vice?'

'Why, hello, Mr Tollemache,' Vachell answered. 'Have one with me. I'm just taking a little time out. Thirsty work, detecting.'

'It must be,' Tollemache said, 'especially when you try to make a poor old codger like Popple into a window-blind lassoo artist who goes about murdering Governors. I once spent six months trying to persuade the old boy to kill off some of the surplus population in his milk cows, but he was too damned soft-hearted. No homicidal instincts at all. Come and join us, what? Table over there.'

Tollemache's party included Maisie Watson and her Imperial Airways pilot, who was still waiting for the southbound to arrive. He was looking a little offended, for Tollemache had just presented him with the slogan, 'Travel Imperial and see the world at your ease', and he wasn't quite sure how he ought to take it. The other couple Vachell didn't know. They were all playing 'Knock,

– 160 –

knock', and drinking large Pimms.

'I've brought the pride of the Force along to tell you all about the great arrest,' Tollemache explained. 'Meet Mr Vachell, the boy detective, folks.'

'I've been longing to meet you, Mr Vachell,' Maisie said brightly. 'I think I can help you a little in your inquiries.'

'I bet you can,' Tollemache remarked. 'Maisie's motto is "inquire within".'

Some one said 'Happy landings' and they all drank. Vachell looked at Maisie and said:

'I'd like a word with you, Mrs Watson, if you have the time.'

'Nice work.' Tollemache raised his glass in her direction. 'Our Maisie's made a Force landing, what. We're not wanted here any longer. Come on, Pat, and hold my hand. I've got to see a woman about a man.'

The pilot and the other couple got up to go. 'Do you know Vachell?' Tollemache said. He put one hand on his hip and spoke in a high falsetto. 'Va—chell me he's a policeman, but *I* think he's an awfully cute boy.' Vachell and Maisie were left alone.

'I'm sorry to horn in like this, Mrs Watson,' he said. 'I have a piece of good news I believe you'll be glad to hear. I guess you must have been pretty worried the last few days, and I reckoned you'd like to know that I think we can fix things now.'

'But it's perfectly all right.' She smiled at him; sweetly was the only adjective. She was still keeping to black chiffon. He could see that she was a little uncertain about what she was supposed to be worrying about. 'You can't imagine how relieved I am that it's all over. It's been a terrible, dreadful experience. But now you've solved the mystery so brilliantly—*every one's* saying how marvellous you are, Mr Vachell, and how, of *course*, you ought to be made Commissioner—at least I have the consolation that poor, dear Malcolm will be avenged.'

'I was thinking of another angle to the case, Mrs

Watson,' Vachell said. He beckoned the waiter and ordered another beer and a gimlet. 'It's this way. I figure that you must have been worrying over what's likely to come out at the trial. You know how the newspapers play these things up. Sir Malcolm's private life is likely to come under pretty heavy fire, on the defence side anyway, if only to suggest alternative motives. Of course you wouldn't like that, and I didn't care to think of you being subjected to an ordeal of that sort.'

'But how sweet of you to think of me!' Maisie cried. 'And how understanding! So few men would worry their heads over *my* feelings, or realize how much a horrid scandal can *hurt*.'

'Why, any man in my place would feel just the same,' Vachell went on. 'My problem was how to get around the situation. Well, I've had a word with Mr Jeudwine, and after what he's told me, I think we can fix things so your name won't come out at all. I'm afraid I didn't realize just how matters stood between you and Sir Malcolm, or—'

'Just what did Jeudwine tell you?' Maisie's sweet and girlish expression had changed to one of bewilderment, not unmixed with irritation.

'Well, he just explained how things had worked out,' Vachell said. He seemed embarrassed. 'That Sir Malcolm had...well, that you and he had come to an arrangement not to...gee, you're making it difficult for me, Mrs Watson. I guess you know what it's all about.'

'I certainly do not,' Maisie snapped back. 'And I'd like to know just what Kenneth Jeudwine thinks he knows about it, either!'

'Why, everything, I should say.' The boy brought the drinks and Vachell paid for them. 'Here's to your happiness, Mrs Watson.' He drank half the beer.

'Just what *do* you mean?' Maisie's face had gone cold and hard, and her eyes had narrowed. She took up the gimlet as though it contained vitriol. 'What did Jeudwine tell you about me?'

'You know, you don't make this any easier,' Vachell complained plaintively. 'If you must have it cold, he told me how Sir Malcolm had decided it was best to quit several weeks before the murder, and how you and he—you and Jeudwine, I mean—were, well, that way about each other.'

Maisie put down her empty glass with a violent slap. Her round baby face was contorted and white with rage.

'He told you that, did he, the lousy son of a bitch!' she said. 'He's a dirty liar, a rotten, sneaking, slimy little louse! Because I wouldn't touch him with the end of a ten-foot pole he—'

'Say, easy, now,' Vachell interrupted. 'I'm only telling you what he said.'

'Said!' Maisie recovered some of her self-control with an effort. 'Lied, you mean, the lousy swine. There isn't a word of truth in it, not one word. He said that, did he? Then *I'll* say something. Do you really want to know the truth about this murder?'

'Well, it would help,' Vachell admitted.

'All right then, I'll tell you who killed Malcolm. And I'll tell you why, too.'

'That's swell,' Vachell said. 'Suppose we go back a bit first. Jeudwine fell for you in a big way, didn't he? And wrote you some letters?'

Maisie was too angry to wonder how he knew this. 'He was disgusting,' she said. 'They were horrid letters. Greasy, like him—obscene. He pursued me. He kept trying to force his attentions on me. At first I was soft-hearted and I was sorry for him. But I soon realized that he was a monster underneath. Nothing but a monster.'

'But a literate one,' Vachell added. 'What did you do with the letters?'

'Of course I meant to destroy them, but I forgot about it, and then, when he kept asking for them back, I didn't see why I should do anything for him, so I just kept them.'

'Very proper sentiments, I'd say. So then Jeudwine got mad and threatened to spill the story to Sir Malcolm, did he? About the period when you were soft-hearted, I mean.'

'You seem to know a lot about it.' Maisie looked at him with a trace of suspicion. 'Yes, he did. Malcolm was insanely jealous, and he would have misunderstood my efforts to be nice to Jeudwine—at first, I mean, when I felt sorry for him. I was really only nice to him because I thought I owed it to Malcolm.'

'Very neatly put,' Vachell said. 'Well, what happened on Tuesday night?'

'Jeudwine behaved like a fiend in the garden,' she went on. 'Nothing but a fiend. He threatened me, and said he'd tell Malcolm that very night. And, of course, I knew he'd invent a lot of lies. I was awfully worried, as I didn't want poor Malcolm upset. So during the evening I slipped into Jeudwine's office and gave him back his filthy letters, to stop him doing anything silly. I was really doing it to spare Malcolm, of course.'

'Of course,' Vachell agreed. 'It was the big-hearted thing to do. I hope Mr Jeudwine was properly grateful?'

'He was tight. Really, I was quite nervous, he acted so wildly. I was afraid he was going to assault me. He kept on saying that if *he* couldn't have me, no one else would, and he was going to kill Sir Malcolm—he did, really. He used the most vulgar expressions. I felt it had smirched my friendship with Malcolm. I really don't like to think of it at all.'

'I bet you hate it like hell,' Vachell said. 'You're being very plucky. Well, then what? You left him mouthing vile threats against Sir Malcolm, and went home to bed?'

'You're a funny man, Mr Vachell. You were so sympathetic at first, and now you're being horrid. I tried to argue with him, but he was too tight to be reasonable, and kept on saying that he was going to end it all, so I left him. And the next thing I knew was that my poor Malcolm was dead.' The black chiffon handkerchief came out of Maisie's bag. Vachell acted as if it had been a signal. He jumped to his feet.

'It's been swell of you to tell me all this,' he said. 'I certainly do appreciate it, Mrs Watson, even though it is about three days too late.' He shook hands quickly and was striding across the room before she had time to collect her indignation. As he reached the door he heard a voice calling 'Yippee!' and singing the first bars of 'O, Canada' out of tune. He waved back at Tollemache and dived through the door.

.   .   .   .   .

It was evening before Vachell succeeded in getting hold of Armitage, and even then the Commissioner refused to see Jeudwine before the following afternoon. Armitage's temper was thoroughly sour. A morning with the Attorney-General had confirmed his worst fears, and Pallett had been exceedingly difficult. A bad blunder had been made, and the Acting Governor had refused to admit it.

The Acting Governor himself was rattled. An indignant mass meeting of settlers on the Ngombe plateau had passed a fiery resolution condemning Popple's arrest as a 'deliberate and provocative slur upon the good faith of the settler community', and demanding that the evidence on which it was based should be made public at once. They had gone on to demand, in much more peremptory terms than usual, a reduction in railway rates on fertilizers, the introduction of an export quota for marrowfat peas, and a further step towards self-government for the European community. There had been a sudden outbreak of cattle raiding among the Timburu on the western frontier, and Moon had received disturbing reports that a renewed movement to demand M'Bola's immediate release was spreading rapidly in the native areas. Pallett said that further proof of Popple's guilt must be obtained at once and without fail, as though he was having trouble about a library book on a guaranteed subscription.

Vachell, back at police headquarters, sent for Janis and put him in charge of the search for Machoka. The young inspector had spent most of the day, on the Commissioner's instructions, in reading through reports of Popple's last political speeches and making abstracts of anything that might be construed as a threat against the Governor.

'There's one small point, sir,' he said, when he had finished his report. 'You remember that file on the sewage system at Mbale that had been marked out to G.H.? When I was down at the Secretariat today I thought I'd have a look at it just to see what made it so important. I got it out of the stacks, and so far as I could make out, there hasn't been any action on it for over a year. I brought it along in case you'd like to see it.' He threw the buff file on to the desk.

Vachell grinned at him. 'You sure do sift over the crumbs,' he said. 'You'll make tops as a detective if you keep going that way.' Janis flushed with pleasure. 'I guess the filing clerk would know about it.'

'I tried to ask Fernandez,' Janis replied. 'I wanted to talk to him anyway, about Popple's visit to the Secretariat on the night of the murder. But Fernandez was out at lunch. I went along to ask Mr Pallett if he knew anything about it, but he said he couldn't remember every file that went through his hands. He was rather annoyed at being disturbed, I'm afraid. He was in a conference with Mr Moon and the Attorney-General.'

Vachell grinned broadly. 'Mr Pallett doesn't care to be disturbed,' he said.

During the afternoon a cable from Scotland Yard came in, which read:

Your cable thirtieth. Major Eric Fripton-Scoresby second son honourable James Fripton-Scoresby of Coates Manor Bilbury Berks. Elder brother killed 1916 has one sister Dorothy married 1928 Sir Bertrand Flower present Governor Totseland. Eric Fripton-Scoresby recently retired Indian army now living Salcombe in apparently modest circumstances. Recently appointed director African

Equities Ltd. salary five hundred per annum. Articles
African Equities require directors hold minimum
twenty thousand shares now standing thirty shillings.
No recent market transactions recorded regarding
company but all stock held by directors market
quotations nominal. No police record Fripton-Scoresby.

Vachell read it through twice and felt his muscles
contract a little inside him from suppressed excitement. He
called up the manager of the Chania railway and made an
appointment for the following morning.

. . . . .

At four o'clock the next afternoon the police Commissioner
and his Superintendent kept an appointment with
Jeudwine at Government House. The Governor's secretary
did not pretend to be glad to see them. Armitage had made
up his mind that the interview would be a waste of time.
Only Vachell remained entirely unruffled.

Jeudwine drew up chairs for them in his office. He
looked more sallow and ill than ever. His collar was too big
for his neck, and Vachell wondered if that was because he
had an unusually big Adam's apple or because his long
arms threw out the fit of ready-made shirts.

'I thought you'd finished your inquisitions,' he said to
Armitage. 'You've got the murderer, haven't you? I can't
say I'm surprised it's Popple. He's got away with the pose
of the pure-hearted crusader in a coat of mail for some
time, but now he'll find that he's gone too far in his
gangster methods.' His voice was bitter and gloating at the
same time.

Armitage cleared his throat, said 'Quite, quite,' and
looked across at his assistant.

'Just one or two things we have to straighten out for the
record, Mr Jeudwine,' Vachell said. 'The situation has
changed a little since we talked it over last. I've had a long
talk with Mrs Watson, for one thing.'

'I should have thought you might have had better things to do than to have heart-to-hearts with a tart,' Jeudwine said coldly. 'I hope she gave you some interesting reminiscences.' Armitage expressed strong disapproval in a cough.

'She told me plenty,' Vachell answered. He leant forward and fixed his eyes on Jeudwine's face. 'Maybe you'd care to hear her story, and tell me if she's got it straight.'

Jeudwine shrugged his shoulders and leant back in his chair. He looked out of the window into the sunlight with an indifferent expression.

'She told me,' Vachell continued, 'that your susceptible heart was busted by her innocent, girlish charm. That you forced your unwanted attentions on her until finally she took pity on you and did what little she could to offer you consolation. And then she regretted her impulsive action and walked out on you, taking with her, however, a bunch of letters you'd been thoughtless enough to write. In other words, that you made a pass at her and she, you poor boob, played you for a sucker.'

'Damn you, shut up!' Jeudwine shouted. His lemon-coloured face was flushed, and he jumped to his feet. 'I won't stand your filthy impudence! Commissioner, I appeal to you, have I got to sit here and listen to this damned Canadian inventing libellous stories about my private life?'

Armitage looked annoyed and embarrassed. 'Come to the point, Vachell; come to the point,' he snapped. 'You can't slander people like this. It's most irregular.'

Vachell took no notice of the interruptions, but continued to stare at Jeudwine.

'So you decided on a desperate step,' he went on. 'You were half crazy with jealousy. You had to stand back and watch Sir Malcolm getting everything you wanted handed to him on a silver platter, and it burned you up. You just couldn't take it. There was only one thing you could think

of to unscramble the situation. You decided to rub Sir Malcolm out.'

'It's a bloody lie!' Jeudwine's voice was cracked with passion. He tried to shake the table with his hands. 'Stop him, damn you, keep him quiet! I'll ram your bloody libels down your — neck till they—'

'Steady, now, Mr Jeudwine, steady,' Armitage said. He had suddenly started to take a lively interest in the proceedings. 'We're not laying any charge against you, you know.' He looked anxiously at Vachell, hoping that his statement was true. 'Keep calm, man; keep calm.'

'Before you killed Sir Malcolm, though, you had to recover the letters you'd been sap enough to write to Maisie,' Vachell continued evenly, without changing his conversational tone. 'You weren't sufficiently nuts to want to swing for the murder, and so long as she had those letters she could use them to pin a motive on you any time she wanted. So you threatened to spill the whole story to Sir Malcolm if she didn't turn in those letters. She tried to bluff you at first, but she got scared the bluff wouldn't stick, and around ten o'clock she slipped into your room—in here—and kicked through with the letters.'

Jeudwine was breathing heavily, as though drunk. Veins stood out on his temples and sweat was trickling down over the lenses of his spectacles. 'It's all lies, she made it up, she's the biggest bitch—'

'Keep quiet, Jeudwine,' Armitage said. He was looking at his assistant with mixed bewilderment and uneasiness. 'Go on, man; go on.'

'Well, Maisie left and you burnt the letters, and then you were all set. You already had the method figured out. You had the poison which you got from some native, and you were going to shoot it into the highball you mixed every night for Sir Malcolm, when he was working late.

'But you reckoned that when it was all over, poison would be strongly suspected, even if it couldn't be traced in the P.M., and that some one might start to pay a lot of

attention to that highball. So you figured it would be a smart idea if the glass in which you fixed the highball carried an extra fingerprint or two that hadn't any right to be there. You reckoned this would bust any police theory that nobody handled the glass but you, even if it didn't give them another suspect to chase after.

'So right after Maisie left you went over to the buffet, and the first person you saw there was Popple. He was known to be riding the Governor all the time, so you reckoned he'd make a swell suspect. You offered him a drink and when he set his glass down on the table you switched his glass for yours and carried it back to your office. Then you wiped off all of the prints except one near the rim, because you figured it would look a bit too careless if the murderer left his prints strewn all over the glass like chicken feed in a poultry yard. That was smart. You might have got by, if you'd kept to the plan.'

Vachell paused, and this time Jeudwine said nothing. He was breathing less heavily, but his throat seemed dry and he swallowed now and then with difficulty.

'But you didn't,' Vachell went on steadily. 'You lost your nerve. You were pretty well tanked. At first the liquor gave you courage, but then your nerve began to run out on you, and by the time the Governor buzzed for his Scotch-and-soda you had a bad case of jitters. The highball was all ready in the glass, with Popple's prints on it, but you just hadn't got what it takes to mix in a little shot of powder. So when the buzzer went your nerve crumbled altogether. And the Governor had his highball straight.

'You sat around and kicked yourself for a while and then, when Moon's message came over and you had to go out, you junked the poison in the flower-bed. But when you got to thinking things over you decided that if you couldn't do the job that way, you'd try out some other method. You weren't going to be beat by your own yellowness. You got yourself all steamed up again, and when you returned to your office from sending off the files

you went right into H.E.'s room, walked around behind his chair, cut the cord off the blind with a pocket-knife, knotted it, and slipped the noose around his neck before you had time to back down on yourself. You pulled it tight till he stopped choking and then you got out just as fast as you could, and got yourself cockeyed.'

Vachell stood up, flexed his long arms, and looked at Armitage. 'I'm sorry, sir, to shoot our case to pieces, but it's better done now than later on in court.'

Jeudwine's face was still livid and his hands were shaking, but he had recovered his self-control. 'I deny everything,' he said, 'and I demand to see a lawyer. The whole of this performance is not only a malicious invention, but it's illegal. You're going to suffer for this.'

Vachell, without replying, lifted the telephone and dialled a number. Jeudwine went on denying the charges angrily until Vachell got Maisie Watson on the wire. Then he suddenly crumpled up. 'Stop that!' he shouted. 'Don't let her come near me! I'll tell you what you want, damn you, if you'll keep her away from me!'

He denied absolutely that he had killed his chief. He swore hysterically that he knew nothing whatsoever about the crime. But he admitted the rest of the story, his face dug into his cupped hands, his voice jerky and incoherent. He'd been driven mad by impotent jealousy and desire. He'd brought some native poison from a Somali, but his insanity had stopped short of the actual crime. It was all as Vachell had said, up to the moment that he threw the poison away in the flower-bed in revulsion, terrified lest he should be driven by his own emotions to make a second attempt on the Governor's life, or perhaps to use it on himself.

After that he didn't enter the Governor's study until after the crime had been discovered, and he never saw the Governor alive again. This was God's truth, he swore; and nothing would shake him. He seemed too broken-up to fight any more. The police authorities left him sitting amid the crumpled ruins of his self-respect, shaking with dry

sobs. Neither of them looked at him when they left, and Armitage did not ask him any questions.

.   -.   .   .   .

The Commissioner exploded as soon as they reached headquarters. His moustache was bristling with indignation.

'Damn it, Vachell,' he said, 'your conduct's impossible. You've absolutely no right to spring your theories without any warning like that, making us look the biggest fools in creation, and breaking the law into the bargain.'

Vachell tipped his chair back against the wall and crossed his legs. 'I'm sorry I had to jump it on you like that, sir,' he said. 'I reckoned you'd never believe my theory about Popple's fingerprint unless I could get Jeudwine to come through.'

Armitage grunted. 'How the devil did you find all that out, eh?'

'I figured it this way. I didn't believe, for various reasons, that Popple did the job. Nor did you, sir, if it comes to that. The whole of the case against him was built up around that one thumb-print.

'Well, it followed that if Popple's record was clean the print was either an accident or a plant. Accident didn't seem to fit, but it looked mighty like a plant. So then I had a problem: who was trying to frame Popple, and why? I figured that if we could get the answer to that one, we'd have the case in the bag.

'The only guy who had the opportunity to monkey around with that glass was Jeudwine. And Popple told me that shortly before the murder took place, Jeudwine had come over to the bar and bought him a drink. Jeudwine wasn't friendly with Popple as a rule, so that surprised Popple enough for him to comment on it. Switching glasses at a bar is an old trick, so it didn't need much midnight oil consumption to figure out how the frame was fixed.

'It began to look like Jeudwine was our man. And I ran into three pieces of evidence that seemed to add up to a

good motive. Miss Brandeis told me she heard Jeudwine and Maisie Watson scrapping on the night of the party over some revelation he threatened to make to Sir Malcolm. I found a cigarette stub with lipstick on it in Jeudwine's room, which suggested he'd had a visit from a lady on the night of the murder. And I found he'd burnt up a whole lot of G.H. writing-paper that same evening. I fitted these facts together and made a guess at the story you heard a little while back. Jeudwine's one of those buttoned-up sort of guys who are liable to fall the heaviest for a dame like Maisie, and when they do, then all hell breaks loose inside of them.'

'Yes, yes, I see that,' Armitage said. His annoyance was drowned in his interest. 'Very odd situation, very odd indeed. And you think he really did it, do you?'

Vachell shook his head. 'No, sir, I don't. I think he was telling the truth. He hasn't the guts, for one thing. And there are several facts that don't square with the theory that he's the killer. In the first place, I'm certain it was the murderer's voice, and not Sir Malcolm's, that Watson heard when he looked into the study at ten-forty-eight. And at ten-forty-eight Jeudwine was out after Moon's files—both Abdi and Miss Brandeis testify to that—so he couldn't have been in the study. Secondly, if Jeudwine had done the job he wouldn't have had to use the window, and I don't see why the catch should have been wiped clean. Thirdly, I'm pretty confident that the papers on Sir Malcolm's bureau were disturbed, and something taken away; and Jeudwine could have taken a paper any time—he wouldn't have had to commit murder for it.

'So I got to the point where I had two sets of facts pointing in opposite directions: towards Jeudwine and away from him. You paid your money and you took your choice. I puzzled over that for a while, and then I realized that both might be right. It was just possible that Jeudwine laid his plans for a murder and then backed down, and that some one else finished the job for him. That seemed far-fetched, but at least it did seem to fit in with my impression of Jeudwine's psychology.

'There were two bits of the puzzle I hadn't got figured out, and I concentrated on them. When Jeudwine heard H.E. was murdered, he said a screwy sort of a thing. He said: "S'impossible. S'flower-bed." And Miss Brandeis had seen him walking away from the car park, and she happened to say he'd been standing near the flower-bed.

'I tried to figure what Jeudwine had meant to say. At first I thought it might be connected with Sir Bertrand Flower. But it might also have meant: "It's impossible, because it's in the flower-bed." In other words, H.E. couldn't be dead, because something that was intended to kill him was in the flower-bed.

'Well, what sort of a lethal weapon could you dispose of in a flower-bed? It couldn't be a gun or a knife. The only thing I could think of that would fill the bill was poison. And poison was a likely choice for Jeudwine on account of his fixing a Scotch-and-soda regularly for H.E.

'So I tried out the first part of the theory on Maisie Watson and she fell for it hook, line and sinker. All I had to do then was to spring it on Jeudwine and hope it would work out. He went in head first. It's tough about Popple, sir, but you know we never had a case that the dumbest jury ever called would swallow.'

Armitage cleared his throat and said: 'Ingenious, Vachell; ingenious, I must admit. Though I cannot approve of your methods. You had no right to force a confession from Jeudwine in that manner. Practically the third degree.' He took off his spectacles, rubbed them, and blinked his eyes. He looked thoroughly upset. 'I don't know what Mr Pallett will say.'

'Mr Pallett can go take a running jump at himself,' Vachell said. 'I have an idea things are going to break in the next few days. If they work out the way I anticipate, there'll be an explosion that will make the niggers down in the palm groves jump so high they'll knock the nuts out of the trees.

'I'd like to make one suggestion. Hold this story for a few days, and then let it break. By that time either Mr Pallett will have bigger game than Popple to hunt, or I shall have flopped so hard you could pin all the murders in Chania for the last ten years on me and it wouldn't make any difference to my reputation. In that case I'll take the rap for Popple and that will put the department in the clear. What do you say?'

Armitage replaced his spectacles and looked at Vachell in shocked surprise. He dismissed the suggestion as outrageous, totally unworthy of an officer of the Chania police. A mistake had been made and an innocent man had suffered. The mistake must be rectified without a moment's delay, and Popple released.

It took Vachell about ten minutes and the exercise of his most persuasive powers to break down the Commissioner's resolve. He only asked for two days. At the end of that time Pallett could be told and Popple released. It might wreck his chances of clearing up the case if the mistake about Popple became public property at once.

At the first sign of a crack in the Commissioner's stonewall attitude, Vachell jumped to his feet and reached for his hat. 'That's fine of you, sir,' he said, 'and thanks a lot. You'll have my report in two days from tonight.' In three strides he was out of the room.

'Hey, Vachell,' Armitage called. 'I didn't say... You must let me know what you propose to do. . . .' His voice echoed down the empty corridor. The Superintendent had gone.

14

The preliminary part of Vachell's scheme, as it turned out, was the most difficult. He wanted a word with Tollemache, and it was harder to get Tollemache alone than to cut a single buffalo out of a cow herd.

He started out on his quest at about six o'clock that evening, and brought it to a triumphant end at four the next morning. The night life of Marula was not usually very pronounced; but it was a Saturday, and the magnet of sensation had brought the more mobile members of the up-country population down to the capital. Here they fused with the flying contingent from the overseas press, and the result was a party.

At six o'clock Vachell located Tollemache at the Mazuri Club. He was drinking sundowners with two London newshawks and the flying correspondent of the London paper, whose name, it appeared, was Toots. She was short, plump, and vivacious, with a snub nose and a mass of blonde curls. The murder story, she said, had gone cold after the first few days—Popple's wife supervised a general store and five children in a small town on the Ngombe plateau, and his home life was unspectacular—so she had stayed on at Dane's and done a series on Lone Women of the Outback instead.

She started the party in a bad temper, on account of a cable she had just received from the Foreign Editor, she explained. One of the subs on the paper had queried her account of life in a mangrove swamp on the higher slopes of Mount Kilimanjaro. He was considered an authority on the tropics since he had once worked on a paper in Mexico City, so the Foreign Editor had rung up some one at Kew Gardens who was very unsympathetic about the mangroves. 'Check up on your botany,' the office had cabled her, 'and soft-pedal highways railroads play sticks angle keeping colonials cornfed lions washed up airplanes okay especially medical.'

As the evening wore on she recovered her good humour and told the story of her solo flight from Reykjavik, Iceland, to St Helena. This was the exploit that first won her fame, coupled with a contract from the Slimforall Corset Company, who signed her on as their Flying Ambassadress. She had flown around the world twice since then, selling Litasare corsets and Aviator brassières with great success, espcially in Japan. This was generally agreed to be rather sinister. 'Shows how air-minded they're getting down there,' she said. 'The Hearst papers ran a story on it. That's how I got my start in newspapers.'

The party dined at Raoul's, danced at Dane's, and ended up at Mazuri dancing to a radio that could get New York. It had swollen to about twenty people by then. Tollemache felt that it was the sort of party old Popple would enjoy, and it was a shame he couldn't join it. The injustice weighed on him a good deal, and at about two o'clock he called for volunteers to storm the jail. They all went off in cars and had gone some way before it was discovered that no one knew where the jail was, except Vachell. He combined, he thought, discretion with tact by directing them to the museum.

Tollemache organized a raiding party which gained triumphant access to the building before any one realized the mistake. Once inside, he delivered himself of a lecture on criminal types illustrated by stuffed fishes, while the B.U.P. man organized a rival party to search for a specimen of virgin bush, whose reputed existence, he said, had always attracted him to Africa. Tollemache recognized with overjoyed affection the features of his friend Popple in the face of a hartebeest on a pedestal. Popple was captured and borne back in a car to Mazuri, where he delivered a racy account of his experiences in jail which cast drastic slurs on the habits of the warders. He ended the evening by unanimous election as first president of Chania and by making, with Tollemache as interpreter, a loudly applauded speech from the throne.

The party broke up about four after refusing, with a sudden display of spirit, to be flown up to Tollemache's farm for breakfast by the owner and Toots, who were anxious to give a demonstration of flying upside down with their wings tied together.

Vachell hung on to the end and got his reward. 'Fly you

somewhere, ol' boy? Delighted,' Tollemache said. 'Absolutely. Any time, any where. Where d'you want to go to? Sydney, Buenos Aires, Peiping, Terre Haute? Only Mbale? That's fine, ol' boy, get you there for breakfast, what?'

Vachell declined firmly and outlined his scheme over a plate of bacon and eggs. Tollemache listened with delight and agreed with enthusiasm.

'For God's sake keep your mouth buttoned up,' Vachell added. 'I'd be fired at the drop of a hat if you spill it to any one. Remember that when your newspaper friends come around.'

'Trust me, old boy, what,' Tollemache said. 'My foundations are dug out of solid discretion. Besides, the newshawks are going tomorrow, thank God. I asked that girl to stay for a month, but by the mercy of providence I didn't tell her where I live.'

A pallid dawn was creeping over the sky when Vachell left the Mazuri Club, his plan complete. It was Sunday morning. He arranged to meet Tollemache at the airport that afternoon at four. By the following evening, he believed, the case would be over.

·   ·   ·   ·   ·

Tollemache was standing by his plane, a dark-red Miles Hawk, when Vachell arrived at the airport. It was a clear, sunlit evening, but heavy cumulus clouds were banking up against the horizon. Long shadows from the hangars fell across the runway. An Imperial Airways northbound Atlanta had just got in and was being put to bed in its shed under the eye of the young pilot, who was still waiting for the southbound to arrive from somewhere in the Sudan. A quarter of a mile away a herd of zebra and gazelle grazed slowly over the plain, undisturbed by the familiar drone of engines.

Vachell climbed into the front cockpit, fastened on a helmet and adjusted the straps. Tollemache took his place behind and revved up the engines. A native pulled the blocks away from under the wheels and the plane taxied out, turned into the wind, and climbed slowly. Marula lay shining beneath them as they headed into the sunset.

In ten minutes the edge of the plain was left behind and they looked down on to the round thatched roofs of native huts which sprawled in tightly stockaded groups over the hillsides. Native gardens stood out in small rectangular patches, brown and dark against the lighter pastures. They climbed steadily to cross a range of mountains. Irregular ridges rose and fell in waves of brilliant green. They looked like rolling pastures, but in reality they were dense forests of bamboo.

An hour later they dropped again over a vast valley lying between tall rocky escarpments, dotted with the dark purple cones of old volcanoes and the gleaming blue of lakes. Here and there a cluster of farm-house roofs stood out like pimples, and they could see two feathery plumes rising from the snouts of converging trains.

The plane rose again to cross the wide, level stretches of the Ngombe plateau, lying shadowless in the evening light except for dark patches thrown by drifting clouds. At intervals they passed over tree-ringed townships whose corrugated iron roofs flashed back the sunlight in twinkling points of light.

They flew over the plateau for an hour, crossed a deep rocky chasm, and approached another rolling range of mountains. As the sun began to dip over a jagged horizon the foothills of the mountains lay below. The plane started to lose height and soon they could see the roofs of Mbale township clustering in a belt of trees. The roofs looked grey and flat now that the sun's rays were no longer reflected from them. They circled once over the town and flattened out neatly on to the runway of an aerodrome. The Hawk made a perfect landing, and came to rest gently about ten yards from the hangar.

'Good trip,' said the pilot. 'Under bogey, what? Nice following wind.' Two natives came out to help wheel the plane into the hangar. Tollemache found his car sheltering under a tarpaulin and drove his passenger through five miles of open, park-like country, dotted with clumps of cedar and podo, to his house. The rains had started north of the Ngombe plateau and the young grass was fresh and green. The sharp tang of wet earth was in the air.

They spent a comfortable evening by a large open stone fireplace and a roaring blaze of cedar logs. Tollemache's house was rambling but designed for comfort, solidly built of stone. They sat in a big cedar-panelled living-room littered with books, magazines, pipes, fishing-rods, polo sticks, and other miscellaneous objects. Wire-haired terriers wandered in and out at will. The house was untidy in a friendly rather than a sordid way. Vachell was relieved to see that there were no sporting trophies on the walls.

They had short drinks and hot baths, and dined, in dressing-gowns and pyjamas, off fresh trout caught that morning in a river running through the farm, lamb chops, fresh salad, and ice-cream with hot chocolate sauce. After dinner the manager came in for a short talk and Vachell tuned in to the radio to the B.B.C. Empire programme. He got the league football results, the latest scores of an M.C.C. Test Match in the Argentine, and a programme of old Kentish songs rendered by Portland Place yokels. Tollemache gave a howl of anguish, and Vachell switched it off. When the manager left they went through their plans thoroughly over a final drink in front of the fire. They went to bed early, for the altitude was over seven thousand feet and the cold, crisp air made them sleepy.

They were up for an early breakfast, and drove down to the airport at 8.30, with three camp-chairs and a folding-table. At nine o'clock Tollemache refuelled and took off in the Miles Hawk. 'Back about five, what?' he shouted above the engine's roar. Vachell waved back and watched the red plane soar overhead and disappear in the blue distance, flying north.

He left the chairs and table in a room partitioned off

from the hangar to form a small, unused office, and drove slowly back to Tollemache's farm. The manager showed him the milking sheds, the electrically operated dairy, the prize Carnation Holstein bull imported from Seattle, and the imported Ayrshire cows. He admired the silo and an experimental grass-drying machine, listened to a lecture on pasture improvement by paddocking and the use of fertilizers, and tried to display proper enthusiasm about a new deep-rooted and ultra-leafy strain of Australian Rhodes grass.

When that was over he borrowed a fishing-rod and wandered off to the wooded banks of a trout stream that rippled down from the mountains immediately above the farm. The water was running rather strong for trout but he had to kill time somehow. There was nothing he could do but wait and worry. He passed a restless morning and caught only two fish.

At three o'clock he drove back to the airport and stood about impatiently watching the sky. It was hell, mooching around with nothing to do. He went through his plans and his theories a hundred times, and thought of as many snags.

At 3.30 a black speck appeared on the horizon, coming from the wrong direction. It grew into a plane, circled over the field, and made a good landing. It was a blue Percival Vega Gull. A slight figure in a sky-blue flying suit and a silver helmet stepped out of the cockpit and Vachell realized, with horror, that it was Toots. There was no mistaking her. He could see a mat of blonde curls as soon as she pulled off her helmet.

He stepped back quickly into the office and closed the door, praying that she hadn't seen him. After an interval he heard her voice calling out, and then a native groundsman answered. They had a jerky conversation, which neither could understand, in two languages. 'Mr Tollemache,' she kept on saying. 'Where?' After an agonizing interval he peered round the door and watched her disappear on foot in the direction of Mbale township.

He sat down on a camp-chair and swore. So Tollemache had double-crossed him after all. The press were in on it, and that was the end. It was too late to do anything now, except think out the wording of his resignation. They might allow him to do it that way, but he doubted it.

At 5.15 Vachell's straining eyes detected a moving speck in the light-blue sky. It swelled steadily in size until he could recognize the Miles Hawk. It banked as it circled and he saw that there was a figure in the second cockpit. Tollemache had his passenger all right.

The plane landed smoothly and ran up to within a few yards of the hangar. The pilot vaulted out as the engine fluttered to a stop. A man in an overcoat and thin linen suit clambered out of the other cockpit, refusing Tollemache's hand. Vachell put on his official helmet with its red badge and walked out briskly to salute the crumpled and irate figure of Sir Bertrand Flower.

'What the devil is the meaning of this, sir!' he shouted at Tollemache. Anger gave colour and animation to his face but Vachell thought again how lined and ill he looked. 'Is this a practical joke? If so, it is the most ill-mannered and impudent jest it has ever been my—'

'Pardon me, sir,' Vachell interrupted. He stood very erect in his uniform, and spoke brusquely. 'Superintendent Vachell, of the Chania Police. Captain Tollemache was acting under the orders of my superior, Commissioner Armitage. I must ask you to be good enough to step this way. There are some questions—'

'By whose authority do you act?' Sir Bertrand Flower stormed. 'Never in all my life have I encountered such infernal insolence, such downright insubordination! I shall report you to Downing Street for this—you, and your Commissioner, and have you dismissed from the service! I demand to be conducted immediately to the nearest telephone. . . .' A fit of coughing overtook the outraged Governor. His face was ashen and his straggling grey moustache was quivering with emotion.

Vachell stood motionless, his helmet tipped slightly over one eye. His face retained a wooden and impersonal expression.

'I am here on His Excellency's instructions, sir,' he said. 'I am instructed to express the regret of the Chania Government, but to put certain questions to you to which they feel compelled to demand an answer.'

Sir Bertrand Flower's hands were shaking as he pulled off his flying helmet. 'You have no power to do this,' he said. 'The Chania Government cannot carry out raids on neighbouring territories and kidnap the King's representative! This is sedition, young man, sedition!'

'No, sir,' Vachell answered. 'Since you are now in Chania territory, I must remind you that you have no legal status other than that of a plain British subject. I must therefore ask you to reply to certain questions in connection with the death of Sir Malcolm McLeod.'

'Require me!' The Governor was beginning to bluster. 'You have no right to do that. I refuse absolutely to answer. Kindly conduct me to—'

'One moment, sir,' Vachell interrupted again. 'My instructions are to inform you that you need not answer these questions unless you wish. But at the same time I must warn you'—he thrust a long hand into an inner pocket of his coat and dragged out a stiff official envelope—'that I have here a warrant for your arrest, countersigned by H.E., for the murder of Sir Malcolm McLeod on the night of the 28th of March.'

Sir Bertrand Flower gave a half-choked gasp, tried to speak, and achieved an incoherent stutter. His face was terrible. It looked as though it was going to fall to pieces.

'My orders are only to execute this warrant,' Vachell went on, 'in the event of your refusing to make a statement. In that case I shall be compelled to place you under arrest and to convey you to Marula. Should you be prepared to make a statement, however, the Commissioner instructed me not to execute the warrant. In that case your safe return to Totseland will be guaranteed. You understand that H.E. is anxious to avoid publicity as far as possible, sir.'

Vachell afterwards ascribed Sir Bertrand Flower's collapse before this atrocious piece of bluff to the final surrender of a moral resistance which had been sapped by weeks of mental torment. His righteous indignation suddenly crumbled. He looked frayed and beaten, like the withered husk of a weather-battered corn-cob.

'Very well,' he said. 'I will make a statement, but not because you have a warrant. I am not guilty of murder.'

Vachell led the way into the bare wooden office. Sir Bertrand Flower slumped into a camp-chair and Tollemache seated himself cockily in another, smoothing his Guard's moustache. Vachell drew his chair up to the table and took a sheet of typewritten foolscap out of his pocket.

'I have a list of questions, sir, which the Commissioner—'

'No,' the Governor said, his eyes on the paper. 'I'm not going to stand an inquisition. I said I'd make a statement, and I will, and I thank God that at last it has come to this. You may make a note of what I say.'

'Suits me,' said Vachell. He pulled out his notebook.

'The first thing I have to say,' the Governor began, 'is that I did not kill Sir Malcolm McLeod. I am not a murderer. I am aware that I cannot prove my innocence, and that my motive, on the surface, may appear a strong one. That, I assume, you know already.'

'I'd like to have it in your own words, sir.'

The Governor kept his eyes on the bare plank floor and turned his flying helmet round and round in his hands. He spoke in a low voice.

'It is extremely painful for me,' he said, 'but in spite of that I am glad that at last it has come to this. The strain was becoming...but I will begin at the beginning.

'About three years ago I began to get into serious financial difficulties. My wife's extravagances and her insistence on keeping up a style of living beyond our means—but I need not go into that. I tried to obtain money to redeem her debts by speculating on the stock exchange, and for a while I succeeded, but a series of unlucky incidents drove me further into debt. I knew that, if information should reach the Colonial Office, I should probably be forced to resign. Then, with my salary gone and my career at an end, my situation would have become desperate. I had two sons at school and...I do not wish to make excuses for my conduct, but at such times I believe that worry and desperation can destroy our normal instincts of self-respect and integrity. One can think only of the present, and one is blinded—foolishly, stupidly, of course—to the inevitable consequences.

'About this time I met Sir Felix Landauer, who had just formed a new company called African Equities Ltd., of which he was chairman, to acquire the control of several African trading concerns. One of these was Blackett Brothers, which, as you know, has a virtual, and very profitable, monopoly of the trade in cheap cotton goods in Totseland. The railway freight on these goods forms a very big proportion of the cost price. It amounts, I believe, to more than the original factory price plus the ocean freight put together. It is therefore a matter of great importance to Blackett Brothers that the cost of railway freights to Totseland should be kept low.

'For some time, as you know, there have been rumours of a federation between Chania and Totseland involving an amalgamation of the two railways. Should this come about, it is highly probable that the Chania policy of high rates on imported goods, balanced by low rates on exports, would be extended to the combined system. This, of course, would lead to a sharp rise in Totseland rates and a corresponding increase in the cost price of cotton-piece goods.

'That, gentleman, was the position when I met Sir Felix Landauer last year. I will not weary you with details of our negotiations. I can only say that I myself honestly believed the Totseland system of rating to be the fairest and best, that I wished to see it preserved, and that as God is my judge I would not have entered into any undertaking with Sir Felix Landauer had I not honestly considered that I was acting in the best interests of the natives for whom we are trustees.

'However, I am not here to defend my actions. It was obviously very much to the interest of African Equities that federation between Chania and Totseland should be postponed, even abandoned altogether; or that, if it could not be prevented, the rates on imported goods charged by the amalgamated railways should be kept as low as possible. To cut a long story short, I undertook to use my influence in this direction, which I myself considered to be the right one, and in return I accepted a block of thirty thousand pounds' worth of stock in African Equities.

'As it would clearly have been impossible to have placed it in my name, the shares were transferred to my brother-in-law, Major Fripton-Scoresby, who was made a director of the company at five hundred pounds a year.'

Sir Bertrand Flower paused to control a fit of coughing. Now that he was well launched some of his self-confidence seemed to have returned. Vachell was scribbling hard in his notebook. Tollemache was staring bug-eyed at the narrator. It was one of the few times in his life that he had ever looked confounded.

'How McLeod first became aware of my association with African Equities,' the Governor continued, 'and with the fact that the company controlled the activities of Blackett Brothers, I do not know. He did find it out, however, and he taxed me with it during the interview I had with him on the night that he met his death. He had received a letter by that morning's air mail from a firm of solicitors in London, tracing the transfer of a block of shares from Sir Felix Landauer to my brother-in-law. I could not deny the facts. McLeod behaved, I think, with generosity. He said that he had no wish to ruin me, and that he would leave my future to my own conscience. I gave him my word not to oppose his proposals in regard to federation at the conference, and, on that, he gave me the letter from the lawyers—James & Durstine was the name of the firm—and said that I could do what I wished with it.

'I retired to my room and considered my situation. I must ask you to believe me, gentlemen, when I say that my position had been preying on my mind to such an extent that I could not sleep and my health was being seriously affected. I had regretted again and again the weakness that had led me to a betrayal of my principles and myself. I now decided, once and for all, to end the matter. That night I wrote to Sir Felix Landauer to say that our agreement was at an end and that I would refund the shares which I held in my brother-in-law's name. At the same time I wrote to the Secretary of State tendering my resignation.

'I had barely finished composing these letters when the shocking news of McLeod's murder reached me. I realized, of course, that my own position would be exceedingly unpleasant should the whole miserable story come out. Fortunately, McLeod had given me the lawyer's letter, which would otherwise have led to an immediate inquiry. At the same time McLeod's death removed the danger of my exposure, since he assured me—and I believed him—that he had mentioned the matter to nobody.

'There was therefore no longer any need for me to sever my connexion with African Equities, but I could stand the sense of guilt, of loss of self-respect, no longer. I decided to stand by my resolution, and I posted the letter I had written the night before to Landauer. I felt as if a burden had been removed from my shoulders, even if ruin was to be the result.'

The Governor finished his monologue and wiped a moist forehead with his handkerchief. Long, thin strips of light from the setting sun fell through cracks in the flimsy door on to the floor-boards. The Governor was breathing heavily, as though he had completed some strenuous physical labour.

Vachell leant back in his chair and stretched his legs. 'How about your resignation?' he asked. 'Did you mail that also?'

'No. I realized that to tender a resignation dated the very night of McLeod's murder, when I was staying in the same house, would almost certainly arouse comment. I tore that letter up. I had a presentiment, even then, that the murder would be the end, for me as well as for McLeod. From the moment that you, Mr Vachell, mentioned African Equities to me the next day, that presentiment strengthened, though I must confess that I never suspected that the Chania authorities would descend to such an undignified trick as they have played on me today. But my preparations are made. I am not guilty of murder, I repeat, but I am guilty of using my public position for my private ends, and my career is at an end. No doubt that merits punishment, but the disgrace...'

The Governor was interrupted by another fit of coughing. His skin looked grey and drawn, his eyes sunken and tired. His hands still gripped the flying helmet in his lap.

Vachell sat back and glanced at Tollemache. The high-pitched tone of a feminine voice reached their ears through the door. Toots was looking for some one and getting closer all the time.

'That dame,' Vachell said. 'You brought her here. For God's sake keep her out.'

Tollemache jumped to his feet. 'Me bring her here? Not in a thousand years.' He slipped quickly through the door, closing it behind him in a cascade of creaks, and Vachell heard his raised voice arguing with Toots outside. 'Full of skeletons,' he said, 'seated on chests of Spanish gold.'

Vachell kept his eyes fixed on the Governor's face. 'What's the idea of denying the murder?' he said. 'You haven't got a case. It's a sure-fire conviction.'

Sir Bertrand shrugged his shoulders. 'Had I committed the murder, I should admit it. I'm tired of deception—worn out, finished. I have no more wish to fight. But murder is something I could never bring myself to do. It never even entered my head as a way out.'

Vachell looked at him for a moment without speaking. Then he handed over a paper. 'Will you sign that, please,' he said.

Sir Bertrand took it wearily and read it slowly through. The voices outside rose several tones and moved nearer. 'I'm going to look,' Toots said shrilly. 'I adore mysteries.'

The Governor slowly pulled a fountain pen from his pocket and drew two crossed lines through the last paragraph of the typescript. 'The facts are correct,' he said, 'but the conclusion false. I did not kill McLeod.'

The door burst open and Toots thrust a blonde curly head into the room. Her eyelashes, liberally mascaraed, stood out like tree-twigs in winter against a pale sky. 'My,' she said, 'if it isn't your pet cop! So that's your secret vice, is it? And who's the boy friend?'

Vachell rose quickly to his feet. 'Good evening, Miss er, uh,' he said. 'This is a pleasure. May I present Mr Rushcliff? Mr Rushcliff and I are just coming to terms about the sale of a pedigree dog. Miss uh, if you'd wait a moment—'

'Nuts,' said Toots. 'You can't fool me that easy. I'm not a newspaper gal for nothing. I got news sense, see? Come on, let's have it. Kick through, Mr Cop.'

'Oh, come on,' said Tollemache. He pulled at her arm from behind. 'I want a drink, and the sun's half down.'

Vachell went out, propelling Toots in front of him. 'Say, you're bugs,' he said. 'There's nothing going on around here. We're just going out to Tollemache's place. Come and join us.' He linked his arm in Toots' and Tollemache, with equal affection, took the other. They walked three abreast towards the car.

'I came to see Tolly,' Toots protested. 'He asked me. He promised to introduce me to the English baronet's daughter that married the black chief and lives in the tree-tops, waited on by gorillas. My paper wants the story. Didn't you, Tolly?'

Tollemache groaned and Vachell said: 'You'll enjoy her. She's a very real person. It's too bad Tollemache has three maiden aunts visiting him just now. There's a good hotel in town, though.'

'Nuts,' said Toots. 'I don't like hotels. They're—hey, what's eating you?'

At the sound of an engine starting up Vachell and Tollemache jerked their heads round simultaneously as though they had been pulled by a string. 'Hey,' said Toots, 'there's a guy trying to swipe your plane.'

Sir Bertrand Flower swung the propeller of the Miles Hawk, and as they started to run he clambered into the cockpit. The propeller made a golden halo round the plane's nose in the last slanting sunrays. The engine's note grew deeper and the machine started to move slowly forward. It made straight towards them, accelerating quickly. It came on without swerving, and they jumped to one side and flattened themselves on the grass. The low blade of one wing swept over their heads. They felt the rush of air against their cheeks as it passed a few feet away. They scrambled up to see the red plane turn at the end of the runway and come racing back. Its wheels rose from the ground, its nose went up, its under-carriage cleared the roof of the hangar, and it roared away into the sky.

'The other plane,' Vachell shouted. They sprinted down the field to the Percival Gull, and Tollemache skidded to a stop and swung the propeller. Toots came pounding up indignantly, crying, 'You can't do that! It's my plane.'

'Can't I though?' said Tollemache, and pushed her over with his arm. She sprawled on to the grass, shrieking imprecations. Tollemache clambered into the pilot's seat and raced the engine. Vachell was already in. The plane, pursued by a shouting figure in blue with arms flying like the blades of a windmill, taxied into the wind, rose over the sheds, and roared after the dwindling speck that was the Miles Hawk.

The Governor was trying to make a getaway back to

Totseland, Vachell supposed. Once there he would become again the presence of the King, legally inviolate. He needn't have been so spectacular about it; the idea was to fly him back there tomorrow anyway, and then let matters take their course. He was keen about flying—that was what the bluff had been based on in the first place—and had taken over the controls of machines occasionally, but he couldn't have flown solo before. If the Gull could guide him down on landing there was just a chance.

Then Vachell realized that they were not headed for Totseland at all. They were making for the range of mountains that lay behind Tollemache's farm—high, craggy mountains covered with dense forest. There was no landing ground that way, anywhere.

They flew straight towards the sunset, into a red, fiery bowl. The sky was a vivid blaze of colour. The Hawk was growing bigger; they were gaining on it. The Gull soared steeply as open pastures with scattered trees beneath them gave way to a dark tangle of forest that lay like a deep shadow across the rising slopes. They were over the mountains now. The crest of the range lay ahead, black and heavy against the blood-red sky.

Vachell kept his eyes fixed on the Hawk, black as a crow against the sunset. He could see the outline of a man's head, a faint bulge midway between the wing-tips. It was getting closer all the time.

Tollemache was climbing above the Hawk to force it down and make it turn. They were approaching the crest of the range. The slopes beneath were staggered with deep and rocky gullies. The Hawk was flying very low.

Suddenly Vachell caught his breath and leaned out of the seat, craning his neck to watch the plane ahead and below. It wasn't rising at all. Jagged peaks towered above it and in front, impassively black, and scarred with bare rock. The Hawk was going directly at them, steady and straight as a flat trajectory bullet.

It made no attempt to rise. The nose of the plane went

into the rock like a torpedo into the side of a battleship. Above the zoom of the Gull's engines Vachell heard the sickening crash of the impact and, a second later, the roar of an explosion. A spurt of orange flame shot up through the trees, and then subsided. In a few seconds tongues of flame flickered up from the shadows below as the fuselage caught alight. Tollemache dipped the nose of the Gull, straightened out, and circled over the smoking and scattered remains of his machine. Of its occupant, nothing remained.

The colour was fading swiftly from the sky as the shadow of night fell quickly over the hills. The forest below looked like a cloak of black velvet with a single ruby shining at the throat. 'Forest fire,' Tollemache shouted. He opened the throttle and headed the plane for home.

15

It started to rain hard at about eight o'clock that evening, and Vachell drove Tollemache's Ford V8 all night through the rain. The roads seemed like melted chocolate. In places he churned through mud up to the axles, making a third rut with the differential. He stuck three times, and got out somehow by cutting bushes to pack in the bottom of the ruts, and jacking up the wheels on a plank which he found in the back. The car lurched and slewed and skated all over the dirty road. Rain lashed unendingly at the windshield, and spat at him through the bellowing side-curtains of the box-body.

He stopped at the first post office on the trunk line telegraph and got through to Armitage's house. Disjointedly he told his chief the news.

'Can you get through to Totseland?' Vachell shouted. 'I guess they'll be looking for Sir Bertrand and—'

'Looking for him, by God, looking for him, that's good from you! The whole R.A.F. squadron went out from here at four o'clock. Do you realize—'

'I'm on my way, sir. I'll be down just as soon as I can make it.'

'You'll be under arrest when you get here! For abduction, if not for murder. Where is he—his body, I mean?'

'Cinders,' said Vachell, and rang off.

It was raining worse than ever. He churned on up hills and slithered down them, twisting the wheel continuously to keep the nose of the car on the road. The loose end of a chain clanked against the wing. The main road was better, and when he reached the turn-off he made good time.

About twenty miles short of Marula he had to climb a steep escarpment. The road became a shelf of rock in the side of a precipice, and a drop of a thousand feet lay below him. Water was pouring down the one-in-five grade and the wheels slipped on stone. At one hairpin bend the car gave a sickening lurch and pivoted on its front wheels, its back swinging out wide over the void. The steering-wheel swung uselessly, and Vachell shut his eyes and waited for the crash. When he opened them again the car was still on the road and, even more surprising, it faced in the right direction.

A cold dawn was struggling with still persistent rain when he got to Marula, soaked to the skin and splashed with gobs of mud. He went straight home for a bath and change, and then to the Commissioner's house. Armitage was waiting for him in dressing-gown and pyjamas. His fury was fluent, bitter, and almost totally out of control.

Vachell was fired twice that morning. He was fired once by Armitage, with profanity, and once by Pallett, with pomposity. He was given until Saturday to clear up at the office and to clear out. After that his fate depended on the Secretary of State's decision. There would almost certainly be an inquiry, and Pallett made it quite clear that the Chania Government would advise prosecution on more than one serious charge.

The rain had cleared off and Marula was flooded with

bright sunlight by the time the Acting Governor had had his say. Vachell drove slowly back to his bungalow. The air was fresh and clean, the rain-wet trees washed free of dust. Birds were twittering brightly on dripping branches in his garden, serenading the warming sun.

'Get the hell out of here, you sanctimonious little bastards,' Vachell said to them. 'Don't you know any dirges?'

.　　.　　.　　.　　.

On Wednesday Vachell had to fly to Totseland for the day to make a statement to the Acting Governor. He was received with cold, silent hostility, and treated with the minimum of civility. In spite of that, the Totseland Acting Governor hated to see him go. He would have liked to have kept the Chania policeman for a long time, in jail. He hated Chania, anyway, with all its works, and this was the final insult. Vachell had a depressing day.

On Thursday morning he went down to his office in Marula to clear up his papers and hand over to Janis, who was to take temporary charge until a new superintendent was appointed. He was very upset over Vachell's dismissal, and attempted, in a tongue-tied way, to express his sympathy.

'I just took a chance and it didn't work out,' Vachell said. He did not seem particularly upset. 'Some one had to take the rap over Popple anyway. It's just one of those things.'

'It isn't fair,' Janis said. 'Not if you were right about Sir Bertrand Flower. *Did* he do it, do you think?'

Vachell massaged his ear-lobe and leant back in his chair. 'Sure, he did it,' he said. 'He admitted everything else. He wouldn't admit that because he knew we couldn't prove it. He had a wife and two boys and he didn't want them to be branded as a murderer's family, so he denied it all and beat the rap. I guess he did it to save them, partly. We'd have pinned it on him if he'd lived. We'll never be able to now.'

– 194 –

'In that case,' said Janis, 'they shouldn't sack you for finding it out. But why ever did you kidnap him like that?'

'Because I wanted proof,' Vachell answered, 'and there wasn't any other way to get it. The Chania police couldn't go into Totseland, and the Totseland police couldn't work on their own Governor because he represents the King. I'm telling you, it puts a policeman in a hell of a spot when he finds he's gotten involved with the constitution of the British Empire. They forgot to put in anything to regulate the procedure when one Governor bumps off another. It was a dead end, and all I could think of was to blast a way out. I guess the idea wasn't so hot after all. Though if it hadn't been for Toots...'

'I still don't understand how you got him to Mbale,' Janis said.

'That part worked out. I knew Tollemache and Sir Bertrand's A.D.C. were close friends—they were in the same regiment, I guess. Tollemache landed at the Totseland airport around noon and called up the A.D.C., and of course he got an invitation to G.H. for lunch. I knew Sir Bertrand was air-minded, too. He's been trying to sell the C.O. on airplanes for the Totseland Administration.

'Tollemache got to bucking about his new plane at luncheon and offered Sir Bertrand a ride. It happened that Sir Bertrand had to open a new mission school that afternoon, and Tollemache said he'd fly him there. Sir Bertrand fell for it, and as soon as Tollemache got him in the air he raced for home and there wasn't a thing Sir Bertrand could do. I bet it left the Totseland people flat.' Vachell grinned in spite of himself.

'Well, if you're satisfied Sir Bertrand killed H.E., I suppose the case is finished,' Janis said.

'It's finished as far as I'm concerned,' Vachell replied, 'and it looks like I'll be finished too—in jail.'

.   .   .   .   .

Until Saturday morning, however, Vachell was still head

of the C.I.D., and Janis insisted on submitting his usual reports. There were several robberies, an assault case, and a raid on a secret still.

'And there's one rather funny thing, sir,' Janis concluded, keeping his titbit for the end. 'You remember the filing clerk at the Secretariat, Fernandez? Well, he's disappeared.'

'Disappeared!' Vachell exclaimed. 'When?'

'Last Friday night apparently. He didn't show up at the office on Saturday morning, but they thought he was sick, and didn't worry. On Monday afternoon, when he still hadn't turned up, they sent a boy round to his house to inquire, and found he hadn't been there since he left for work on Friday morning. The Secretariat reported it on Monday night, and I heard about it first thing Tuesday.'

'Well, that is something,' Vachell said. 'Haven't his family any idea where he is?'

'No, none. His wife was away on a visit, and that's why it wasn't reported earlier. He was stopping with his wife's parents, and they thought he'd decided to spend the weekend with friends or something. But he'd said nothing to them about going off anywhere, and nothing at the office to suggest he wouldn't go to work as usual on Saturday. He's been in Government service for about fifteen years and they say he's always been a very steady, reliable chap, so it's all rather mysterious.'

'You're telling me,' Vachell remarked. He reached for a piece of gum in the desk drawer. 'Who saw him last?'

'Several people at the Goan club. Apparently he always plays billiards on Tuesdays and Fridays. He went there as usual last Friday after knocking off work at four o'clock. I spoke to a couple of his Goan pals who'd seen him there, and they said he seemed just as usual, and didn't mention anything about going away. As far as I can make out he left about six-thirty to go home—his family say he always come back by bus—and hasn't been heard of since. It's queer, isn't it, sir?'

'It's queer as hell,' Vachell agreed.

'I had two Indian constables out making inquiries all yesterday, but they don't seem to have got any forrarder. Of course he may have been robbed and assaulted, but that doesn't seem likely. I don't see how it can have any connexion with the big case, do you, sir?'

'That's the hell of it,' Vachell said. 'It doesn't make any sense. We must find him somehow. Use everything you've got.'

Vachell found himself forgetting that he wasn't in charge any longer. He frowned at the blotter and tried not to think about Fernandez. It didn't fit into the pattern. It was just plain nuts. Forget it, he thought.

When a messenger came in with a telegram from Tollemache telling him succinctly: 'Toots escaped,' he knew there'd be plenty to worry over. For he suspected strongly that Toots, more of a newshawk than a lady, had listened to most of Sir Bertrand Flower's confession with her ear glued to the door of the airport office. Tollemache had volunteered to keep her imprisoned on his farm until Flower's death had ceased to rate as front-page news. At all costs, Vachell had told him, she must be prevented from connecting with the London papers. The Totseland Government's official *communiqué* had stated that the Governor had met his death in an air smash. A rigid censorship had been clamped down to prevent the true story from reaching the public or the press. But now, it seemed, Toots had got through.

The story broke in the London papers on Friday morning. Furious cables started coming in from the C.O. shortly after lunch. For the next few days the Chania Government was in a turmoil. Pallett denied the story *in toto*. No one believed him. The *Courier* flew a reporter to Mbale in a chartered plane, only to find that Tollemache and Toots had disappeared in the Percival Gull, no one knew where. (They were heard of two days later in Khartoum, and later on in Kano.) Pallett issued an order forbidding all Government servants to interview the press or to mention the subject to any non-official. Askaris were posted round the Secretariat to turn back reporters. Only the man who held a watching brief for the Government of India got through, demanding to know what steps were being taken to safeguard the lives and property of British Indian subjects.

In Totseland the white community, making up in indignation what it lacked in size, accused the Chania settlers of inventing the whole story in order to discredit Totseland and cover up their own Government's inability to catch the real murderer. Sharp practice they expected, they said; but when Chania kidnapped their Governor and hounded him to suicide it was going too far. The death of Sir Bertrand Flower, it was implied, had been skilfully engineered by the Chania farmers as part of a plot to retain low export rates on maize and continue to charge high import rates on imported Totseland necessities such as ginger beer.

In England, the story made the front page. It was the biggest case of corruption in high quarters that had been revealed for a long while. Questions appeared in droves on the order paper of the House. The Labour party used the incident to illustrate the irrefutable fact that British imperialism was rotten to the core. They demanded that the colonies should be handed over immediately to the League of Nations. The German press seized on the case as proof positive of the corruption of effete British rule and the justice of Germany's demands for the return of her colonies. A group of young Tories formed a deputation to wait on the Prime Minister with the request that, in view of the disturbed conditions now prevailing in certain African territories, he would issue a Cabinet ultimatum to Germany that in no circumstances would the British Government consider the transfer of the Tanganyika mandate to any foreign power.

A correspondence started in *The Times* on the need to introduce restrictions on the printing in the press of irresponsible rumours deleterious to imperial security and injurious to British prestige in India, Africa, and the East. Several English weeklies called for a world conference on international freedom of access to raw materials, and one newspaper, in no uncertain terms, accused the United States of having stolen a British island in the Pacific for a seaplane base. Mr Winston Churchill accused the Government of dangerous vacillation in strengthening the defences of the African colonies. Mussolini announced that he was moving fresh troops to Ethiopia in view of disturbed conditions threatening the security of the Italian Empire. 'The prestige of the white races,' he cried, 'must be preserved! Italy, in the name of Western civilization, will never shirk her share of that great responsibility bequeathed by the Cæsars!'

Practically the only country where the story was not printed, after the first Reuters' messages appeared, was Chania. Pallett ordered the *Courier* to suppress all reference to Sir Bertrand Flower's death, on penalty of prosecution under an obscure clause of the Incitement to Racial Enmity Ordinance.

.   .   .   .   .

In the middle of the turmoil on Friday afternoon Janis came into Vachell's office with news.

'Machoka's been found,' he said excitedly. 'The D.O. Taritibu has just rung up to say they've got him—apparently he was hiding in Taritibu all the time—and he's on the way to Marula now. Mr Pallett is going to question him as soon as he arrives. And Miss Brandeis is on the way back to hospital, with fever.'

'How about the clerk?' Vachell asked.

'I've got some news there too. It's awfully queer. One of Fernandez' fellow-members of the Goan club turned up here this morning with a story. He's been away since last Saturday and only just heard about Fernandez' disappearance, and that's why he didn't come forward before. He says he left the Goan club just after Fernandez on Friday night—a week ago today—and walked along the street a little way behind him. The Goan club's in Parkside Avenue, you know, just beyond the turn-off to the aerodrome. Fernandez was making for the bus stop, towards the town.'

'By himself?' Vachell queried.

'Yes. Well, this Goan says that, about a hundred yards from the club, a car going the same way pulled up beside Fernandez, who stopped and spoke to the driver. Then Fernandez got into the car and was driven off towards the town. The other Goan assumed that some one had recognized Fernandez and offered him a lift home.'

'Did he see the driver of this car?'

'No, that's the trouble, he didn't see him at all, because it was a saloon car and it had gone right past him before it stopped. He didn't notice the licence number either.'

'Does he know if Fernandez has any friends with cars like the one that stopped?'

'He said he didn't know of any one. He thought it was a European's car, though when I asked him why, he didn't seem to know. He doesn't think he'd recognize it again, so there's nothing to go on there, I'm afraid. The only point he seemed sure of was that Fernandez must have known the driver.'

'Looks like a tough assignment,' Vachell commented. 'Maybe he just skipped out on account of some personal trouble. Good luck, anyway, and I hope you hit his trail.'

Janis suddenly looked crestfallen and upset. 'I keep on forgetting,' he said. 'Are you really going?'

'My last day,' Vachell said.

On the way to the office on Saturday morning Vachell stopped at the B.I. office and booked a passage to Lourenço Marques. He hoped the Government would let him use it. He'd decided on Johannesburg next; they said it was full of money, and he ought to be able to pick up something. It was good-bye to police work after this. What the hell, he thought, I've been a policeman long enough. He drew £50 from the bank and cleaned out his account with a cheque to Tollemache to go towards the cost of a new plane.

Armitage was gruff and uncomfortable, and jerked out a few sentences of sympathy when he went in to say good-bye. 'Very sorry, Vachell, very sorry indeed,' he grunted, 'but you asked for it, you know. Discipline must be maintained. Though personally, I...' He got up and shook hands. The shadow of Mr Pallett was in the room.

Janis was really upset. He stammered out some awkward phrases of thanks. 'Major Armitage thinks you've solved the case,' he added. 'He thinks it was Flower all right. I believe he tried to get your case reconsidered, but Mr Pallett wouldn't listen. It's a shame.'

The little office looked bare and deserted when the Indian rugs and paintings had been removed. As an afterthought Vachell took away a spare copy of the typewritten summaries he had made of his last case. It was finished, of course, but there were one or two points that still didn't seem to fit in quite squarely, and he might like to look them over some time. He filled his pockets with an assortment of personal letters, pencils, snapshots, gum, and cigarettes from the drawers of the desk, took a final look round, and walked down the steps of the wooden building for the last time, no longer superintendent of the Chania C.I.D.

.   .   .   .   .

That afternoon Vachell went down to the hospital to see Olivia Brandeis. It wasn't a bad go of fever and she was very annoyed with the D.O. Taritibu for sending her to Marula. She was getting up the next morning, she said, and going back to Wabenda in a few days. Her frizzy hair made a halo against the pillow, and her black beady eyes were like two currants set in a round of dough. There was a large bowl of roses on the bedside-table and violets on the washstand. Mark Beaton, she said, had brought them down the night before. He was going to take her out for a drive the next day.

Vachell listened attentively to the story of her adventures with the Plaindweller's League.

'There's no doubt my interpretation is the right one,' she said. 'Moon and Pallett did me the honour of coming down this morning to hear about it first hand. Apparently the meeting I saw fits in with some vague suspicions Moon has had for some time, and now they've managed to catch Machoka at last, he's confirmed my theories.'

'They made him squeal, did they?' Vachell asked.

'They brought him in last night, and he was scared out of his wits. Moon and the D.O. between them got a confession out of him. He admitted he was a member of this League, and said they used to meet in a beer-hall down at Chinyani. Some one—he didn't seem to know who—had told them that in a very short time the white men would clear out to fight a great war in Europe. Their magic would be destroyed, and they wouldn't come back, so that the Africans would take over the country. It's the same story that was at the bottom of the Congo society—it seems to be going all round Africa, in the mysterious way things do. These Plaindwellers evidently thought that dressing up in white men's uniforms would help them to acquire white man's magic. Much the same mentality as that of General Goering, if you stop to consider it.

'Machoka said he didn't want the white men to go at all, himself, nor did the others, but they had been told it was going to happen, so they thought they'd better get ready for it. The same idea as the rearmament programme, really. The society caught on and spread to the reserves and then, like all political societies before it, I gather it developed into a sort of racket on the side. The members frightened old men into parting with some of their wealth under the influence of sinister threats—much as political parties raise money for campaign funds in America, I believe.'

'How about the murder?' Vachell asked. 'Did Machoka come through with any confessions there?'

'Very much not, I gathered. He was a great disappointment to your friend Mr Pallett, I'm afraid. He denied all knowledge of it and swore that the story he told before was the absolute truth. When you questioned him and mentioned the Plaindwellers, he was so frightened he simply ran away—a perfectly straightforward reaction. Personally, I believe he's speaking the truth. From what I know of African mentality, he'd much rather confess to a murder than give away the deadly secrets of a semi-magical society, an action which no doubt carries with it all sorts of fearful curses. The uncertain sentence of a European judge isn't half as terrifying to a native as the certain and horrible vengeance of his ancestral spirits.'

'So the Plaindweller theory of the crime has flopped,' Vachell said. 'That's too bad.'

'Yours flopped too, I understand,' Olivia said maliciously.

'Flopped is right,' Vachell agreed. 'That is, the theory didn't, but I flopped hard enough to flatten the rock of Gibraltar, if I'd happened to hit it.' He told her the story briefly.

'It's bad luck,' Olivia commented. 'It must have been Flower, I suppose, although you've left one or two points unexplained. That dialling sound I heard in the study, for instance. A true scientific theory should leave no loose ends.'

'Well, maybe we'll have to call in one of your witchdoctor friends to settle it after all,' Vachell said, getting up to go. 'I've shot my bolt.'

'I've found one who says he's solved it,' Olivia replied. 'A man called Silu. He says he knows who murdered McLeod.'

'That's swell,' said Vachell heartily. 'Send him along. There's an opening for a new head of the C.I.D. right now.'

'Silu told it to me in a riddle,' Olivia persisted. 'I suppose it was just a bluff, but he was a curiously impressive old man. I can't help feeling that he *did* know something, though I've no idea how he could have.'

'Well, let's have it, then.'

'I don't know the answer. I believe there must be one, even if it's only facetious, and I've been puzzling over it all day. "What is it that swallows at noontime he who is swallowed by night? He who swells and grows little." Those were the words.'

'Nuts,' said Vachell. 'He was taking you for a ride. An old man like that couldn't know anything.'

'He knows a great deal more about vegetable poisons,' Olivia retorted, 'than most Ph.D.s probably. And he's worked for Europeans in his youth, in Marula and the western frontier and all over the place. He knows much more than you'd think.'

'He's been around, the old son of a gun,' Vachell remarked. 'Well, send him along to the police department. They can use him, I guess. Maybe if I'd spent more time fooling around with goats' entrails I'd have made out better as a detective.'

'He was a very nice old man,' Olivia said firmly. 'I believe he knows something.'

'I'll stop by tomorrow and tell you the answer to the riddle,' Vachell said. 'Be seeing you.'

16

Vachell's conversation with Olivia nourished a little demon of doubt that had been hopping about in his brain ever since Sir Bertrand Flower had crossed out the last paragraph of the confession. That night, eating a solitary dinner, he mulled over the case again and again. Everything pointed to Flower, and yet...The trouble was, Flower hadn't acted like a guilty man. There was something strangely convincing about his denials. Tough break he put himself out that way.

Just good acting, of course. But what was it Olivia had said? 'A true scientific theory should leave no loose ends.' Well, the loose ends didn't amount to much. The dialling sound Olivia had heard, the shuffling of the files on H.E.'s bureau, the file on the Mbale sewerage system, and now, maybe, Fernandez' disappearance. Could that have any connexion? It didn't seem to have, and yet, Fernandez had been involved. . . .

'The hell with it,' Vachell said aloud. He decided to go out and buy himself a drink. If things had worked out right he'd intended to write to Marvin McLeod and tell her that everything had been cleared up. That was out now, and he hadn't been able to see her off on the plane. Writing letters was a crazy idea, anyhow. What he needed was a drink.

Popple was giving a party at Dane's to celebrate his release from jail. He came over to the bar to ask Vachell to join it. Just like Popple, Vachell thought; on Monday he was going to start proceedings against the police for wrongful arrest and defamation of character.

For some reason, Vachell refused the invitation. He sat down alone at a small table and moodily considered his drink. Maybe the only guy who knows the answer is that crazy old heathen wizard Olivia's teamed up with, he thought. Maybe he rides around on a broomstick and turns his enemies into mosquitoes. What was the riddle again? 'What is it that swallows at noontime he who is swallowed by night? He who swells and grows little.' Just plain nuts. . . .

All of a sudden the answer flashed on to his brain like the opening shot of a picture on to the blank surface of a screen. His hand, holding a double-whisky, was paralysed in mid-air. Thoughts whirred through his brain like racing planes. He lowered the glass slowly. 'How in hell,' he said aloud, 'did the old spell-seller get that idea?' What could he know about it? Could he, conceivably, be right?

Vachell sat for about ten minutes without moving, going over every detail of the case in his mind. Gradually, as he did so, the pattern formed. He pieced it together bit by bit. Everything fitted, except one thing. he didn't see how that could be squared with the theory. If it couldn't, the theory wouldn't stick. If he could get around it, then old Silu was right. He'd have to wait until the morning; and then, one way or the other, he would know.

.   .   .   .   .

At eight o'clock on Sunday morning Vachell hauled Janis out of bed and took him down to police headquarters, unshaven and amazed, to look at a map. It was a large-scale map of Marula and the suburbs. He put his finger on the Goan club, and said:

'If you started out from here with a live Goan and you wanted to ditch a dead one, where would you go?'

Janis looked startled. 'I say, sir! Do you think...?' He felt a rising excitement. He thought for a moment, and said: 'You could turn off down the road to the airport and get on to the plains in ten minutes. There are no houses beyond the hangars and there are lots of bushy gullies near the road, farther on.'

'Right,' Vachell said. 'And plenty of hyenas. Get hold of a bunch of askaris and meet me down at the airport as soon as you can make it.' Janis disappeared in the direction of the police lines, and Vachell, illegally dressed in police uniform, drove down to the airport immediately at full speed.

Marula stood on a slight hill, but plains ran up to the municipality's lower boundary. Beyond the airport the open veld stretched away to a far flat horizon. Now it was flushed with the first vigorous growth of the rains, and lay green and smiling in the clear golden light of the early morning sun. Here and there it was scarred with sandy gullies in which dense thorn scrub grew. Herds of zebra, wildebeest and antelope grazed over the flats, and lions sometimes hunted up to the outskirts of the city. The road, deteriorated into a rutted sandy track, continued beyond the airport and in places it dropped into the gullies and climbed out again. At these spots thick bush came right up to the road.

Vachell made brief inquiries at the airport without much hope, for a week had gone by since Fernandez' disappearance. No one remembered any cars passing the airport on the Friday night. Fifteen minutes later Janis arrived in a police lorry with twelve askaris. Vachell gave him full instructions and the lorry rattled away down the road, the askaris swaying from side to side with the motion and evincing no curiosity as to their destination.

Vachell drove straight back to Marula and called up the telephone exchange. No, the operator said, the supervisor wasn't there. After much persuasion she revealed his address. Vachell found him having breakfast on the veranda of his bungalow with his wife, dressed for golf. He led his visitor reluctantly into the sitting-room and sat down. Vachell asked him one question.

'How did you hear of that?' the supervisor asked.

'Never mind how I heard. Can it be done?'

'Yes, it can,' the supervisor answered, 'but for heaven's sake don't spread it about.' He explained further with diagrams. 'I didn't know any one out here knew about it,' he said. 'They had some trouble in England and the engineers have been working on it; I believe they've stopped it now.' Vachell thanked him and took a deep breath. 'That puts the case in the bag,' he said.

The morning dragged on interminably. Vachell went home and mulled over his notes of the case. He had to make sure there was no mistake this time. Everything worked out. There were no loose ends. He paced up and down his sitting-room, smoking endless cigarettes. He had no lunch, but made himself a quart of black coffee.

At two o'clock Janis rang up from the airport.

'I think we've got him,' he said. 'What there is to get.'

'Swell,' Vachell said. 'Whereabouts?'

'In one of those gullies, about two miles beyond the

aerodrome. We drew each one in turn, keeping close to the road. It's hot as blazes, and I'm torn to bits. I've got a skull and a thigh-bone and some bits of vertebræ and two chewed-up ribs. They were scattered all round the place over about a square mile of bush. The hyenas have had a field day. I can't find any more, but that's quite a good bag.'

'Anything you could use for identification?'

'I found one shoe near the skull, and we've collected a few bits of torn clothing and a pocket-knife. The men are still down there hunting for more.'

'Fine. Bring the rags up here right away and leave the bones; I'll go over and get the wife.'

He fetched Mrs Fernandez in his car and took her to his bungalow. Janis arrived and spread the tattered and pathetic remains on the dining-room table. Fernandez' wife burst into tears when she saw them, and sobbed that she recognized the shoe and the pocket-knife. Vachell was doubtful, but she turned the shoe over and pointed to a new patch on the sole and relapsed into a fresh fit of weeping. Vachell drove her home again while Janis went back to continue the search. At four o'clock he rang up to say that they had found a watch with R.F. on it, and that seemed to clinch the matter.

Vachell decided to go down to the hospital to tell Olivia he had solved the riddle. The sister in charge said that she was much better today and that she had gone out about five minutes ago with a gentleman for a short drive. No, she'd no idea who it was.

Vachell got back into his car and drove slowly towards his house. It was terrible, having to wait around like this. Half-way there an idea gripped him suddenly like a cold and clammy hand. He said: 'Gee!' aloud, and jammed his foot down on the accelerator. A cold wave of fear made his flesh tingle. He should have thought of that before. He was dumber than an ostrich. But it might still be all right.

The wheels screeched on the gravel as he jolted to a

violent stop in front of his bungalow. He sprinted across the lawn and up to the steps. He dialled a number frantically on the telephone in the hall. The disk seemed to move as slowly as a bus in a traffic jam. 'Bwana not here,' said a native voice, in bad English. 'He go out in motor-car. Yes? I think—ten minutes gone.'

Vachell slapped down the receiver and sprinted back to the car, thinking as he went. He jumped into the car and let the clutch in with a bang. Gravel scattered as the wheels kicked off and the car got under way.

There were four trunk roads leading out of Marula. One ran through a closely settled district, small farms with houses near the road. Another went up into a thickly populated native area, huts within sight all the way, and a stream of native foot traffic. Rule those out. The third went down to the plains past the airport, and the fourth was the main up-country road that led to the Ngombe plateau.

He'd been seen leaving the hospital with Olivia in the car. He couldn't just dump her and come home. He'd have to think up some story. An automobile crash. . . . Vachell thought of the escarpment five nights ago. A skid on a wet road on the edge of the precipice. The drop was on the left, the driver's seat on the right. One wheel over, the car teetering on the edge, the driver jumping out on the offside, the car crashing down into the chasm with its passenger. It could be done.

The road went past the police lines, and as Vachell approached them he saw an askari in uniform wobbling out of the gate on a bicycle. He trod on the brake and skidded to a stop. 'Get in,' he ordered. 'In here. Quickly.' He pushed open the door of the car and the askari, recognizing a police officer, obeyed mechanically in a daze of surprise. The native gazed back at his abandoned bicycle with dismay as the car shot forward and raced along the shady street.

The road forked and they swung to the right, dodging among the Sunday evening traffic. Angry drivers honked

and leant out to shout at them as they cut in. The askari
cowered into his seat with round, frightened eyes. The car
skidded violently round a bend, bounced against the bank,
shot sideways across the road with a dented wing, and
straightened out in a series of sickening swerves. A cyclist
dived into the ditch just in time, and a group of native
women carrying loads of firewood scattered in front like a
covey of startled partridges. It was twenty miles to the top
of the escarpment, and the others had about fifteen
minutes' start.

Ten miles out it started to rain. The storm blotted out
the road like a blanket and Vachell had to slow down. The
sky was black and menacing in front and soon the road
became a shining ribbon and mud splashed up over the
doors. They started to climb steadily and the car lurched
heavily round corners, its back wheels swinging out at each
bend, so that they took the curves sideways on. The askari
jittered in the passenger's seat.

They reached the summit and saw the vast valley, dark
under thunderclouds, stretching away in the distance
below. Three separate storms were sweeping across it, but
on top the rain had lightened to a steady drizzle and a shaft
of diffused sunlight struggled through lowering clouds.

The road started to drop into the valley, two thousand
feet below. The first grade was easy, but soon it steepened
and the road twisted and turned like the trail of a hunted
hare. It narrowed also, and steep crags of rock began to
tower above it on the right. Vachell dropped into second
and roared down, crashing over bumps, hugging the right-
hand side of the road.

Vachell was getting worried. No sign of the other car,
and they were dropping rapidly. It might be too late. Or
they had taken another road. 'Look below for a fallen car,'
he yelled to the askari. 'Look well.'

They came to the start of the precipice. A wall of rock
rose above them on the right and the road seemed to hang
out into space. On the left was a drop, steep but not sheer,

of about four hundred feet into a gully, and then a deeper chasm beyond. Scrubby bushes, grass, and loose stones straggled up the uneven face of the cliff. Fear was rising in Vachell's heart. The fourth murder...and through his negligence. His blunders were like Abraham's offspring, without number.

They swung round a sharp bend. Beyond it the road ran straight for about a hundred yards. At the far end was a bay scooped out of the cliff to provide a level space for cars to park. Poised on the edge was a stationary saloon car. A man was standing beside the driver's seat, his hand resting on the door.

Vachell felt his taut muscles loosen in a wave of relief. He recognized the man. It was the right road, and he had arrived in time.

He drew up behind the stationary car and slid out, his arms aching from their grip on the bucking wheel. The askari was still cowering down in his seat, gripping his knees.

'Good evening,' said the man standing by the car. 'Is there anything wrong?'

'An urgent message for Miss Brandeis,' Vachell answered. 'I've been sent to fetch her back.' He walked forward towards the car.

'I am just about to take Miss Brandeis back,' her escort said. 'I was not aware that you had been appointed her nurse.' Olivia leaned over the wheel and said, 'Hello, who on earth wants me?'

'It's a cable from England,' Vachell said. He dug his hand into his tunic pocket and felt for a piece of paper. He looked steadily at the man's face and their eyes met. For a moment neither of them moved. Vachell knew that his bluff had failed at the same instant as the man's hand darted to his coat pocket. Vachell threw himself forward, struggling to free his right arm. There was a blinding flash in his eyes and roar in his ears. He felt a punch in his chest like the impact of a charging buffalo, and then a red stab of pain.

The shot caught him off his balance and knocked him sideways. He spun for a split second on the tip of the road, darkness roaring in his head. Then he toppled slowly over into space. As he fell a crash like thunder filled his ears and he was dimly conscious of the black shape of the car in front heeling over the edge. A vision of spinning up-turned wheels imprinted itself on his brain and was blotted out by red lightning and then enveloped in blackness.

Vachell dropped twenty feet on to the crown of a small flat-topped acacia that grew on a slight ledge jutting out of the rock-face. He crashed through it and hung there limply, upside down, his head on the rock below and his legs caught in a jungle of branches. He felt something wet and sticky creeping over his face. It was as if he had been crushed flat by a steam-roller, but he wasn't unconscious.

He jerked his legs convulsively and was dimly surprised to find that they responded. It sent waves of pain through his body, but he went on kicking until he shook himself down on to the rock and lay there, gasping for breath.

A stone rattled past and he tipped his head back until he could see the line where rock and sky met above. A black bulge appeared on the edge and then subsided. He realized that it was a man lowering himself over the rim and starting to scramble towards him. A sharp twitch of fear revived his senses like a cold shower. The askari! His one hope. He raised himself on one elbow to shout for help.

The man crouching just above on the side of the precipice saw him move and raised one arm, clinging with the other to the root of a bush. There was a gun in his hand. Vachell rolled over, gripping a branch with one hand, and shouted with all his strength. The man straightened his arm and shifted his aim. The end of the barrel glared down at Vachell like a round, ferocious eye.

Vachell looked up in a last despairing hope. He saw a black figure against the sky. The askari was standing on the edge of the cliff with a rock in his hand.

'Throw!' Vachell yelled. At the same instant the askari

hurled the rock on to the figure ten feet below him. It struck on the side of the head and the man swayed, slipped, and grabbed on to a tree-root with both hands to save himself. The gun clattered down the cliff, bouncing on the rocks, and came to rest against a bush twenty feet farther down.

Vachell called on every ounce of his strength for a last effort. He launched himself over the ledge and slid down the wet rock, clutching at bushes and roots with hands and feet. His left arm wouldn't work. His body was burning with pain. He landed against another tree as a rock crashed by him and thudded into the gully below. The man was clambering down too in a wild rush for the gun, and the askari was pelting him with heavy stones.

The gun lay precariously a few yards from Vachell's right foot. He spreadeagled himself against the cliff and slid towards it like a snake, using his teeth to grip the straggling bush. With a final effort he leant over and grasped its butt in his hand.

The gun's owner stood poised on the ledge just above him, his back to the slope, clinging on with both hands. His face was wild and distorted, like a cornered animal. Vachell dug his toes into the loose soil and bush roots, braced his body against the slope and lifted his right arm, pointing the gun at the other's chest. His head was swimming and his voice was hoarse.

'Victor Moon,' he said, 'I arrest you for—'

Moon's muscles tautened and his knees bent slightly for a spring. Vachell squeezed the gun and heard the thud of the echo roaring back at him from the rocks above. Moon swayed for an instant on the ledge. His body gave a convulsive twist and crumpled at the knees, then he toppled forward and pitched into space. There was a crash of branches, and below that a heavy thud: then silence.

Vachell's head swam dizzily and he knew he was going to faint. He dropped the gun and wedged his right wrist between a root and a stone. Falling debris rattled past him into the chasm below. There were crashes from the rocks above. He felt himself sliding down as though heavy weights were tied to his body: slowly at first, then faster, the earth crumbling beneath his feet. Something hard pressed against his two shoulders, and then blackness swallowed him up.

17

The next thing Vachell became aware of was a white dome over his eyes and a tight, constricted feeling over his body. He tried to move, but couldn't. He decided he must be stretched out stiff in a coffin. That was why he couldn't move. Corpses never could.

He discovered that he could move his head, and found himself gazing at a bowl of red roses on a table. Beyond that was more white. It moved, and a woman's voice said: 'Don't talk now. Lie quiet, and you'll feel better in a moment.' Things started to come back, and he asked: 'Was she killed too?' His voice sounded very strange and distant.

'No,' the nurse said. 'She's going to be all right. You mustn't talk. Be a good boy now, and go to sleep.'

When Vachell woke again his head was clearer, but his body was still immobile. He learnt later that he had broken an arm and three ribs. The bullet had gone through the side of his chest, missing a lung by a hair and doing no permanent damage. He had lost a lot of blood.

He kept on asking about Olivia, and as soon as he was stronger they told him the part of the story he didn't know. When Moon fired at Vachell, it seemed, he had leant his weight against his car and pushed it forward over the edge of the precipice. It was a low-built saloon, and the strength of the body saved Olivia's life. The spinning car crashed into the gully below, but the force of its fall was broken by small trees. Olivia was found under the wreckage with a fractured skull, crushed ribs, and both legs broken, but still, by some miracle, alive.

The askari's presence of mind saved two lives. He crouched down in Vachell's car when the shot was fired, and so escaped notice. Moon scrambled over and down the cliff in order to finish Vachell off at close quarters. The askari seized a stone from the side of the road and hurled it on to Moon's head below. Then he came down in pursuit and reached Vachell just in time to save him, as he fainted, from slithering off to certain death below.

The askari wedged his officer's limp form behind a stunted acacia and climbed up to fetch help. He stopped the first car that passed, carrying a settler and his wife home from Marula. Between them they hauled Vachell up and the woman drove him at once to Marula hospital.

The settler and the askari went down the cliff again in search of Olivia. It took half an hour to clear the wreckage enough to reach her, and then they thought she was dead; but they carried her by stages up the gully and on to the road and got her to hospital. For three days life fought uncertainly to retain its hold, and then her strength began to return. She was out of danger in a week. After that her recovery amazed the doctors by its speed.

As soon as Vachell was allowed visitors, Armitage came down to see him, bringing the Acting Governor along. Janis, who had already visited his ex-chief and rounded off the investigation by clearing up two final points, came too.

'In view of the special circumstances,' Pallett said, cleaning his glasses in an unaccustomed embarrassment, 'your—er—resignation from the Chania police has not yet taken effect. I am anxious to hear your explanation of the most—ah—unfortunate incident that occurred last Sunday. It is just possible that I may feel able to—ah—reconsider the whole question of your status in the light of that information.' Vachell realized that the Acting Governor was trying to be gracious.

The four men sat in wicker chairs on a cool, cement-floored balcony outside Vachell's private room on the first floor. The bright grass lay flooded with sunlight beneath them and a breeze stirred the trees that sheltered the hospital from the road. Vachell's arm was in splints and his ribs were tightly bound in plaster, but his bones had almost ceased to ache and he was allowed to walk a few paces. He had one black and orange eye, and strips of plaster across his cheeks gave his face a sinister look. Tea and cigarettes stood on a table between them. Vachell was eating jam puffs, for which he had a weakness he was rarely able to indulge. He had given a special order to a Marula baker for a daily delivery while he remained in hospital.

'Thanks, sir,' he said to Pallett. 'There isn't a lot to explain. I got the case all balled up at the start and didn't even straighten it out at the end. An old African witch-doctor, way out in the sticks, had to do that for me. And I used to think I'd make a detective!'

He shook his head sadly and offered his visitors more tea. Then he finished off the last jam puff, lit a cigarette, and began to talk.

'That trick with the telephone fooled me,' he said. 'From the start it was obvious that one of the objects of the crime was to get possession of something Sir Malcolm had on his bureau. The killer replaced whatever it was he took with a file from the stack at Sir Malcolm's side. It just happened to be the one file that wasn't in use at the time, so instead of covering up the fact that something had been swiped it made the set-up look just a little bit off centre.

'I was fooled, though, just the same. As soon as I heard of the letter Sir Malcolm described as "stinking fish"—the one that turned out to come from James and Durstine in London and to tell what was in back of Sir Bertrand Flower's opposition to the Chania-Totseland federation proposals—I leapt to the conclusion that it was the missing document. Right there was where I jumped the track. I picked Flower for the murderer and went after him as hard as I knew. His motive was a honey and if he didn't kill Sir Malcolm he should have—it isn't fair on a dick to get motive, opportunity, and a lot of circumstantial evidence all sewn up together like that and then to find the case won't stick.

'I spent so much time chasing after that letter I never thought to make one investigation that would have led right up to the guy we wanted as straight as the road to Rome. I had the whole case in the bag two days after the murder and never knew it. I'm a hell of a detective.'

Vachell groaned and swallowed a cup of lukewarm tea. Pallett was leaning back in his chair with an expressionless face, the tips of his fingers pressed together. Armitage was smoking a cigar, and Janis watched a blue and gold humming-bird that had perched on the balcony rail eyeing the tea-table with mixed feelings of yearning and fear.

'Janis here spotted the hole in Moon's plan, and it was a hole you could drive a truck through once you knew about it,' Vachell went on. 'I had Fernandez, the filing clerk at the Secretariat, make a list of all the files that were supposed to be up at G.H. at the time of the murder, and Janis traced each one of them. I wanted to make sure they could all be accounted for. They could, and everything seemed okay. Now one of those files was all about a plan to install a new sewerage system in a little hick town called Mbale, and it hadn't been out of the stacks in a year. All the other files dealt with hot subjects like the Chania-Totseland federation. You wouldn't expect an old file about sewers to get all the way up to the big shots at G.H., any more than you'd expect to hear of a bubble dancer being asked to join the Junior League. It was wrong; and that's where I should have got my start. But I was busy chasing moonbeams, and I let it alone.

'When I did get around to asking how a file on sewers got up to H.E. at Government House, I got the solution. The reference number on that Mbale file is B/329. Take a crimp out of the B and what do you get?'

He stretched out his hand for a file that Janis had brought with him at Vachell's request, and held it up.

'P/329. And that's the number of Moon's personal file.'

'Then the sewerage file never went to G.H. at all!' Janis exclaimed.

'No. I'll come to that in a moment. There was one other thing that bothered me all along. I believed from the start that the killer got in by the window and out through Jeudwine's room. Well, it seemed like a pretty good break for him to pick on the only five minutes that Jeudwine was out of the room to make his getaway. The phone call from Moon that cleared Jeudwine out of the path came through while the murderer was actually next door working on the job. It seemed remarkably opportune, and I did wonder whether there was any way Moon himself could be mixed up in it; but the exchange record showed a call from Moon's house at ten-forty-four and no call from the Governor's study, so I reckoned that let Moon out.

'Then Miss Brandeis came through with a piece of information that bothered me a lot. She'd been standing right outside the Governor's study at the time of the murder and she heard some one dialling a number inside. She fixed the time exactly at ten-forty-four.

'The exchange had no record of that call. I couldn't figure it out at all. I didn't get the answer to that one until I interrupted the supervisor's breakfast last Sunday. If I hadn't had Flower on my mind so much I should have got around to that before.

'It's a trick. Seems they had trouble in England at one time with it, through people gypping the Post Office by using it in the public call boxes, and now the engineers have figured out a way to stop it. But they haven't got the latest system installed in Marula yet, so it works all right here.

'You work it this way. You know how when you dial "O", that puts you through to the operator at the switchboard in the exchange. Now if you twist the dial right around as far as it will go, and dial your number backwards without letting the disk slide back into the resting position, you'll get your number direct on the operator's line without bringing into action the mechanism that records your call.'

'What do you mean, backwards?' Armitage interrupted.

'You start by dialling "O",' Vachell said, 'but instead of letting the disk slide back, you keep your finger on it and you keep it twisted right around as far as it will go. Then, if the first number you want is five, you move the disk five points back and then return it to the position you started from. You don't let it slide back to the resting position at all. You simply dial from the other side of the disk. It's as easy as pie when you know the trick, and it gives you your number without leaving any trace at the exchange, so you get your call free. I don't understand the mechanism of the thing myself, but that's the way it works. That's how Moon made two calls from the Governor's study without leaving any record at the exchange.'

He paused for breath, and lit another cigarette. His audience looked thoroughly bewildered. Janis was waggling one finger in the air to keep pace with mental dialling.

'Very—ah—interesting,' Pallett commented. 'You must on no account mention this to any one else, Vachell. It would never do if the public were to practise frauds on the Post Office by means of this—ah—device.'

'I'm still in the dark as to what actually took place, Vachell,' the Commissioner said. 'Why should Moon want to murder Sir Malcolm? They always seemed on very good terms.'

'So they were, I guess,' Vachell answered. 'They had a lot in common, I'd say. Until Sir Malcolm found out that Moon had murdered his brother.'

'His brother!' Armitage exclaimed. 'What do you mean? Explain, Vachell; explain.'

'Here's the set-up,' Vachell said, 'as I see it. Twenty years ago Moon was a cadet on the western frontier, and Alistair McLeod, Sir Malcolm's elder brother, was his superior officer. Moon was an ambitious youngster, but for some reason—I guess we'll never know—he blotted his copybook and got in bad with his boss. At the end of every cadet's first period of service the D.O. has to submit a report to headquarters; and if it's a bad one the cadet is liable to get fired from the service and shipped home as a failure.

'Well, suppose young Moon suspects that his boss is going to send back a report that will kill his career stone-dead. And suppose his D.O., McLeod, falls sick about that time with malaria. They're out on safari and he has to be nursed by Moon. They're literally hundreds of miles from the nearest Government post, remember, and there's no one around to ask questions. It's probably a thousand to one against being found out.

'Let's say the temptation is too strong for Moon. He slips a shot of native poison into McLeod's soup one night and watches his boss pass out from a combined attack of fever and alkaloids. Then he buries McLeod and reports another death from blackwater. He turns in the report on himself rewritten in highly complimentary terms, and gets off to a good start in his career on the strength of it. Let's check that from the file.'

He turned to the bottom of a sheaf of papers on Moon's personal file, to the earliest report in the series. It occupied one page and a quarter of foolscap. He studied it carefully and handed it over to Armitage.

'Take a look at that,' he said. 'Look at those two sheets. Do you notice they're typed on different quality paper? I'd lay a thousand to one an expert would find they were typed by different operators.'

Armitage examined the typescript and grunted agreement. The report was a glowing one. The last paragraph, which ran over on to the second page, read:—

"In addition to these qualities, indispensable to a good District Officer, of presence of mind, good humour, sound judgment and resource, Moon has displayed a more than usual intellectual capacity. He is

keen and quick-witted, and thorough in his atten-
dance to detail. He undoubtedly has a good brain and
has shown unusual facilities in the acquisition of native
languages. Were brains the only consideration, I
should not hesitate to recommend him for confirma-
tion in the service.

> *I have the honour to be,*
> *Sir,*
> *Your most obedient servant,*
> *A. McLeod,*
> *D.O. Sabuni"*

'That second page carries McLeod's signature,' Vachell
pointed out. 'I'd say it was genuine. Take a look at the first
page. It reads like Dr Goebbels' opinion of Adolf Hitler.
But let's suppose that the first couple of paragraphs of the
original report poured it over Moon like Dr Goebbels on
Joseph Stalin, and that the last paragraph of the first page
read something like this:—

> *"I have, therefore, the honour to report that for the*
> *reasons stated above I do not consider that Mr Moon is*
> *qualified to hold the responsible position of District*
> *Officer. I should not, however, like to be unjust, and*
> *there is no doubt that Mr Moon possesses certain good*
> *qualities which should be placed to his credit. He is*
> *quick-witted, and thorough in his attendance to detail.*
> *He undoubtedly has a good brain and has shown*
> *unusual facilities in the acquisition of native languages.*
> *Were brains the only consideration, I should not*
> *hesitate to recommend him for confirmation in the*
> *service."*

'Most likely that was the way it read originally; that, or
something like it. The file shows how Moon changed it
around. He got away with it all right.

'But there was one thing Moon overlooked. Alistair

McLeod kept a diary, and after he died Moon went through it and it seemed okay, so he turned it in with the rest of McLeod's personal effects, and in due course it was shipped home to his mother in England. Maybe she read it and maybe she didn't, but anyway nothing happened until she died twenty years later. Then her junk was inherited by her only surviving son, who by that time was Governor of the colony his brother died in; and Moon had got to be the Secretary for Native Affairs.

'This next bit is just guess-work, and we'll never be able to check it now, but this is how I think it worked out. Sir Malcolm went through his brother's effects and got interested in his old diary, and tucked away in a flap in the back of the cover he found a scrawled deathbed message from his brother. Alistair McLeod had realized from his symptoms that he'd been poisoned, and before he went out he scrawled the name of his murderer and a last appeal to be avenged. For twenty years that appeal lay undelivered; and then Sir Malcolm ran across it and realized that his Secretary for Native Affairs had killed his brother.

'That must have been pretty tough to take. Sir Malcolm checked up as far as he could from Moon's personal file, and he probably spotted that Alistair's report was phony. His next actions are pure surmise, but I imagine he decided that he couldn't let the thing ride and allow an unconvicted murderer to hold down a senior job in the colonial service. So he resolved to spill the story of his find to Moon, and to give him a chance to explain away the note.

'He did this, I believe on the evening he was bumped, when Moon went along to the study at nine-forty-five p.m. I believe Sir Malcolm had only run across the note in the previous day or two; he was the sort of guy who wouldn't lose any time when he had an unpleasant job to clean up. He laid it all on the line: showed Moon the note and the file report and told him that there'd have to be a C.O. inquiry.

'Moon was in a tough spot. An inquiry would bust his chances of promotion skyhigh anyway, and at the worst it would land him in the dock. He felt desperate as hell, and he made up his mind to take a desperate way out.

'Around ten-thirty he sneaked along the front of the house to peek through Sir Malcolm's window, to see how the situation stood. The window was open and the blind up, so he could see the room was empty except for Sir Malcolm, who sat at the bureau with his teeth well into his work. Moon had no gun, but he noticed the cord swinging from the blind, and an idea hit him. He reached up and cut the cord and tied it in a slipknot so it made a noose. Then he put his leg over the sill—it's only waist-high—and climbed very quietly into the study. Sir Malcolm was concentrating so hard he didn't hear a thing. Moon slipped the noose over his head, jerked it tight, and held on till the job was done. Sir Malcolm never had a chance.

'The next thing Moon did was probably to close the window and pull down the blind, and wipe his fingerprints off the catch. He was only just in time, for Miss Brandeis must have come along about half a minute later, and she and Popple had quite a conversation out there while Moon was looking around for two things—his file and the diary. He found the file all right—I think Sir Malcolm was studying it when he was bumped, and Moon replaced it with another one so as not to arouse suspicion—but he couldn't find the diary.

'That knocked him for a loop, but he hadn't time to hang around and worry. He had to get clear. When Popple moved his car away that left the window so exposed he didn't dare to get out that way; there were people moving around outside all evening. He knew there was an askari on guard in the passage and Jeudwine was blocking the only other line of retreat, so things were in pretty bad shape.

'He decided the only chance was to get Jeudwine out of the way, and this was where he did some fast thinking. He remembered that trick with the telephone. It would enable him to call Jeudwine from the Governor's study without the call being traced back; but he knew that if the police were smart we'd check on the calls, and if there wasn't anything chalked up against his own telephone account we'd be able to bust his story wide open. On the other hand, if the exchange record proved he'd been talking on his own line about the time the murder was committed, he'd have a swell alibi. It was pretty smart, and it fooled me.

'He grabbed the Governor's telephone and called his own home first, dialling backwards. His Somali boy answered. I'll ask Janis to tell the next part of the story, because he talked to the Somali boy a couple of days ago.'

Janis turned slightly pink with pleasure at finding himself drawn into the saga, and cleared his throat nervously.

'Of course Mr Vachell told me what to ask,' he said. 'The Somali said that his master had told him, over the telephone, to ring up the hospital at once and inquire how Mrs Jenkins was. I asked him if he didn't think it was rather an odd message, but he shrugged his shoulders and said it was not for him to question his master's orders, he just obeyed them. He's been with Moon for years. He rang up the hospital, and they said they didn't know anything about a Mrs Jenkins, so he gave Moon the message on his return shortly afterwards. Moon said he'd made a mistake about the hospital, and gave the boy strict orders not to say anything about having made the call. The boy didn't, either, when I questioned him a day or two later.'

Vachell took up the tale again. 'Moon was smart, because he knew the hospital would answer a call that late, and it wouldn't bother them at all. So that was the way he got a call registered on his own line. Then he called Jeudwine in the next room, dialling backwards again, and asked him to send along the files he'd left in the men's wash-room. It so happened he'd brought them along that night, and, of course, they were still there. That cleared the path through Jeudwine's office.

'But he still hadn't got the diary. He risked discovery to

make a final search, and he nearly lost out, because he was still in the study when Watson knocked on the door. It was a tough break, but he had the nerve of the devil. I'd have hated to get into a poker game with that guy. He swivelled the reading-lamp around and crouched down behind the bureau. When Watson looked in he saw a corpse with a telephone in its hand—only he didn't know it was a corpse. The play fooled him, and he stayed out.

'Even Moon had enough by then, and, diary or no diary, he decided to beat it. He grabbed his personal file and sneaked out through Jeudwine's room and across the hall while Abdi was handing the Chief Justice his hat. Then, I guess, he picked up his car and drove like the devil to his home, and just made it before the G.H. driver got down there with the files.

'He must have been scared as hell about that diary. If the police found Alistair McLeod's note he knew it was daisies for him. The next thing was that Beaton called him up and fetched him back to G.H. He waited around until I was ready to grill him, and the first thing he saw when he came into the study was the diary. We found it in the private safe, remember, and I put it down on the bureau because Mr Pallett objected to my taking charge of it. It says a lot for Moon's nerve that he never made a sign. He had to sit within a foot of it while I fired questions at him, and like it.

'But he wasn't finished yet. He did some more fast thinking and reckoned that, once we started to check on every one, his connexion with Alistair McLeod would be liable to come out. Anyway we'd get it from the diary. So he spilled the yarn about serving under McLeod twenty years before, and he told how he'd collected some of the native daggers and swords and what-have-you that were lying around in the room. Then he used an old play, and I fell. He drew my attention to one of the daggers. I walked over to look at it and turned my back on Moon.

'Of course, I'm guessing now, but this is the only story I can build that fits the facts. There's a little pocket in the back of the diary, and I guess Sir Malcolm had tucked this note in there, where we found it. While I was examining the dagger Moon pulled the note out of the diary flap, and when I looked around again he was knocking his pipe out in the ash-tray. He must have walked out of that room feeling like a million dollars. It was his one real break. He certainly used it to make a monkey out of me.

'He only had one thing left to do. He had to get his personal file back into the stacks without being spotted. That was easy, because next morning he found himself Acting Colonial Secretary, and Mr Pallett handed over the keys of the secret file room. That's right, sir?'

Pallett nodded. 'That is correct, yes. As I recollect, Moon asked me for them, but as he was stepping into my place this was a perfectly natural request and it did not—ah—excite any suspicions in my mind.'

'He probably waited until Fernandez had gone out, and then slipped the file back into its place. There was one more difficulty, though. Fernandez had entered the reference number of the file on his list when it left the registry. There was just a chance tht the police might start to check on the files to see that there was nothing missing, and if he discovered Moon's personal file had gone up to G.H. the day before the murder we might ask why, and that would be a tough one to answer.

'So he had another smart idea. He turned up Fernandez' list and put an extra crimp in the P, so the entry became B/329. That eliminated all trace of the trip his personal file had made to G.H. He ticked off the entry to show it had come back to the registry, and then, I imagine, he went out and bought himself a drink. He deserved one. He'd covered his tracks just about as deep as a two-weeks' snowstorm covers a trail in Northern Quebec.

'After that all he had to do was to sit back and laugh while we hunted butterflies. It seemed he had everything soldered up so tight there just wasn't any place a leak could get started.

'Well, that was how things stood up a week last Friday. Then Moon got a bad jolt. Janis here decided to do a little research into the problem of why the file on sewers, B/329, went up to G.H. He went down to ask Fernandez about it, but Fernandez was out, so he crashed a conference between Mr Pallett, Moon, and the A.G. to ask if any one knew what it was all about.

'Now Fernandez was the one loose tile in the roof of Moon's water-tight shelter. Fernandez knew that Moon's file had gone up to G.H. the day before the murder—in fact, he'd got it out of the stacks and sent it up himself. It was just a matter of routine, so there wasn't a chance he'd think enough of it to bring the matter up on his own hook; but once the police started to make inquiries about the file on sewers, he'd turn up his records and find that some one had tampered with his list, and things would start to get serious.

'There were only two alternatives for Moon; to take the rap, or to put Fernandez out. Moon knew about Fernandez' habit of playing billiards twice a week at the Goan club, and that happened to be a Friday. So Moon waited around in his car until Fernandez came out of the club, and then he drove by and offered the Goan a ride home. But Fernandez never got home. Moon took the airport road and when they got far enough out he shot Fernandez and dumped him in the bush for the hyenas. He knew that by the time a serious search got under way they would have distributed the bits around so thoroughly that identification would be difficult, and in any case the police would never be able to find out what killed the Goan.

'So Moon stopped the leak, and after that he was sitting pretty again. And he'd have got clean away with it, too, if Miss Brandeis hadn't happened to team up with an old witchdoctor down in the Wabenda country. This old guy had been sitting around taking snuff and throwing bones and eating goats' insides, knowing perfectly well all the time who knocked off Sir Malcolm, while the police chased themselves in circles like six-day bicycle racers in Madison Square Garden.

'Miss Brandeis got fever and came back to town with a red-hot story about the Plaindweller's League and their fancy-dress party. Moon went down to hospital to hear the story, full of good cheer. The more red herrings the police chased after, the better he felt. But this time he got a jolt that meant something. Miss Brandeis told him all about her old friend Silu and how he'd solved the mystery, and she wound up with a recitation of the riddle. Moon must have felt the stars had turned back in their courses just to crack down on him. He read the riddle, of course, and realized it was just a question of time before Miss Brandeis saw it too, or told it to someone who did. Then the police would put old Silu on the stand and the past would give up its dead.

'It was that fool riddle that put me on the trail. I got to puzzling over it, for something to think about, I guess, and then suddenly I saw it. "What is it that swallows at noontime he who is swallowed by night? He who swells and grows little." You know how some natives say the sun is swallowed by night and that makes the darkness, so "he who is swallowed by night" obviously meant the sun. And the only thing that puts out the sun in the daytime is an eclipse. And the thing that causes an eclipse is the moon. Silu worked for Europeans in his youth and probably picked up a lot of general information, including the truth about eclipses. The sun isn't a bad, if flattering, simile for a Governor, the big shot; and eclipse is good enough for murder. And, of course, "he that swells and grows little" is the moon, that waxes and wanes. Silu sounds like a cagey old guy who knows a lot, more than he'll admit, and if he once worked for Moon it's quite likely that some one told him what the name meant in English.

'I didn't know then whether Silu had worked it out with oracles and omens and things, or whether he had some inside dope we hadn't picked up. But I assumed he had some reason for his riddle and I went to work on the case from that angle. It fitted, all except that telephone call, and then, when I got the explanation for that, I had it in the bag.

'Even then I missed the obvious. It didn't occur to me that Miss Brandeis might have told Moon the riddle, and I never thought to ask her. It was only after I got down to the hospital Sunday afternoon, and heard she'd gone out for a ride, that the idea she might be in danger hit me. From the moment she told him, of course, her life wasn't worth a cent. From Moon's point of view she was loose with a stick of dynamite. It had to be him or her.

'Well, you know the rest. There's only one more point to clean up, and that's how old Silu got mixed up in the thing. Janis here contacted the D.O. Taritibu and he went out to see if he could make the old man talk. He did; and it seems that Silu was with Alistair McLeod's outfit up on the western frontier in 1916, when Moon was a cadet. Silu was a witchdoctor even in those days, though just a young one. He knew a lot about poison, and most likely he's the guy who sold Moon whatever it was he used to kill McLeod, although Silu naturally won't admit it. Anyway, he knew that Alistair McLeod had died of poison. When Alistair's brother came out to the country he just naturally assumed that the living brother would avenge the dead. It's an old native custom, and he didn't think that Sir Malcolm would be such a rat as to pass up his family responsibilities. When it went the other way he thought that Moon had got his blow in first, which is exactly what did happen. Which goes to prove that it you want to be a good detective all you have to do is to stop a hundred miles away from the scene of action, take a lot of snuff, and use psychology.'

Vachell came thankfully to the end of his long recital, and leant back in his chair, exhausted. He looked white and tired, and his limbs felt heavy as wet meal. Armitage cleared his throat and jerked out a little speech of congratulation. Pallett rose to his feet and picked up his hat. It was getting late and he had a bridge appointment.

'We must not tire you further,' he said. 'Thank you, Vachell, for your very—ah—illuminating statement. Allow me to congratulate you on the final—ah—elucidation of this very distressing, indeed shocking, series of events, although I must confess that your methods have been—ah—unorthodox and in some respects highly injudicious. However, in the circumstances, I think that it may be possible to reconsider the matter of your—ah—resignation, although, of course, the final decision must rest with the Secretary of State. Should I feel able, on mature consideration, to take a lenient view of your undoubted indiscretion, it is possible that he may be willing to regard the most displeasing incident in connexion with Sir Bertrand Flower as—ah—a very regrettable but, nevertheless, pardonable instance of excess of zeal.'

The Acting Governor shook hands and departed. Vachell reflected that he was the only man he knew whose exit could properly be described in the words, 'He withdrew'.

'Extraordinary show,' he heard the Commissioner remark as he followed Pallett through the door. 'Can't understand it. Moon seemed a decent feller. Must have been out of his mind. Matter of fact, I always had my doubts about whether he was really a pukka sahib. . . .'

Janis lingered long enough to shake Vachell warmly by the hand and say: 'Congratulations, sir. Jolly good show. Let me know if I can do anything, won't you?'

'Thanks a lot,' Vachell said. 'All I can think of right now is to shoot up a female newshawk for me, but I guess she'd beat you to it on the draw.'

Janis grinned and said it was only her way of saying she loved him. Vachell, he knew, was referring to Toots, who had cashed in on the final chapter of the Strangled Governor case by splashing her personal impressions of Vachell on a centre page under the head: 'Canadian Wonder—Chania's Death-Dealing Dick'.

Janis departed, and Vachell was left in peace on the balcony to watch the evening shadows creep over the lawn.

It was nearly time for bed. Two nurses came towards him along the balcony, wheeling a prostrate figure on a rolling stretcher. Only a round white face, with two black beads for eyes, was visible in the centre of a corona of bandages.

'Well!' he said. 'You picked a nice boy-friend to ride with.'

'He *was* nice,' Olivia said. Her voice was weak and faint, but still full of spirit. She was cased in plaster of Paris, but she was already beginning to recover her mental grip. 'He was only following the instincts of self-preservation,' she went on. 'I wanted to thank you—'

'For getting you pushed three hundred feet over a precipice,' Vachell said. 'It must have been a lot of fun.'

'I think I shall stick to anthropology after this,' Olivia said, 'if I ever get out of all these damned bandages and casts. It's less exciting, but I like it better. Old Silu's much more restful, and he seems to get the same results.'

Vachell watched a sister carry a large vase of red roses through the door of Olivia's room. They were fresh blooms that looked as though they had just been picked.

'Silu's got me hipped on riddles,' he said. 'Who is it that sends letters to she who is in Paris but flowers to she who is in plaster of Paris? He who walks at Government House. You see, it's catching.'

'What *do* you mean?' Olivia asked. What was visible of her face seems to express annoyance.

'There's a strange tribal custom of the Wa-British you ought to study some time,' Vachell answered. 'When young men wish to express favourable interest in a female, they send offerings of flowers. Now among the Wa-bolony—'

'Oh, nuts,' said Olivia.